Riotous Assembly

Tom Sharpe was born in 1928 and educated at Lancing and Pembroke College, Cambridge. He did his National Service in the Marines before going to South Africa in 1951, where he did social work for the Non-European Affairs Department before teaching in Natal. He had a photographic studio in Pietermaritzburg from 1957 until 1961, when he was deported. From 1963–72 he was a lecturer in history at the Cambridge College of Arts and Technology. His second novel, the sequel to *Riotous Assembly*, is called *Indecent Exposure*. His *Wilt*, *Porterhouse Blue* and *Blott on the Landscape* are also available in Pan. Tom Sharpe is married and lives in Cambridge.

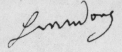

Tom Sharpe

Riotous Assembly

Pan Books London and Sydney

First published 1971 by Martin Secker & Warburg Ltd
This edition published 1973 by Pan Books Ltd,
Cavaye Place, London SW10 9PG
8th printing 1979
© Tom Sharp 1971
ISBN 0 330 23423 4
Printed and bound in England by
Hazell Watson & Viney Ltd, Aylesbury, Bucks

For all those members of the
South African Police Force whose
lives are dedicated to the
preservation of Western Civilization
in Southern Africa

Chapter 1

Piemburg is deceptive. Nothing about it is entirely what it seems to be. Huddled among the foothills of the Drakensberg and crouching at the feet of a great flat-topped hill it has few of the marks of a capital city. Travellers whose trains to Johannesburg stop, if they bother, beneath the rusting sheet-metal gingerbread of its station roof, or who whisk past on the National Highway, glimpse a tiny town that seems to have died and been embalmed. For Piemburg is by popular accounts quite dead. Sleepy Hollow they call it, and an American visitor is reported to have looked at Piemburg and said, 'Half the size of New York Cemetery and twice as dead.' And certainly at a first glance the city's lack of animation seems complete. It lies curled in its valley under the African sun and sleeps. Its red iron roofs and wrought-iron balconies bespeak a distant age of long-forgotten enterprise. Its roads are lined with jacarandas and its gardens are lush with flowering dark verandahs. Everything grows immediately and just as immediately stands still. Time and the climate both combine to growth and growth's suspension.

And Piemburg grew with the garrison, and with the garrison's departure died. Or fell asleep. The capital of Zululand, it sprang up with the British Empire's conquest of the Zulu nation. In the first flush of that resounding victory, Piemburg was transformed from a tiny settlement long deserted by its Afrikaaner founders into a capital city. Civic buildings multiplied in a rash of colonnade and red Victorian brick. The Governor's mansion bloomed with Italian marble floors, Venetian glass and all the trimmings of Imperial splendour. The railway station, a paragon of metal fretwork and faïence, provided a suitable staging post for the Viceregal trains that passed through Piemburg on their way to farther and less attractive Imperial dominions in the hinterland of Africa. And

7

as the great steam engines blustered up the winding gradient to Empire View, the hill above Piemburg, carrying with them their august burden to an early death by tsetse fly or malarial mosquito, monocled and moustached men would gaze serenely down on the capital of Zululand and murmur, 'A gem, a gem set in a green and yellow ring,' and then turn back to study the wholly inaccurate survey maps of their new territories.

Piemburg would salute their passing with a Governor's greeting on the station platform and an exchange of statesmanlike admonitions made inaudible by the military band playing under the iron roof. And Piemburg would pay its respects a few months later when the Viceregal coffin borne in a carriage draped in black and drawn by a locomotive adorned with wreaths halted a moment while the band played a death march with a gusto that made once more inaudible the Governor's condolences to the Aide-de-camp. And in the intervals between Imperial progress and Imperial retreat, the capital of Zululand would adorn itself with new bandstands and botanical gardens and the amusement of a tiny metropolis. In Fort Rapier the great parade ground would echo to the bellowed commands of sergeant-majors. Thousands of putteed legs would stamp or turn about, and the glittering bayonets would eddy to and fro across the brilliant square.

In the town itself the streets were prickly with waxed moustaches. Blanco and brass polish stood high on the list of life's necessities. In the Imperial Hotel the mornings and afternoons were liquid among potted plants and wicker chairs with the music of a Palm Court orchestra. Sam Browne belts and whalebone waist-pinchers restrained the officers and their wives who listened to the whine of the violins and recalled the shires and parishes of England with thankful melancholy. Many would never return and those who stayed and were not buried in the military cemetery in Fort Rapier would build their houses as close to the Governor's mansion as their seniority and overdrafts allowed.

While the garrison stayed Piemburg prospered. Piemburg was even, briefly, gay. The Garrison Theatre was made brilliant by performances of plays and revues that bred one great English actor and playwright and charmed the Governor and his wife.

Bazaars and garden parties were bright with the parasols and bustles of wives who had been swept from the terraced suburbs and semi-detached houses of South London to the grandeur of the lawns and shrubberies of Piemburg by the surprising good fortune of having married husbands whose mediocrity won for them the reward of being posted to this distant sliver of the Empire. The taste of the Victorian lower middle class imposed itself indelibly upon Piemburg and has stayed there to this day. And with the taste there came an immutable sense of hierarchy. Viceroys, governors, generals, vice-governors, colonels, down the ranks swept, broadening as they went, through nuances too subtle to enumerate, where schools and wives' fathers' professions and a dropped aspirate or one retained 'g' could cause a major to step in an instant up above a lieutenant-colonel. At the bottom of the scale came private soldiers in the pay corps. Below these pariahs there was nothing left. Zulus competed with Pondos, Coloureds with Indians. What happened down there was simply nobody's concern. All that one had to know was that somewhere even lower than the loyal Zulus and the treacherous Pondos there were the Boers. And so it went until the war. Boers didn't wash. Boers were cowards. Boers were stupid. Boers were an excrescence that blocked the way to Cairo. Piemburg ignored the Boers.

And then came the Boer War and as the Boers shot the monocles out of the eyes of the officers of Fort Rapier, waiting deliberately for a semaphore reflection of the sun to signal a suitable monocled target, a new respect was born in Piemburg. The Boer could shoot straight. The Boer was cunning. The Boer was now the enemy.

And but a moment later the Boer was the enemy no more. The obstacle to Cairo and the gold mines quite removed, Piemburg began its swift decline. As the garrison departed and the bands played *Goodbye Dolly Gray* for the last time, Piemburg fell asleep. Like a replete puff-adder coiled and bloated it lay under the African sun and dreamt of its brief days of glory. Only a sense of precedence remained to multiply in the luxuriant climate of its own mediocrity. The houses stood and gazed at the ring of hills and on their stoeps the sons and grandsons of the sergeant-majors, quartermaster sergeants and warrant officers pretended to a grandeur their ancestors had never known. In Piemburg time stood still, marked only by the dust that gathered on the heads of the stuffed lions that mouldered in the Alexandra Club and by the drip of snobbery. Piemburg's mediocrity was venomous and waited gently on events.

Chapter 2

Kommandant van Heerden had few illusions about himself and a great many about everything else. And it was thanks to his illusions that he found himself in charge of the Police station in Piemburg. It was not a very onerous position. Piemburg's mediocrity was not conducive to more than petty crime and it had been felt at Police Headquarters in Pretoria that, while Kommandant van Heerden's appointment might push the city's crime rate up, it would at least serve to lower the waves of violence and theft that had followed his posting to other more enterprising towns.

Besides, Piemburg deserved the Kommandant. As the one town in the Republic still to fly the Union Jack from the Town Hall, Piemburg needed to be taught that the Government could not be challenged without taking some revenge.

Kommandant van Heerden knew that his appointment was not due to his success in the field of criminal investigation. He fondly imagined it had come to him because he understood the English. It was in fact due to the reputation of his grandfather, Klaasie van Heerden, who had served under General Cronje at the Battle of Paardeberg and had been shot by the British for refusing to obey the order of his commanding officer to surrender. He had instead stayed put in a hole in the bank of the Modder River and shot down twelve soldiers of the Essex Regiment who were relieving themselves there some forty-eight hours after the last shot had been fired. The fact that Klaasie had been fast asleep throughout the entire battle and had never heard the order to cease fire was discounted by the British during his trial and by later generations of Afrikaans historians. Instead he was accounted a hero who had been martyred for his devotion to the Boer Republics and as a hero he was revered by Afrikaans Nationalists all over South Africa.

It was this legend that had helped Kommandant van Heerden to his present rank. It had taken a long time for his incompetence to live down the reputation for cunning that had been bequeathed him by his grandfather, and by that time it was too late for Police Headquarters to do anything about his inefficiency except put him in command of Piemburg.

Kommandant van Heerden imagined that he had got the post because it was in an English town and certainly it was just the post he wanted. The Kommandant believed that he was one of the few Afrikaaners who really understood the English mind. In spite of the treatment the British had meted out to his grandfather, in spite of the brutality the British had shown to the Boer women and children in the concentration camps, in spite of the sentimentality the British wasted on their black servants, in spite of everything, Kommandant van Heerden admired the British.

There was something about their blundering stupidity that appealed to him. It called out to something deep within his being. He couldn't say exactly what it was, but deep called to deep and, if the Kommandant could have chosen his place of birth, its time and nationality, he would have plumped for Piemburg in 1890 and the heart of an English gentleman.

If he had one regret, it was that his own mediocrity had never had the chance to express itself with anything like the degree of success that had attended the mediocrity and muddle-headedness of the rulers of the British Empire. Born an English gentleman in Victorian Britain he might well have risen to the rank of field-marshal. His military ineptitude would surely have been rewarded by constant and rapid promotion. He was certain he could have done as well as Lord Chelmsford, whose forces had been massacred by the Zulus at Isandhlwana. Stormberg, Spion Kop, Magersfontein, might have been even more appalling disasters had he been in command. Kommandant van Heerden had been born out of nation, time and place.

The same could not be said of the Kommandant's second-in-command, Luitenant Verkramp, nor of Konstabel Els. That they should never have been born at all, or, if their births could not have been aborted, that their nation, place and time should have been as distant as possible from his own, was Kommandant van Heerden's most fervent and frequent wish.

Luitenant Verkramp hated the English. His grandfather had not suffered as had the Kommandant's for the sake of the Boer Republics. Instead he had proclaimed peace and friendship for the British Empire from the pulpit of his church in the Cape and had made a small fortune on the side by supplying the British Army with the Basuto ponies it needed for its mounted infantry. Verkramp's childhood had been spent in the shadow of that pulpit and little Verkramp had inherited a marked eschatological bent from his grandfather and a hatred for all things English from his father who had spent his life trying to live down the name of 'traitor' which had clung to the Verkramp family long after the Boer War. Luitenant Verkramp brought both inheritances with him to his work. He combined his inquisitorial tendencies with his antipathy for the English by becoming head of the Security Branch in Piemburg, a post which allowed him to send reports on the political reliability of the citizens of Piemburg to his superiors in BOSS, the Bureau of State Security in Pretoria. Even Kommandant van Heerden was the subject of Luitenant Verkramp's suspicions and the Kommandant had taken good care to read the reports about himself that Verkramp had submitted. In one of these he had detected the innuendo that he was insufficiently active in pursuit of Communist cells.

In the week following, the Kommandant had sought to rebut the accusation by a series of lightning raids on likely Communist groups. A playreading of Shaw's *Arms and the Man* at the Piemburg Amateur Dramatic Society had been interrupted by the entrance of the Kommandant and his men who confiscated all copies of the play and took the names of all present. *Black Beauty* had been removed from the shelves of the Public Library on the Kommandant's orders. The showing of the film

The African Queen had been banned at the local cinema, as had an article on weather forecasting in the Piemburg News entitled 'Red Sky at Night'.

All in all the Kommandant felt satisfied that he had made significant moves to combat the spread of Marxism in Piemburg and the public outcry that followed would, he felt, go a long way to convince BOSS that he was not as soft on Communists as Luitenant Verkramp's report had suggested. Besides he had Verkramp's report on Konstabel Els to fall back on.

The gulf that separated fact from fiction in all the Luitenant's reports on political life in Piemburg widened to a cosmic abyss in the report he had submitted on Konstabel Els. In it Els was described as a regular attendant at the Dutch Reformed Church, an ardent member of the Nationalist Party and a determined opponent of 'liberalistic and communistic tendencies to pollute racial purity by social, economic and political methods of integration'. Since Els neither went to church nor belonged to the Nationalist Party and was a living exponent of mixed sexual intercourse, Kommandant van Heerden felt that he had Luitenant Verkramp's reputation for accuracy by the short hairs.

With Konstabel Els matters stood rather differently. For one thing Els constituted no sort of threat to the Kommandant though a very considerable one to nearly everyone else in Piemburg. His natural aptitude for violence and particularly for shooting black people was only equalled by his taste for brandy and his predilection for forcing the less attractive parts of his person into those parts of African women legally reserved for male members of their own race. Kommandant van Heerden had had to speak quite severely to him about the illegality of this last tendency on several occasions, but he had put Els' taste for black women down to the undoubted fact that the Konstabel was of mixed race himself.

No, Konstabel Els had his virtues. He was conscientious, he was an excellent shot and he knew how to operate the electrical-therapy machine which had proved such a boon in extracting confessions from suspects. Luitenant Verkramp had brought it back from one of his visits to Pretoria and Els had immediately made himself extraordinarily proficient with it. It had originally been intended for political suspects only, but Luitenant Verkramp's efforts to find any saboteurs or Communists in Piemburg to try the gadget out on had failed so hopelessly that Els had finally had to arrest a native boy he had caught early one morning with a bottle of milk in his hand. The fact that Els knew him to be the milk-delivery boy hadn't prevented the Konstabel proving the efficacy of electric-shock therapy and after five minutes' treatment the boy readily confessed that he had stolen the milk, while after ten minutes he admitted administering poisoned milk to fifty European households that very morning. When Els proposed transferring the terminal from the boy's toe to his penis, the suspect admitted to being a member of the Communist Party and agreed that he had been trained in milk sabotage in Peking. At that point Luitenant Verkramp confessed himself satisfied with the experiment and the milk-delivery boy was charged with being out without a Pass, obstructing the police in the course of their duties and resisting arrest, which charges got him six months hard labour and satisfied the magistrate that his injuries were justified if not actually self-inflicted. Yes, Els had his virtues, not the least of which was a deep if obscure sense of devotion to his commanding officer. Not that Kommandant van Heerden was in the least interested in Konstabel Els' regard for him, but it made a change from the abiding dislike that emanated from Luitenant Verkramp.

All in all Kommandant van Heerden felt well satisfied with life in Piemburg. Things would go on as they had in the past and he would have time to continue his private hobby, the intellectual puzzle of trying to understand the English, a puzzle he knew to be impossible to solve but for that very reason endlessly fascinating.

If Piemburg was the garden of Kommandant van Heerden's soul where he could wander happily dreaming of great men and great deeds done, Miss Házelstone of Jacaranda Park was the key plant, the corner tree of this interior landscape. Not that she was young or beautiful or charming or even in any sense likeable. She was none of these things. She was old, ugly, garrulous and abrupt to the point of rudeness. Hardly alluring qualities but to the Kommandant they were filled with extraordinary attractions. These were all the attributes of the English. To hear Miss Hazelstone's voice, high-pitched, loud and utterly unself-conscious, was to hear the true voice of the British Empire. To be chided, nay, trounced by Miss Hazelstone for infringing his authority by cautioning her chauffeur for driving at 80 mph through a built-up area in a 1936 Hudson Terraplane with defective brakes was a pleasure almost too great to be borne. He treasured her refusal to grant him any title. 'Van Heerden,' she would snarl from the back of the sedan, 'you exceed your authority. Driver, proceed', and the car would drive off leaving the Kommandant marvelling at her *savoir-faire*.

Then again on the rare occasions that he could find an excuse to visit Jacaranda House, Miss Hazelstone would receive him, if she deigned to see him at all, at the servants' entrance and would dispatch him with an economy of incivility and an abundance of implicit contempt that left the Kommandant breathless with admiration.

With Luitenant Verkramp she was even ruder, and when the Kommandant could endure the Security Branch man's insolence no longer he would invent reasons for him to call at Jacaranda House. Luitenant Verkramp had made the mistake on his first visit of addressing Miss Hazelstone in Afrikaans and ever since she had spoken to him in Kitchen Kaffir, a pidgin Zulu reserved only for the most menial and mentally retarded black servants. Luitenant Verkramp returned from these penitential trips speechless with rage and vented his spleen by submitting security reports on the Hazelstone family accusing the old woman of subversion and of fomenting civil disorder. These memoranda he sent to Pretoria with the recommendation that Miss Hazelstone's activities be brought to the attention of the State Attorney.

The Kommandant doubted that the reports enhanced Verkramp's reputation for accuracy or for political reliability. He had forgotten to tell his second-in-command that Miss Hazelstone was the only daughter of the late Judge Hazelstone of the Supreme Court who was known in the legal world as Breakneck Bill and who, in a Minority Report of the Commission on Traffic Congestion, had advocated that flogging be made mandatory for parking offences. With such antecedents, it seemed unlikely to the Kommandant that BOSS would question Miss Hazelstone's patriotism. English she might be, subversive and criminal never.

It came therefore as all the more of a shock when he heard Konstabel Els answer the phone in the outer office and the strident tones of Miss Hazelstone vibrating from the receiver. Interested to see how Els would suffer at her hands, the Kommandant listened to the conversation.

Miss Hazelstone was telephoning to report that she had just shot her Zulu cook. Konstabel Els was perfectly capable of handling the matter. He had in his time as a police officer shot any number of Zulu cooks. Besides there was a regular procedure for dealing with such reports. Konstabel Els went into the routine.

'You wish to report the death of a kaffir,' he began.

'I have just murdered my Zulu cook,' snapped Miss Hazelstone.

Els was placatory. 'That's what I said. You wish to report the death of a coon.'

'I wish to do nothing of the sort. I told you I have just murdered Fivepence.'

Els tried again. 'The loss of a few coins doesn't count as murder.'

'Fivepence was my cook.'

'Killing a cook doesn't count as murder either.'

'What does it count as, then?' Miss Hazelstone's confidence in her own guilt was beginning to wilt under Konstabel Els' favourable diagnosis of the situation.

'Killing a white cook can be murder. It's unlikely but it can be. Killing a black cook can't. Not under any circumstances. Killing a black cook comes under self-defence, justifiable homicide or garbage disposal.' Els permitted himself a giggle. 'Have you tried the Health Department?' he inquired.

It was obvious to the Kommandant that Els had lost what little sense of social deference he had ever possessed. He pushed Els aside and took the call himself.

'Kommandant van Heerden here,' he said. 'I understand that there has been a slight accident with your cook.'

Miss Hazelstone was adamant. 'I have just murdered my Zulu cook.'

Kommandant van Heerden ignored the self-accusation. 'The body is in the house?' he inquired.

'The body is on the lawn,' said Miss Hazelstone. The Kommandant sighed. It was always the same. Why couldn't people shoot blacks inside their houses where they were supposed to shoot them?

'I will be up at Jacaranda House in forty minutes,' he said, 'and when I arrive I will find the body in the house.'

'You won't,' Miss Hazelstone insisted, 'you'll find it on the back lawn.'

Kommandant van Heerden tried again.

'When I arrive the body will be in the house.' He said it very slowly this time.

Miss Hazelstone was not impressed. 'Are you suggesting that I move the body?' she asked angrily.

The Kommandant was appalled at the suggestion. 'Certainly not,' he said. 'I have no wish to put you to any inconvenience and besides there might be fingerprints. You can get the servants to move it for you.'

There was a pause while Miss Hazelstone considered the implications of this remark. 'It sounds to me as though you are suggesting that I should tamper with the evidence of a crime,' she said slowly and menacingly. 'It sounds to me as though you are trying to get me to interfere with the course of justice.'

'Madam,' interrupted the Kommandant, 'I am merely trying to help you to obey the law.' He paused, groping for words. 'The law says that it is a crime to shoot kaffirs outside your house. But the law also says it is perfectly permissible and proper to shoot them inside your house if they have entered illegally.'

'Fivepence was my cook and had every legal right to enter the house.'

'I'm afraid you're wrong there,' Kommandant van Heerden went on. 'Your house is a white area and no kaffir is entitled to enter a white area without permission. By shooting your cook you were refusing him permission to enter your house. I think it is safe to assume that.'

There was a silence at the other end of the line. Miss Hazelstone was evidently convinced.

'I'll be up in forty minutes,' continued van Heerden, adding hopefully, 'and I trust the body—'

'You'll be up here in five minutes and Fivepence will be on the lawn where I shot him,' snarled Miss Hazelstone and slammed down the phone.

The Kommandant looked at the receiver and sighed. He put it down wearily and turning to Konstabel Els he ordered his car.

As they drove up the hill to Jacaranda Park, Kommandant van Heerden knew he was faced with a difficult case. He studied the back of Konstabel Els' head and found some consolation in its shape and colour.

If the worst came to the worst he could always make use of Els' great gift of incompetence and if in spite of all his efforts to prevent it, Miss Hazelstone insisted on being tried for murder, she would have as the chief prosecution witness against her, befuddled and besotted, Konstabel Els. If nothing else could save her, if she pleaded guilty in open court, if she signed confession after confession, Konstabel Els under cross-examination by no matter how half-witted a defence attorney would convince the most biased jury or the most inflexible judge that she was the innocent victim of police incompetence and unbridled perjury. The State Attorney was known to have referred to Konstabel Els in the witness box as the Instant Alibi.

Chapter 3

It was with these thoughts in mind that Kommandant van Heerden drove down the drive to Jacaranda House. They interrupted only briefly the aesthetic pleasure he always felt in the presence of relics of the British Empire, for Jacaranda House was pure Cecil Rhodes and Bishop Colenso.

Rambling and stuccoed, the massive edifice had been jerry-built to last. In style it managed to combine elements of both East and West. In Jacaranda House the twain had met. At first sight it looked as though Windsor Castle had been used for the artificial insemination of the Brighton Pavilion and from its crenellated gables to its tiled and columned verandah it succeeded with an eclecticism truly English in bringing more than a touch of the durbah to a building as functionally efficient as a gents. Whoever had built Jacaranda House might not and almost certainly did not know what he was doing, but he must have been a positive genius even to have known how.

As the police car drew up, the great Gothic front door was opened by an Indian butler, wearing white gloves and a red sash, who led the Kommandant and his assistant through a vast hall whose walls were patinaed with the mouldering heads of one wart-hog, sixteen buffaloes, ten lions and numerous lesser fauna, which heads the late Judge Hazelstone had purchased at an auction to sustain his totally unwarranted reputation as a big-game hunter. To add to the impression that they were in the jungle a profusion of potted plants and ferns reached their dusty fronds up to the plaster fan-vaulting. The corridor and the great sitting-room through which they passed were similarly decorated with the portraits of long-dead Hazelstones, and when at last they came out on to the verandah at the back of the house, Kommandant van Heerden's regard for Imperial Britain had increased by leaps and bounds.

Miss Hazelstone had chosen the scene of her crime with a sense of propriety and occasion which belonged to a distant and leisurely age. The body of Fivepence lay on an immaculate lawn and was huddled in a suitably obeisant rigour at the foot of a pedestal on which had stood the bust of Sir Theophilus Hazelstone, GCR, GCSI, GCIE, DSO, and one-time Governor of Zululand and Viceroy of Matabeleland; which bust had been erected at the conclusion of the Zulu Rebellion to commemorate Sir Theophilus' victory at Bulundi over seventeen thousand unarmed Zulus who had misguidedly assumed that Sir Theophilus had invited them there for an indaba as the representative of the Great White Queen. The ensuing massacre was noted in military history as the first occasion on which ten-inch naval guns had been fired at the point-blank range of twelve yards with the resultant deaths by shrapnel of half their gun crews. In later stages of the battle this mistake had been rectified and the naval guns had been used at long range to decimate the fleeing Zulus to such good effect that they had destroyed four farmhouses and a British blockhouse on the Tugela River some seven miles beyond the actual battlefield. These innovations in the art of military strategy had earned Sir Theophilus his knighthood and a bar to his DSO, not to mention the admiration of his surviving officers and men, and had added to his reputation for scrupulous honesty and fair play among the tribesmen who, maimed and mutilated, managed to survive the holocaust. During his reign as Governor, Zululand knew a decade of untroubled peace and on his death a generation of Zulu widows came out of mourning.

It was on the reputation of such heroes as Sir Theophilus that Kommandant van Heerden's admiration for the British and their Empire had been formed. Reputation, it seemed to the Kommandant, was all that remained to Sir Theophilus. Certainly his bust had disappeared from its pedestal and lay fragmented over half an acre of otherwise spotless lawn. Beyond the lawn the trunks of the gum trees were gashed and splintered and the azalea bushes looked as though they had been the subject of the concentrated attention of some very large and desperately hungry animal. Branches and leaves lay scattered and torn in a gap some twenty yards across.

For a moment the Kommandant drew fresh hope that Fivepence's sudden death must have been the result not of any human agency but of some natural cataclysm in the order of a freak tornado which had passed without a shadow of a doubt well noticed through Jacaranda Park but unremarked in the rest of Piemburg. This brief spasm of optimism died almost as soon as it was born. It was all too obvious that whatever other gifts Miss Hazelstone had inherited from her illustrious Imperial forebears, Sir Theophilus had left her with a marked propensity for enormous firearms and their use at quite unnecessarily close range.

She sat, a thin, angular, almost frail, elderly lady dressed in dark chiffon with lace to her throat, in a frail, elderly wicker

20

chair complete with an unnecessary antimacassar and cradled in her lap lay a weapon which startled Kommandant van Heerden and even Konstabel Els and which explained all too readily the scene of devastation that lay beyond the contorted figure of Fivepence and the bustless pedestal. It was a four-barrelled rifle, some six feet in length and its bore was of a diameter so large that it suggested one of Sir Theophilus' favourite weapons, the ten-inch naval gun. Kommandant van Heerden's experienced eye told him immediately that this was no standard firearm licensed for self-defence.

'This is the murder weapon,' said Miss Hazelstone, evidently reading his thoughts. She patted the four barrels and van Heerden noted that she was obviously determined to leave no part of the gun free of fingerprints.

The Kommandant eyed the rifle cautiously. 'What is it?' he inquired at last.

'It's a magazine-loaded multi-barrelled elephant gun,' Miss Hazelstone replied. 'It was designed by my father, the late Judge Hazelstone and made to his own specifications. Its rate of fire is forty bullets a minute and it can incapacitate a charging elephant at a thousand yards.'

Van Heerden volunteered the opinion that it seemed un-necessary to kill elephants at a thousand yards. He couldn't bring himself to use the word 'incapacitate'. It seemed in-appropriately modest. Evaporate seemed more likely.

'My father was a lousy shot,' Miss Hazelstone continued. 'Besides, he was a dreadful coward.'

'No man who fired that gun could be called a coward,' said the Kommandant both gallantly and truthfully. He was beginning to find the interview quite relaxing. Murder had evidently brought a new touch of humanity to Miss Hazelstone. She was treating him with unaccustomed civility. The Kommandant decided that the time had come to resume his defence of Miss Hazelstone's innocence.

'That rifle is far too heavy for a woman ... I beg your pardon ... for a lady to use,' he said and regretted the remark almost as soon as it was made. It was evident that Miss Hazelstone would respond to any challenge. She rose from her chair and aimed the great rifle into the garden.

The Kommandant had discounted any possibility that she might fire the thing. Konstabel Els, for once, acted with greater resourcefulness and threw himself to the ground. That the ground he chose was already occupied by a large Dobermann Pinscher and that the dog chose to dispute the right of Konstabel Els to lie prone on it and that in any case all South African dogs are trained to bite persons of Negro extraction and that Konstabel Els was of sufficiently mixed blood to justify biting on suspicion, all this was lost to Kommandant van Heerden as Miss Hazelstone, aiming now at the ground and now at the sky, pulled the trigger.

The Kommandant, who was standing some eighteen inches to the right of the four barrels and almost level with their muzzles and who, but an instant before, had been a rational-thinking human being in full possession of his senses, found himself as it seemed to him, in a vast and rapidly expanding bubble of flame. The sensible world of garden, sky, twittering birds, even the screams of Els being savaged by the Dobermann, all disappeared. Kommandant van Heerden knew only the absolute silence at the still heart of an enormous explosion. There was no pain, no anxiety, no thought, only the certain realization, not that the end of the world was at hand, but that it had already been irremediably accomplished. For one brief, illuminating moment Kommandant van Heerden experienced the highest form of mystical understanding, total bodily dissolution. It was some time before he returned to the world of physical sensation and too late for him to hear anything of the thunderclap that volleyed forth from Jacaranda Park in the direction of the Drakensberg Mountains. With the glazed eyes of an awakened sleepwalker and the singed moustache that comes from standing too close to an enormous gun barrel, he looked at the scene around him. It was not one to reassure a man doubtful of his own sanity.

Konstabel Els' contretemps with the Dobermann had been exacerbated, to put it mildly, by the broadside. It was doubtful which of the two animals had been more maddened by the roar of the elephant gun. The dog, which had at first bitten Konstabel Els' ankle to the bone, had transferred its attentions to his groin and once there had developed all the symptoms of lockjaw. Els, conservative as ever, and having nothing else to bite on except the Dobermann's backside, was applying his knowledge, gained in several thousand interrogations of Africans, of what he cheerfully called 'ball-bashing' but which in the autopsy reports on some of his patients was termed severe contusions to the testicles.

Kommandant van Heerden turned what remained of his attention away from this unpleasant spectacle and tried to look at Miss Hazelstone who lay stunned but satisfied in the wicker chair where the kick of the rifle had thrown her. Through his singed eyelashes the Kommandant could partially see that she was addressing him because her lips were moving but it was some minutes before he recovered his hearing sufficiently to be able to make out what she was saying. Not that he found her remarks at all helpful. It seemed positively gratuitous to repeat, 'There you are. I told you I could fire the gun,' and the Kommandant began to wonder if he had not been a trifle unjust to Luitenant Verkramp. Miss Hazelstone was after all a woman who would stick at nothing.

Her second firing had destroyed what remained of the pedestal on which Sir Theophilus' bust had stood and, being aimed at ground level, had almost obliterated all traces of Fivepence's recently obeisant corpse. Almost but not entirely, for the fragmentary and dispersed remains of Sir Theophilus' bust had been joined on their widely separated patches of lawn by the no less fragmentary and dispersed remains of the late Zulu cook, while patches of black skin had attached themselves limpet-like to the blasted trunks of the gum trees that fringed the once-immaculate lawn. Kommandant van Heerden couldn't bring himself to focus on the round black object that kept trying to draw attention to itself by swinging wistfully from a branch in the upper reaches of an otherwise attractive blue gum. Down the centre of the lawn the elephant gun had cut a straight trench some eight inches in depth and fifteen yards long from whose serrated edges arose what the Kommandant despairingly hoped was steam.

Feeling that the afternoon's work and his recent transcendental experience had released him from the standards of politeness he had previously maintained in Miss Hazelstone's company, the Kommandant sat down uninvited in a chair well outside any likely arc of fire from the terrible elephant gun, and watched Konstabel Els' gladiatorial conflict with the Dobermann with the air of a connoisseur.

On the whole he thought they were pretty well matched both in physique and in intellectual grasp of the situation. Certainly Els suffered the disadvantage of a smaller jaw and fewer teeth, but what he lacked in biting power he made up for in concentration and experience in castration. The Kommandant did think, momentarily, of intervening but Miss Hazelstone had already acted with that decisiveness he had always found so admirable in persons of her class. She sent the Indian butler into the house and a moment later he returned with a bottle of ammonia and a large wad of cotton wool.

'The best way of separating dogs,' she shouted above the growls and groans, 'is to hold a pad of cotton wool soaked with ammonia over their muzzles. They gasp for air and you pull 'em apart,' and so saying she clamped the wad over Konstabel Els' already purple face. The Kommandant wondered at her choice of Els as the first to be forced to release his grip, but he put it down to the English love of animals and, to be fair to Miss Hazelstone, he knew her to be particularly fond of the Dobermann.

It was immediately apparent that the method was remarkably efficacious. With a muffled scream and all the symptoms of imminent asphyxia, Els released his grip on the dog's reproductive organs and was assisted in discontinuing the struggle by the Indian butler who, hanging on to his ankles, attempted to drag the Konstabel away.

Unfortunately for Els the Dobermann was less intimidated by the threat of death by suffocation, or else it had developed an immunity to ammonia and it took several minutes to persuade the beast not to pursue the advantage it naturally assumed it had won by the intervention of its mistress. It may well have thought that Miss Hazelstone had joined it on the ground because Konstabel Els had transferred his quite appalling mandible attentions to her, which would at least have been more natural although, considering her age and lack of physical charm, not altogether understandable. Whatever the reasons for the Dobermann's continuing attachment to Els' groin, the interval allowed the Kommandant to concentrate his attention, interrupted only by the agonized screams of his assistant, on the case he had been forced to investigate.

By the time peace and tranquillity had once more been restored to Jacaranda House and Miss Hazelstone had sent Oogly, the Indian butler, to serve tea in the drawing-room, Kommandant van Heerden had sufficiently recovered his faculties to begin the investigation of the case. But first he ordered Konstabel Els to retrieve the remains of Fivepence from the lawn and from what was clearly an unscaleable blue gum, an order which the Konstabel tended to dispute on the grounds that he was in need of immediate and prolonged hospital treatment for multiple and severe dog bite, not to mention battle fatigue and shell shock.

In the end the Kommandant was able to resume his interrogation of Miss Hazelstone to the accompaniment of an old-fashioned tea with smoked-salmon sandwiches and cream scones and the almost equally enjoyable observation of Konstabel Els suffering severe vertigo some forty feet up the blue gum.

'Now about this cook,' the Kommandant began. 'Can I take it that you were dissatisfied with his cooking?'

'Fivepence was an excellent cook,' Miss Hazelstone declared emphatically.

'I see,' said the Kommandant, though he didn't, either literally or metaphorically. He had been having difficulty with his vision ever since he had been enveloped in that ball of flame. It sort of came and went and his hearing was behaving erratically too.

'Fivepence was a culinary expert,' Miss Hazelstone went on.

'Was he indeed?' The Kommandant's hopes were raised. 'And when did he do this?'

'Every day of course.'

'And when did you first discover what he was up to?'

'Almost from the word "Go".'

The Kommandant was amazed. 'And you allowed him to go on?'

'Of course I did. You don't think I was going to stop him, do you?' Miss Hazelstone snapped.

'But your duty as a citizen—'

'My duty as a citizen fiddlesticks. Why in the name of heaven should my duty as a citizen oblige me to sack an excellent cook?'

The Kommandant groped in the recesses of his shell-shocked mind for a suitable answer.

'Well, you seem to have shot him for it,' he said at last.

'I did nothing of the sort,' Miss Hazelstone snorted. 'Fivepence's death was a *crime passionelle*.'

Kommandant van Heerden tried to imagine what a Cream Passion Nell looked like. Fivepence's death had looked more like an exploded blood pudding to him and as for the portions that Konstabel Els was still attempting to dislodge from the blue gum, even a dog butcher would have been hard put to it to think of an adequate description for them.

'A Cream Passion Nell,' he repeated slowly, hoping that Miss Hazelstone would come to his rescue with a more familiar term. She did.

'A crime of passion, you fool,' she snarled.

Kommandant van Heerden nodded. He had never supposed it to have been anything else. Nobody in his right mind would have inflicted those appàlling injuries on Fivepence in cold blood and without some degree of feeling being involved.

'Oh I can see that,' he said.

But Miss Hazelstone had no intention of allowing him to remain under this comforting misapprehension. 'I want you to understand that my feelings for Fivepence were not those which normally obtain between mistress and servant,' she said.

Kommandant van Heerden had already reached that conclusion off his own bat. He nodded encouragingly. Miss Hazelstone's old-fashioned and formal way of expressing her thoughts delighted him. Her next remark had quite the opposite effect.

'What I am trying to tell you,' she continued, 'is that I was in love with him.'

It took some time for the full implications of this statement to sink into the Kommandant's overloaded mind. By compari-

26

son his experience of bodily dissolution at the muzzle of the elephant gun had been a mere sighing of the breeze in distant meadow grass. This was a bombshell. Speechless with horror he gazed unfocused in Miss Hazelstone's direction. He knew now what the face of madness looked like. It looked like a frail elderly gentlewoman of illustrious and impeccable British descent sitting in a winged-back armchair holding in her delicate hands a china teacup on which in gilt transfer the crest of the Hazelstones, a wild boar rampant, was underlined by the family motto '*Baisez-moi*', and openly confessing to an Afrikaans policeman that she was in love with her black cook.

Miss Hazelstone ignored the Kommandant's stunned silence. She evidently took it for a mark of respect for the delicacy of her feelings.

'Fivepence and I were lovers,' she went on. 'We loved one another with a deep and undying devotion.'

Kommandant van Heerden's mind reeled. It was bad enough having to try, however hopelessly, to comprehend what, in God's name, Miss Hazelstone could have found in any way attractive in a black cook, let alone trying to imagine how a black cook could be in love with Miss Hazelstone, but when to crown it all, she used the expression 'undying devotion' while what was left of Fivepence was splattered over an acre of lawn and shrubbery or hung sixty feet up a blue gum tree as a direct result of his lover's passion for him, then Kommandant van Heerden knew that his mind was seriously in danger of utter derangement.

'Go on,' he gasped involuntarily. He had intended to say, 'For God's sake shut up,' but his professional training got the better of him.

Miss Hazelstone seemed happy to continue.

'We became lovers eight years ago and from the first we were delightfully happy. Fivepence understood my emotional needs. Of course we couldn't marry, because of the absurd Immorality Act.' She paused and held up a hand as if to silence the Kommandant's shocked protest. 'So we had to live in sin.' Kommandant van Heerden was past shock. He goggled at her. 'But if we weren't married,' Miss Hazelstone continued, 'we were happy. I must admit we didn't have much of a social life, but then by the time you reach my age, a quiet life at home is all one really wants, don't you think?'

Kommandant van Heerden didn't think. He was doing his best not to listen. He rose unsteadily from his chair and closed the french doors that led out on to the stoep. What this ghastly old woman was telling him must on no account reach the ears of Konstabel Els. He was relieved to note that the redoubtable Konstabel had finally made it to the top of the tree, where he seemed to be stuck.

While Miss Hazelstone mumbled on with her catalogue of Fivepence's virtues, the Kommandant paced the room, frenziedly searching his mind for some means of hushing the case up. Miss Hazelstone and Jacaranda House were practically national institutions. Her column on refined living and etiquette appeared in every newspaper in the country, not to mention her frequent articles in the glossier women's journals. If the doyenne of English society in Zululand were known to have murdered her black cook, or if falling in love with black cooks was to come into the category of refined living and the fashion spread, as well it might, South Africa would go coloured in a year. And what about the effect on the Zulus themselves when they learnt that one of their number had been having it off with the granddaughter of the Great Governor, Sir Theophilus Hazelstone, in Sir Theophilus' own kraal, Jacaranda Park, freely, practically legally, and at her insistence? Kommandant van Heerden's imagination swept on from wholesale rape by thousands of Zulu cooks, to native rebellion and finally race war. Luitenant Verkramp had been right in his reports to Pretoria after all. He had shown astonishing perspicacity. Miss Hazelstone and her Zulu bloody cook were indeed capable of ending three hundred years of White Supremacy in Southern Africa. Worse still he, Kommandant van Heerden, would be held responsible.

At last, after gazing long and prayerfully into the face of a moth-eaten hyena which, in his distracted state of mind, he assumed to be a portrait of Sir Theophilus in his younger days, the Kommandant mustered his last remaining faculties and turned back to his tormentor. He would make one last attempt to make the old bitch see her duty as a lady and a white

28

woman and deny that she had ever entertained anything more lethal or passionate than mildly critical thoughts towards her Zulu cook.

Miss Hazelstone had completed her catalogue of Fivepence's virtues as a sentimental and spiritual companion. She had begun to describe the cook's attributes as a physical and sensual lover, a sharer of her bed and satisfier of her sexual appetites which were, the Kommandant was to discover to his disgust, prodigious and, in his view, perverse to the point of enormity.

'Of course, we did have our little difficulties to begin with,' she was saying. 'There were little incompatibilities in our attitudes, not to mention our physical attributes. A man of your experience, Kommandant, will naturally know what I mean.'

The Kommandant, whose experience of sex was limited to an annual visit to a brothel in Lourenço Marques on his summer holiday, but whose experience of Zulus was fairly extensive, thought that he knew what she meant and hoped to hell that he didn't.

'To begin with Fivepence suffered from *ejaculatio praecox*,' Miss Hazelstone continued clinically. For a brief, all too short moment the Kommandant's lack of Latin and his limited knowledge of medicine spared him the full implications of this remark. Miss Hazelstone hastened to explain.

'He used to have emissions prematurely,' she said, and when the Kommandant ventured to suggest incomprehendingly that, in his humble opinion, Fivepence could not have gone to mission prematurely enough considering his filthy habits in later life, Miss Hazelstone stooped to the level of the stable and explained in language the Kommandant was forced, however unwillingly, to recognize as all too intelligible.

'He used to ejaculate almost as soon as I touched him,' she continued remorselessly, and mistaking the Kommandant's look of abject horror for an indication that he still didn't grasp her meaning, she administered the *coup de grâce* to his dumb-founded sensibilities.

'He used to come before he could get his prick into me,' she said, and as she said it, the Kommandant seemed to be aware, as in some ghastly nightmare, that the corners of Miss Hazelstone's mouth turned upwards in a slight smile of happy remembrance.

He knew now that Miss Hazelstone was clean out of her mind. He was about to say that she had blown her top, but the phrase, being all too reminiscent of Fivepence's disgusting propensity, not to mention his ultimate fate, was throttled on the threshold of his consciousness.

'In the end we got over the problem,' Miss Hazelstone went on. 'First of all I got him to wear three contraceptives, one on top of the other, to desensitize his *glans penis* and that was quite satisfactory from my point of view though it tended to restrict his circulation a teeny bit and he did complain that he couldn't feel very much. After an hour I would get him to take one off and that helped him a bit and finally he would take the second off and we would have a simultaneous orgasm.' She paused and wagged a finger mischievously at the stupefied Kommandant who was desperately trying to raise enough energy to call a halt to these appalling disclosures. 'But that wasn't the end of it,' she went on. 'I want you to know that I finally arrived at an even better solution to dear Fivepence's little trouble. I was having my six-monthly check-up at the dentist and Dr Levy gave me an injection of local anaesthetic to deaden the pain.' She hesitated as if ashamed to confess to a weakness. 'Of course in the old days we never bothered with such nonsense. A little pain never hurt anyone. But Dr Levy insisted and afterwards I was so glad I had had it. You see I suddenly realized how I could stop Fivepence being overcome by the intensity of his feelings for me.' She paused. There was indeed no need for her to continue.

Kommandant van Heerden's lightning intellect had raced ahead and had grasped the point quite firmly. Besides he was beginning to understand, though only fitfully, the train of thought that Miss Hazelstone was bound to follow.

At this moment he visualized the scene in court which would follow the disclosure that Miss Hazelstone had made it a habit to inject her black cook's penis with a hypodermic syringe filled with novocaine before allowing him to have sexual intercourse with her. He visualized it and vowed that it would never happen, even if it meant he had to kill her to prevent it.

Despairingly his gaze wandered round the assembly of long-dead Hazelstones adorning the walls of the drawing-room and he hoped they appreciated the sacrifices he was prepared to make to save their family name from the shame that Miss Hazelstone seemed hell-bent on bestowing on it. The bit about the novocaine injections was an innovation in sexual techniques of such a bizarre nature that it wouldn't just hit the national headlines. The newspapers of the world would splash that titbit in foot-high letters across their front pages. He couldn't begin to think how they would actually word it, but he had every confidence in their editors' abilities to make it sensational. He tried to imagine what sort of sensation Five-pence had found it to be and reached the conclusion that the cook's death at the muzzle of that awful elephant gun must have seemed a relatively comfortable release from the continual practice of Miss Hazelstone plunging the needle of her hypodermic syringe into the top of his cock. The Kommandant wondered idly if Fivepence had had a foreskin. It was a fact that they would never be able to ascertain now.

The thought caused him to glance out of the window to see how Konstabel Els was getting on. He noted, with what little astonishment Miss Hazelstone's confession had left in him, that Els had regained his head for heights, not to mention Fivepence's, and had somehow managed to reach the ground where he was busily seeking promotion by kicking the Indian butler into collecting the scattered remains of the Zulu cook and putting them into a pillowcase. Els was, as usual, the Kommandant thought, being a bit optimistic. They didn't need anything as large as a pillowcase. A spongebag would have done just as well.

Chapter 4

Behind him Miss Hazelstone, evidently exhausted by her confession, sat back silent in her armchair and gazed happily into
her memories. Kommandant van Heerden slumped into a chair
opposite her and gazed with less satisfaction into his immediate future. What Miss Hazelstone had revealed to him he
had no doubt she would reveal to the world if he gave her half
a chance and at all costs those revelations had got to be
stopped in their tracks. His own career, the reputation of
Zululand's leading family, the whole future of South Africa
clearly depended on Miss Hazelstone's silence. His first duty
was to ensure that no word of the afternoon's events leaked
out of Jacaranda Park. Kommandant van Heerden had little
faith in his own ability to prevent that leak. He had none
whatsoever in Els'.

The Kommandant knew from bitter experience that Konstabel Els was incapable of keeping anything, money, wife,
penis, prisoners, let alone gossip, to himself. And what Miss
Hazelstone had to recount wasn't in the nature of mere gossip.
It was political, racial, social, you name it, dynamite.

It was just at this point in his musings that the Kommandant
caught sight of Konstabel Els approaching the house. He had
the air of a good dog that has done its duty and expects to be
rewarded. Had he possessed a tail he would undoubtedly have
been wagging it. Lacking that appendage he dragged behind
him a terrible substitute which, Kommandant van Heerden
noted thankfully, he had the decency not to wag. What remained of Fivepence were not things that anybody, not even
Els, would wish to wag.

Kommandant van Heerden acted swiftly. He stepped out on
to the stoep and shut the door behind him.

'Konstabel Els,' he commanded. 'These are your orders.'
The Konstabel dropped the pillowcase and came to attention

eagerly. Tree-climbing and body-snatching he could do with-out, but he loved being given orders. They usually meant that he was being given permission to hurt somebody.

'You will dispose of that . . . that thing,' the Kommandant ordered.

'Yes sir,' said Els thankfully. He was getting tired of Five-pence.

'Proceed to the main gate and remain there on guard until you are relieved. See that nobody enters or leaves the grounds. Anybody at all. That means Europeans as well. Do you under-stand?'

'Yes sir.'

'If anyone enters you are to see that they don't get out again.'

'Can I use firearms to stop them, sir?' asked Els.

Kommandant van Heerden hesitated. He didn't want a bloodbath up at the main gateway to Jacaranda Park. On the other hand the situation was clearly such a desperate one and one word to the Press would bring hordes of newspapermen up – that he was prepared to take drastic measures.

'Yes,' he said at last. 'You can shoot.' And then remembering the fuss there had been when a wounded reporter had been taken to Piemburg Hospital, he added, 'And shoot to kill, Els, shoot to kill.' Complaints from the morgue were easier to refute.

Kommandant van Heerden went back into the house and Konstabel Els started off to guard the main gate. He hadn't gone very far when the thought crossed his mind that the elephant gun would certainly ensure that nothing larger than a cockroach got out of Jacaranda Park alive. He turned back and collected the gun from the stoep and then, after adding several packets of revolver ammunition from the police car, set off up the drive with a light heart.

Back in the house Kommandant van Heerden was glad to see that Miss Hazelstone was still in her stupor in the arm-chair. At least one problem had been solved. No word of the injections would reach Konstabel Els. The thought of what would follow should Els get wind of that diversion had been haunting the Kommandant's mind. There had been enough

33

complaints lately from local residents about the screams that came from the cells in Piemburg Police Station without Konstabel Els practising penal injections on the prisoners. Not that Els would have been content to use novocaine. He would have graduated to nitric acid before you could say Apartheid.

With Els out of the way, the Kommandant decided on his next step. Leaving Miss Hazelstone in her chair, he made his way to the telephone which lurked in the potted jungle in the hall. He made two calls. The first was to Luitenant Verkramp at the Police Station.

In later life Luitenant Verkramp was to recall that telephone conversation with the shudder that comes from recalling the first omens of disaster. At the time he had merely wondered what the hell was wrong with his Kommandant. Van Heerden sounded as though he were on the brink of a nervous breakdown.

'Verkramp, is that you?' his voice came in a strangled whisper over the phone.

'Of course it's me. Who the hell did you think it was?' Verkramp couldn't hear the answer but it sounded as if the Kommandant was trying to swallow something very unpleasant. 'What's going on up there? Is something wrong with you?' Verkramp inquired hopefully.

'Stop asking stupid questions and listen,' the Kommandant whispered authoritatively. 'I want you to assemble every single officer in Piemburg at the police barracks.'

Luitenant Verkramp was appalled. 'I can't do that,' he said, 'the rugby match is on. There'll be a riot if—'

'There'll be a fucking riot if you don't,' the Kommandant snarled. 'That's number one. Second, all leave including sick leave is cancelled. Got that?'

Luitenant Verkramp wasn't sure what he had got. It sounded like a frantic Kommandant.

'Assemble them all at the barracks,' continued the Kommandant. 'I want every man jack of them fully armed up here as soon as possible. Bring the Saracens too, and the guard dogs, oh and bring the searchlights too. All the barbed wire we've got, and bring those rabies signs we used in the epidemic last year.'

'The rabies signs?' Luitenant Verkramp shouted. 'You want the guard dogs and the rabies signs?'

'And don't forget the bubonic plague signs. Bring them too.'

Luitenant Verkramp tried to visualize the desperate outbreak of disease that had broken out at Jacaranda Park that necessitated warning the population about both rabies and bubonic plague.

'Are you sure you're all right?' he asked. It sounded as if the Kommandant was delirious.

'Of course I am all right,' snapped the Kommandant. 'Why the hell shouldn't I be all right?'

'Well, I just thought—'

'I don't care a stuff what you thought. You're not paid to think. You're paid to obey my orders. And I'm ordering you to bring every bloody sign we've got and every bloody policeman and every bloody guard dog ...' Kommandant van Heerden's catalogue continued while Verkramp desperately searched his mind for the reasons for this emergency. The Kommandant's final order trumped the lot. 'Come up here by a roundabout route. I don't want to attract any public attention.' And before the Luitenant could inquire how he thought it possible to avoid public attention with a convoy of six armoured cars, twenty-five lorries and ten searchlights, not to mention seventy guard dogs, and several dozen enormous billboards announcing the outbreak of bubonic plague and rabies, the Kommandant had put down the phone.

Kommandant van Heerden's second call was to the Commissioner of Police for Zululand. Standing among the flora and fauna of the hall, the Kommandant hesitated some time before making his second call. He could see a number of difficulties looming up ahead of him when he made his request for Emergency Powers to deal with this situation, not the least of which was the sheer disbelief that was certain to greet his considered opinion as a police officer that the daughter of the late Judge Hazelstone had not only murdered her Zulu cook but that prior to this act had been fornicating with him regularly for eight years after rendering his reproductive organs totally numb and insensitive by intramuscular injections of massive doses of novocaine. Kommandant van Heerden knew what he would do to any subordinate officer who rang him up in the middle of a hot summer afternoon to tell him that sort of cock-and-bull story. He decided to avoid going into the details of the case. He would stress the likely consequences of a murder case involving the daughter of an extremely eminent judge who had, in his time, been the country's leading exponent of capital punishment, and he would use Luitenant Verkramp's report to Pretoria on Miss Hazelstone's subversive activities to justify his need for Emergency Powers. Plucking up courage, Kommandant van Heerden picked up the telephone and made his call. He was surprised to find the Commissioner raised no objections to his request.

'Emergency Powers, van Heerden? Of course, help yourself. You know what you're doing. I leave the matter entirely in your hands. Do what you think best.'

Kommandant van Heerden put down the phone with a puzzled frown. He had never liked the Commissioner and he suspected that the feeling was reciprocated.

The Commissioner in fact nourished the ardent hope that one day Kommandant van Heerden would perpetrate an error so unforgivable that he could be summarily reduced to the ranks and it seemed to him now from the Kommandant's hysterical manner on the phone that his day of vengeance was at hand. He immediately cancelled all appointments for the next month and took his annual holiday on the south coast, leaving orders that he was not to be disturbed. He spent the next week lying in the sun in the certain knowledge that he had given van Heerden enough rope with which to hang himself.

Armed now with Emergency Powers that made him the arbiter of life and death over 70,000 Piemburgers and gave him authority to suppress newspaper stories and to arrest, detain and torture at leisure all those he disapproved of, the Kommandant was still not a happy man. The events of the day had taken their toll of him.

He turned for relief from his problems to a full-length portrait of Sir Theophilus Hazelstone in the full panoply of his regalia as Knight of the Royal Victorian Order and Viceroy of Matabeleland that hung at the foot of the great staircase. Sir Theophilus stood, robed in ermine, his scarlet uniform encrusted with jewelled stars and the medals of disastrous campaigns, each medal representing the deaths through their General's incompetence of at least ten thousand enlisted men. The Viceroy's left hand rested arthritically upon the hilt of a sword he was far too pusillanimous ever to have withdrawn from its scabbard, while his right hand held the thonged leash of a wild boar which had been specially imported from Bohemia to share the honour of representing the Hazelstone family in this great work of art. Kommandant van Heerden was particularly struck by the wild boar. It reminded him of Konstabel Els and he was not to know that the poor beast had had to be strapped to an iron frame before the Viceroy would enter the same room as the animate family emblem, and that only after being cajoled by the artist and the administration of half a bottle of brandy. All this escaped the Kommandant and left him free to hold firmly to his faith in the great qualities of the Imperial statesman whose granddaughter he had made it his mission to save from the consequences of her own folly. Spiritually resuscitated by his perusal of this portrait and a similar one of the late Judge Hazelstone looking as remorseless as the Kommandant could remember him to have looked in court on the day he had sentenced eleven Pondo tribesmen to death for stealing a goat, the Kommandant slowly ascended the staircase to look for somewhere to rest until Luitenant Verkramp arrived with reinforcements.

Once the Park had been isolated from the outside world, he would set about the business of convincing Miss Hazelstone that she had never murdered her cook and that she had invented the whole business of the injection needle and the love affair. He felt sure that he could bring the old lady to see reason and if that failed the Emergency Powers entitled him to hold her indefinitely and without recourse to a lawyer. If need be he would invoke the Terrorist Act and keep her incommunicado for the rest of her life, which life could be shortened by suitable treatment and a regimen of necessary harshness. It was hardly the method he would like to have applied to a lady of her descent but for the moment he could think of nothing better.

He paused at the top of the staircase to regain his breath

and then made his way along the gallery that ran the length of Jacaranda House. If the hall downstairs had been filled with stuffed heads and portraits, the gallery walls were likewise lined with trophies of past battles. On either side of him the Kommandant was startled to find weapons of all shapes and sizes, weapons of all ages and types, united by only one common feature as far as the Kommandant could make out, that they were all in perfect working order and lethal to a degree he found positively hair-raising. He stopped and examined a machine pistol. Well-oiled and complete, it hung beside an ancient blunderbuss. Kommandant van Heerden was amazed. The gallery was a positive arsenal. Had Miss Hazelstone not telephoned to acknowledge her contretemps with Fivepence and had she decided to defend Jacaranda House, with these weapons at her disposal, she could have held the entire Piemburg police force at bay for weeks. Thanking his lucky stars for her cooperation, Kommandant van Heerden opened one of the doors that led off the gallery and looked inside.

As he had expected, it was a bedroom and was furnished with a sense of taste and delicacy appropriate to the home of South Africa's leading expert in soft furnishings. Chintz curtains and a matching bedspread gave to the whole room a gay and floral air. What lay on the bed had the opposite effect. There was nothing tasteful or delicate about it at all and nobody could call it furnished. For there, its incongruity emphasized by the daintiness of the other appointments, lay the body of a large, hairy and completely naked man. Worse still, for the Kommandant's disturbed state of mind, the body bore all the signs of having only recently bled to death. It was practically coated with blood.

Shaken by the appalling discovery of yet another corpse, the Kommandant staggered into the gallery and leant against the wall. One body in an afternoon he could just about cope with, particularly if it was black, but two, and one of them white, filled him with despair. Jacaranda House was taking on the qualities of an abattoir. Worse still, this second corpse destroyed any chances of hushing the case up. It was one thing to persuade Miss Hazelstone that she hadn't murdered her black cook. The disappearance of Zulu cooks was a routine matter. The murder of a white man would simply have to be made public. There would have to be an inquest. Questions would be asked and one thing would lead to another until the full story of Miss Hazelstone and her Zulu cook came out into the open.

After a moment's agonizing thought, Kommandant van Heerden recovered his nerve sufficiently to peer round the door into the murder room again. The corpse was still there, he noted miserably. On the other hand it had certain attributes which Kommandant van Heerden found unique in his experience of corpses. One quality in particular struck his attention. The corpse had an erection. The Kommandant peered round the door again to confirm his suspicion, and as he did so the corpse stirred and began to snore.

For a moment Kommandant van Heerden was so relieved by this evidence of life, that he felt inclined to laugh. The next moment he realized the full importance of his discovery and the smile died on his face. He had no doubt at all that the man whose body lay before him on the bed was the true murderer of Fivepence. The Kommandant peered down at the figure on the bed and as he did so he became aware of the smell of brandy in the air. A moment later his foot banged against a bottle lying on the floor. He reached down and picked it up. Old Rhino Skin brandy, he noted with disgust. It was a brandy that Konstabel Els was partial to and if anything was needed to confirm his suspicion that the fellow on the bed was a dangerous criminal it was the knowledge that if he shared one of Konstabel Els' depraved tastes, he was almost certain to share others even more vicious.

With the bottle still in his hand Kommandant van Heerden tiptoed from the room. Outside in the passage he tried to consider how this discovery affected his plans. That the man was a murderer, he had no doubt. That he was now drunk to the world, no doubt either. What remained a mystery was why Miss Hazelstone had confessed to a crime she had never committed. More of a mystery still, why she had embroidered her confession with the gratuitous filth that she had been sleeping with her Zulu cook and injecting him with novocaine. Kommandant van Heerden's head reeled with possibilities and, not wishing to remain in the vicinity of a dangerous killer, he made his way along the passage to the landing at the top of the stairs. He wished now that he hadn't sent Els off to guard the main gateway and at the same time he began to wonder when Luitenant Verkramp would arrive with the main force. He leant over the balustrade and stared down on the tropical mausoleum in the hall. Hard by him the head of a stuffed rhinoceros peered myopically into eternity. Kommandant van Heerden peered back and wondered which of his acquaintances it reminded him of, and as he did so he had the sudden insight into the true meaning of Miss Hazelstone's confession which was to alter his life so radically.

He had suddenly realized that the face of the murderer on the bed reminded him of someone. The realization sent him stumbling down the stairs to stare up at the great portrait of Sir Theophilus. A moment later he was back in the bedroom. Tiptoeing to the edge of the bed Kommandant van Heerden peered cautiously down at the face on the pillow. He saw there what he had expected to find. In spite of the gaping mouth and the bag-bottomed eyes, in spite of years of dissipation and sexual over-indulgence and gallons of Old Rhino Skin brandy, the features of the man on the bed bore an unmistakable resemblance to those of Sir Theophilus and to the late Judge Hazelstone. He knew now who the man was. He was Jonathan Hazelstone, Miss Hazelstone's younger brother.

With new understanding dawning on him, Kommandant van Heerden turned to leave the room. As he did so the murderer stirred again. The Kommandant froze in his tracks and watched with a mixture of fear and disgust as a bloodstained hand groped up the man's hairy thigh and grasped the great erection. Kommandant van Heerden waited no longer. With a gasp he dashed from the room and hurried along the corridor. A man who could put away a bottle of Old Rhino Skin and still survive in no matter how comatose a state was undoubtedly a maniac, and if on top of all that he could lie there with an erection while his body fought off the appalling injuries being inflicted on it by the brandy, he was undoubtedly a sex fiend whose sexual appetite must be of such an intensity as to leave nothing safe. Kommandant van Heerden remembered Fivepence's posture at the foot of the pedestal and he began to think he knew how the Zulu cook had died and in his calculations there was no place for the elephant gun.

Without a moment's hesitation he hurried down the stairs and left the house. He must fetch Konstabel Els before he tried to arrest the man. As he strode up the drive, he understood why Miss Hazelstone had made her outrageous confession and with this understanding there grew in the Kommandant's breast a new and deeper respect for the old family ties of the British.

'Chivalry. It's pure chivalry,' he said to himself. 'She is sacrificing herself to protect the family name.' He couldn't quite see how confessing to murdering your black cook was saving the family name, but he supposed it was better than having your brother confess to having buggered the said cook into an early grave. He wondered what the sentence for that sort of crime was.

'Deserves to be hanged,' he said hopefully, and then remembered that no white man had ever been hanged for murdering a black. 'Buggery's different,' he thought. Anyway they could always get him for 'actions calculated to excite racial friction', which crime carried with it ten strokes of the heavy cane, and if buggering a Zulu cook wasn't calculated to excite racial friction, then he for one didn't know what was. He would have to ask Konstabel Els about it. The Konstabel was more experienced in that sort of thing than he was.

Chapter 5

At the main gateway to Jacaranda Park, Konstabel Els was not finding the afternoon as enjoyable as he had expected. Nobody had tried to enter or leave the Park and Els had had very little to shoot at. He had taken a pot shot at a native delivery boy on a bicycle, but the boy had recognized Els in time and had thrown himself into the ditch before Els had time to take proper aim. Missing the native hadn't improved Els' temper.

'Miss one and you miss the fucking lot,' he said to himself, and it was certainly true that once word got round that Kaffir-Killer Els was in the district, white housewives could scream blue murder at their servants and threaten them with every punishment in the book, and still no sane black man would venture out of the house to water the lawn or fetch the groceries.

So, for want of anything better to do, Els had explored the area round the gateway and had closed and bolted the great wrought-iron gates. In the course of his explorations he made the exciting discovery that what he had at first sight taken to be a well-clipped square privet hedge concealed in fact a concrete blockhouse. It was clearly very old and just as clearly very impregnable. It dated in fact from the days of Sir Theophilus who had ordered its construction after the Battle of Bulundi. The Governor's victory on that occasion had done nothing to diminish his natural cowardice and the accusations of treachery levelled against him by the Zulus and by the next of kin of the officers killed by their own shells had turned what had been previously natural anxiety into an obsessive phobia that thousands of vengeful Zulus trained in the use of ten-inch naval guns by the surviving members of his old regiment, the Royal Marines Heavy Artillery Brigade, would storm Jacaranda Park one awful night. Faced with this imaginary threat, Sir Theophilus had begun the collection of weapons that had so startled Kommandant van Heerden in the gallery of Jacaranda House, and also the construction of a series of formidable blockhouses around the perimeter of the Park, all of which had been designed to withstand a direct hit from a ten-inch naval shell fired at point-blank range.

It was a tribute to the Governor's skill as a military engineer that the blockhouses were still standing. Judge Hazelstone, as great a coward as his father but more convinced of the deterrent effect of capital punishment, had once employed a demolition firm to remove the blockhouses. After blunting scores of drills, the demolition crew had decided to try blasting, and conscious that the bunker was no ordinary one they had practically filled it to the roof with dynamite before lighting the fuse. At the inquest that followed the survivors of the demolition crew described the resulting explosion as being like four gigantic tongues of flame issuing from the gun ports of the blockhouse and the noise had been heard in Durban thirty-five miles away. In view of Judge Hazelstone's legal standing the firm had replaced, free of charge, the gateway their zeal had destroyed, but had refused to continue the work of demolishing the blockhouse. They suggested hiding the unsightly building by planting a privet hedge round it as being a less costly way of getting rid of the thing, and contributed to the cost of the operation as a tribute to the men they had lost in the dynamite explosion.

Konstabel Els knew nothing of all this, but having found the doorway to this impregnable fortress, amused himself by mounting the elephant gun in a gun port and aiming it down the road. He wasn't optimist enough to suppose that anything worthy of the fearful weapon was likely to try to enter the Park, but the tedium of his duties persuaded him that there was no harm in being prepared for the most unlikely eventualities.

He had no sooner done this than he spotted an Alsatian dog which had stopped for a pee against one of the gateposts. Konstabel Els was not one to miss opportunities and besides he was still feeling the effects of his encounter with the Dobermann Pinscher. One well-aimed revolver shot and the Alsatian lost all interest in the events of the afternoon. Other people in the neighbourhood of Jacaranda Park were not so fortunate. Five plain-clothes detectives whom Luitenant Verkramp had sent straight up to Jacaranda Park, and who were walking with the utmost discretion and at intervals of twenty-five yards between them, heard the shot, consulted together and began to approach the main gate with drawn revolvers and a degree of furtiveness calculated to excite the suspicions of Konstabel Els in the blockhouse.

Kommandant van Heerden, trudging happily up the drive, also heard the shot, but he was so engrossed in calculating the exact number of strokes Jonathan Hazelstone would receive before being hanged that the sound of one shot coming from Els' direction hardly penetrated his consciousness. He had besides never solved a case before with such rapidity and he had just discovered fresh reasons for justifying his assumption that Jonathan Hazelstone was the murderer. He had recalled that Luitenant Verkramp's report on the Hazelstone family had included the information that Miss Hazelstone's brother had a criminal record involving embezzlement and fraud, and that the family had paid him to live in a remote part of Rhodesia.

It was only when the Kommandant heard a volley of shots ring out from the direction of the gate, followed by the screams of wounded men, that he began to suspect that Els was exceeding his instructions. He hurried on in an attempt to reach the gate before the situation got wholly out of hand, but the density of the firing had by that time reached such danger-ous proportions and its aim was so wild that he was forced to take cover in a hollow beside the drive. Lying there out of sight Kommandant van Heerden began to regret that he had given Els permission to shoot to kill. The agonized screams suggested that Els was having at the very least some moderate degree of success. As stray bullets ricocheted overhead, the Kommand-ant racked his brains to imagine who on earth was trying to shoot it out with his assistant.

In the blockhouse Konstabel Els was faced with the same problem. The five sinister figures who had crept round the corner of the road with revolvers in their hands had been so clearly bent on entering the Park illegally that he had shot the first two without hesitation. The answering spatter of bullets through the privet hedge had seemed fully to justify his action and, safe within the blockhouse, Konstabel Els broke open the ammunition packs and prepared for a long battle.

After ten minutes the plain-clothes men were reinforced by a dozen more and Els settled down to the business of defending the gateway with a relish that fully justified his early expecta-tions that the afternoon would prove interesting.

Luitenant Verkramp had been having his own troubles. In trying to put into effect Kommandant van Heerden's orders he had run into a host of problems. It had been difficult enough to marshal the entire complement of the Piemburg Police force, including the sick and the walking wounded, at the barracks on their rugby afternoon. But when that had been accomplished he was faced with the problem of explaining where they were going and why, and since Kommandant van Heerden had omitted to explain the purpose of the expedition he was left to draw his own conclusions. The only two certain facts he had gleaned from the Kommandant's garbled instructions were that an outbreak of rabies at Jacaranda Park had coincided with the appearance of bubonic plague, a combination of disease so lethal that it seemed positively insane to send six hundred healthy men anywhere near the place. Far better in his opinion to send them in the opposite direction. Nor could he understand why six armoured cars were necessary to help abate the outbreak unless it was that the Kommandant thought they might be useful to control the riot that would certainly break out when the news became public knowledge. The order to bring the searchlights added to the Luitenant's confusion and he could only suppose that they were to be used to search out any infected animals at night so that they could be hunted across country by the armoured cars.

The speech that Verkramp finally made to the assembled policemen was not one to inspire them with any confidence in their own futures and it was only after he had stamped out several incipient signs of mutiny that the column of lorries and the expedition finally got under way. As it was the entire force, headed by six armoured cars bedecked with signs announcing the epidemic of bubonic plague and the rabies outbreak, wound its way slowly along side roads and through the country town of Vlockfontein exciting a degree of attention exceedingly gratifying to the policemen crowding the lorries, but hardly achieving the purpose Kommandant van Heerden had hoped for.

The bubonic plague signs caused a degree of alarm in Vlockfontein only surpassed by the rabies billboards which immediately preceded the lorries containing the untrained German guard dogs, one of which in the excitement broke loose and leapt from the lorry to bite a small boy who had been pulling faces at it. In the panic that ensued the guard dog went berserk, bit a number of other people, several other dogs and finally disappeared up a back alley in pursuit of a cat. Within minutes the convoy had been halted at the request of the Mayor who had insisted that the dog be shot before it could infect anyone else. Verkramp's assurances that the animal was perfectly healthy convinced no one and there was a delay of some twenty-five minutes until it was finally shot by an irate householder on the other side of town.

By that time its desperate search for safety had driven it through back gardens and across lawns, and for almost all the time it had managed to stay out of sight so that its pursuers could only judge its probable whereabouts by the barks and snarls of the dogs belonging to the householders of Vlockfontein. It was therefore not altogether surprising that the notion gained ground that the guard dog had infected the entire canine population of the town, a belief that was confirmed beyond any shadow of doubt by the strange behaviour of the Vlockfontein dogs who, sharing in the general excitement, yelped and barked and strained at their leashes and in general behaved in just that unusual manner that the rabies notices had warned people to look out for.

As the police convoy moved out of Vlockfontein the afternoon quiet was punctuated by the sound of shots as the massacre of the entire dog population began, while the boy who had caused the whole business was testifying to the extremely painful nature of the anti-rabies injections by adding his screams to those of the dying dogs. The discovery later that evening of several dead rats, which had been killed by dogs desperately trying to prove their utility, only added to the general sense of impending disaster among the Vlockfonteiners. Dead rats, they had learnt from the bubonic plague notices, were the first sign that the Black Death had arrived. By nightfall Vlockfontein was a ghost town littered with the corpses of unburied dogs while the roads into Piemburg were jammed with cars whose drivers were exhibiting all the symptoms of mass hysteria. It was clear that the aim that Kommandant van Heerden had hoped to achieve by the detour was not being realized.

The same thing could hardly be said of Konstabel Els. His aim, always accurate, had by this time become positively unerring. The casualties among the plain-clothes men were mounting so rapidly that they fell back from their more advanced positions and huddled in the hedgerow trying to think of some way of circumventing the deadly privet bush which was obstructing them so successfully in the course of their duty. Finally while some of them crept into the thick bushes that covered the hillside directly facing the gateway and far enough away to ensure the deadly revolver couldn't reach them, others decided to try to outflank the murderous bush.

To Konstabel Els it was beginning to become fairly clear that this was no ordinary gun-battle, but something quite new in his experience as an upholder of law and order. He listened with quiet confidence to the hail of bullets that flattened themselves against the walls of the blockhouse. Every now and again he peered out of the gun port that overlooked the Park to make sure that no one had worked his way round behind him, but the Park was clear. He need not have worried. Sir Theophilus had prepared for such an eventuality by constructing an extremely deep ditch which ran between the blockhouses that fringed the Park. As with so many of the Governor's devices this defensive haha was unexpectedly treacherous and so well camouflaged that anyone approaching it from the road was quite unaware of its existence until he was already impaled on the terrible iron spikes that lined its concrete bottom. The plain-clothes men lost two of their number in the haha before they gave up the attempt to outflank the concealed blockhouse.

The screams that followed this attempt heartened Konstabel Els who imagined that he had scored two new hits in what he had no doubt were extremely painful portions of the human anatomy. He was a little surprised at his success as he had not fired for several minutes and certainly not in the direction from which the screams came. He decided to check his rear again, and peering out of the gun port that overlooked the Park was just in time to see Kommandant van Heerden leave his hollow and scuttle towards the house with an astonishing turn of speed for a man of his age and sedentary habits. Kommandant van Heerden had also heard the screams that came from the haha and had reached the frantic conclusion that the time had come to leave the security of his hollow at no matter what cost to life and limb and return to Jacaranda House to try to find out what had happened to the cretinous Luitenant Verkramp.

Whatever the Kommandant's reasons, and they were unknown to Konstabel Els, the sight of his only possible ally scuttling away and leaving him in the lurch convinced the desperate Els that the time had come to use the elephant gun if he were not to die alone and deserted at the hands of the desperados down the road. He could see movement in the bushes on the hillside opposite him and he decided to try a volley there. He mounted the great multi-barrelled rifle in the gun port, aimed at the bushes concealing the plain-clothes men and gently pulled the trigger.

The detonation that followed was of an intensity and had about it a seismic quality which came, when he could pick himself off the floor of the blockhouse where the recoil had thrown him, as a complete surprise to Konstabel Els. Not that he hadn't heard it before, but on that occasion he had been slightly distracted by the attentions of the Dobermann. This time he could appreciate the true qualities of the weapon.

With a white face and with his eardrums reverberating quite astonishingly, he peered through the gun port and observed his handiwork with a sense of satisfaction that he had never known before, not even on the day he had shot two kaffirs dead with the same bullet. That had been a triumph. This was a masterpiece.

The four barrels of the elephant gun erupting simultaneously had opened up a vista before him he would never have believed possible. The great wrought-iron gates of Jacaranda Park lay a twisted and reeking heap of partially molten and totally unidentifiable metal. The stone gateposts had disintegrated. The boars rampant sculpted in granite that had surmounted the posts would ramp no more, while the roadway itself bore witness to the heat of the gases propelling the shells in the shape of four lines of molten and gleaming tarmac which pointed down to what had once been the thick bushes that had obscured his view of his adversaries. Konstabel Els had no need now to complain that he couldn't see what he was shooting at.

The cover his enemies had used was quite gone. The hillside was bare, barren and scorched and it was doubtful if it would ever regain its original look. There was no such doubt about the five objects that remained littering the ground. Bare, barren and horribly mutilated, the five plain-clothes policemen who had sought cover from Els' fire in the bushes needed far more cover now than mere bushes could provide. Dying instantaneously, they had in some sense been luckier than their surviving comrades, some of whom, Els noted with satisfaction, were wandering about naked and blackened and clearly in a state of mental confusion. Els took advantage of their defenceless and shocked state to wing a couple with his revolver and wasn't very surprised that they seemed to take little notice of these new wounds which were obviously an anti-climax after the ravages of the elephant gun. The rest of the plain-clothes men who had been spared the effects of the volley, having dragged their naked and bemused colleagues out of the way of Els' gratuitous target practice, fell back down the hill and awaited the arrival of the main convoy before resuming their attack on the privet bush.

Standing in the turret of the leading armoured car, Luitenant Verkramp had heard the enormous explosion and had immediately jumped to the conclusion that the magazine at the police barracks had been blown up by saboteurs. Coming as it did in the wake of the chaos and panic that had marked the progress of the convoy through the countryside, it came as no great surprise. But looking down over the town he could see nothing to support this supposition. Piemburg lay in its quiet and peaceful hollow under a cloudless and azure sky. The only unusual feature he could spot through his binoculars was an unbroken chain of cars moving slowly along the main road from Vlockfontein.

'Funeral down there,' he muttered to himself, and, puzzled by the enormous length of the cortège, wondered what great man had died. It was only when he turned the next corner and saw the tiny group of naked and hysterical plain-clothes men that he realized for the first time that Kommandant van Heerden's frantic instructions had not after all been unwarranted. Whatever was going on at Jacaranda Park deserved the extraordinary show of force the convoy presented.

He held up his hand and the task force ground to a halt.

'What the hell has been going on?' he asked. There was no need to ask what had been coming off. Naked and blackened, the little group of plain-clothes cops presented a pitiful sight.

'Something has been shooting at us,' one of them managed to blurt out at last.

'What do you mean, something?' Verkramp snarled.

'It's a bush. A bush up by the gateway. Every time anyone goes anywhere near it, it shoots them.'

'A bush? Someone hiding behind a bush you mean. Why didn't you fire back at them?'

'What the fuck do you think we've been doing? And it's not anyone behind a bush. I'll take my oath on that. We've pumped hundreds of rounds into that fucking bush and it still goes on firing back. I tell you it's bloody well bewitched, that bush.'

Luitenant Verkramp looked up the road uncertainly. He certainly wasn't going to fall for any crap about bewitched bushes but on the other hand he could see that something pretty extraordinary had reduced the men to their pitiful condition. It was on the tip of his tongue to say, 'You're out of your minds,' but since they were out of just about everything else he thought it better not to. The question of morale was important and it had been at the back of his mind ever since they had left the station. One false move now and there would be a panic in the convoy. He decided to set the men an example.

'I want two volunteers,' he told Sergeant de Kock and while the Sergeant went off to dragoon two mentally retarded konstabels into volunteering, Luitenant Verkramp turned back to the plain-clothes men.

'Where is this bush?' he asked.

'Just inside the gateway. You can't miss it,' they told him, adding, 'And it won't miss you either.'

'We'll see about that,' muttered the Luitenant and clambering off the Saracen he began to prepare for the reconnaissance. Luitenant Verkramp had attended an anti-guerrilla course at Pretoria and was well versed in the art of camouflage. By the time he had finished the three men who began crawling up the ditch towards Konstabel Els' privet bush resembled nothing so much as three small bushes themselves. They were not so well trimmed, it was true, and certainly not so bullet-proof, but whatever else their camouflage served to conceal it was quite impossible to tell even at close range that here were three uniformed men of the South African Police.

Chapter 6

Kommandant van Heerden had just paused for breath under an oak tree in the middle of Jacaranda Park and was trying to pluck up courage to return to the house when Konstabel Els fired the elephant gun. In the wake of the detonation that followed the Kommandant had his mind made up for him. For one thing a vulture which had been waiting with evident prescience in the branches above him was startled into flight by the roar of the gun and flapped horribly up into the sky. For another the Kommandant reached the immediate conclusion that the company of Jonathan Hazelstone was infinitely less murderous than the holocaust Konstabel Els was generating at the main gate. He left the cover of the tree and raced ponderously towards the house, looking for all the world like the maddened pachyderm the elephant gun had been designed to incapacitate.

Behind him the silence of recent death hung sombrely over Jacaranda Park. Ahead he could just make out the tall elegant figure of Miss Hazelstone standing on the stoep. She was looking tentatively up into the cloudless evening sky. As the Kommandant plunged past her into the drawing-room he heard her say, 'I thought I heard a clap of thunder just now. I do believe it's going to rain.' It was good to be back in a world of sanity, the Kommandant thought, as he dropped limp and exhausted into an easy chair.

Presently Miss Hazelstone turned from her study of the sunset and entered the room. She carried with her an atmosphere of tranquillity and an acceptance of life as it came to her unique, or so it appeared to Kommandant van Heerden, among the people who were living through the events of the afternoon at Jacaranda Park. The same could hardly be said of Konstabel Els. Whatever life was coming his way he certainly wasn't accepting with anything faintly approaching tranquillity. The only consolation Kommandant van Heerden could find was the thought that by the sound of it Els had blown himself and half the neighbouring suburb up.

Miss Hazelstone moved pensively and with an air of gentle melancholy to her wing-backed armchair and seating herself in it turned her face with a look of the profoundest reverence towards a painting that hung above the fireplace.

'He was a good man,' she said at last in a low voice.

Kommandant van Heerden followed her gaze and studied the painting. It portrayed a man in long robes and carrying a lantern in his hand at the door of a house, and the Kommandant supposed it to be yet another portrait of Sir Theophilus, painted this time, to judge by the robe he was wearing, while the great man had been serving in India. It was entitled, 'The Light of the World', which even the Kommandant for all his admiration of the Viceroy, thought was going a bit far. Still he felt called upon to say something.

'I'm sure he was,' he said sympathetically, 'and a very great man too.'

Miss Hazelstone looked at the Kommandant gratefully and with new respect.

'I had no idea,' she murmured.

'Oh, I practically worship the man,' the Kommandant continued, adding as an afterthought, 'He knew how to handle the Zulus all right,' and was surprised when Miss Hazelstone began to sob into her handkerchief. Taking her tears to be a further indication of her devotion to her grandfather, van Heerden ploughed on.

'I only wish there were more of his sort about today,' he said, and was gratified to notice Miss Hazelstone once more gazing at him gratefully over her handkerchief. 'There wouldn't be half the trouble there is in the world today if he were back.' He was about to say, 'He'd hang them by the dozen,' but he realized that hanging wasn't a tactful subject to bring up considering the likely fate of Miss Hazelstone's own brother, so he contented himself by adding, 'He'd soon teach them a thing or two.'

Miss Hazelstone agreed. 'He would, oh, he would. I'm so glad, Kommandant, that you of all people see things his way.'

Kommandant van Heerden couldn't quite see the need for her emphasis. It seemed only natural that a police officer would want to follow Sir Theophilus' methods of dealing with criminals. After all, Judge Hazelstone hadn't sucked his known preference for hanging and flogging out of his thumb. Everyone knew that old Sir Theophilus had made it his duty to see that young William early developed a taste for corporal punishment by inflicting it on the boy from the day he was born. The thought of duty recalled the Kommandant to his own distasteful task, and he realized that this was as good a moment as any to break it to her that he knew that Fivepence had been murdered not by her, but by her brother Jonathan. He rose from his chair and relapsed into the formal jargon of his office.

'I have reason to believe . . .' he began, but Miss Hazelstone wouldn't let him continue. She rose from her chair and gazed up at him enraptured, a reaction van Heerden had hardly expected and certainly couldn't admire. After all, the fellow was her own brother, and only an hour before she had been willing to confess to the murder herself just to shield him.

He began again, 'I have reason to believe—'

'Oh, so have I. So have I. Haven't we all?' and this time Miss Hazelstone gathered the Kommandant's large hands into her own tiny ones and gazed into his eyes. 'I knew it Kommandant, I knew it all the time.'

Kommandant van Heerden needed no telling. Of course she had known about it all the time, otherwise she wouldn't have been covering up for the brute. To hell, he thought, with formalities. 'I suppose he's still upstairs in the bedroom,' he said.

The expression on Miss Hazelstone's face suggested a certain wonder which the Kommandant assumed must be due to her sudden recognition of his talents as a detective.

'Upstairs?' she gasped.

'Yes. In the bedroom with the pink floral bedspread.'

Miss Hazelstone's astonishment was obvious. 'In the pink bedroom?' she stammered, backing away from him.

'He's not a very pleasant sight, I'm afraid,' the Kommandant went on. 'He's as drunk as a lord.'

Miss Hazelstone was verging on hysteria. 'As the Lord?' she managed to gasp at last.

'Soused,' continued the Kommandant. 'Blind drunk and covered with blood. Guilt's written all over him.'

Miss Hazelstone could stand no more. She made for the door but Kommandant van Heerden was there before her.

'Oh no you don't. You're not going upstairs to warn him,' he said. 'He's got to take what's coming to him.' Kommandant van Heerden had private doubts if the fellow was still upstairs. Even a blind drunk must have been jerked awake by that explosion. Still the man was a maniac and one never knew with lunatics. Their actions were likely to be unpredictable. There were symptoms too, he now noticed, of irrationality and unpredictability in Miss Hazelstone's behaviour, and signs that she could behave in a manner neither sweet nor gentle.

'Come, come, my dear Miss Hazelstone. There are some things we must learn to accept,' he said reassuringly, and as he said it, Miss Hazelstone knew only one thing for certain, that nothing on God's earth would persuade her to come anywhere within striking distance of this fat perspiring policeman who thought that Jesus Christ was lying dead drunk and covered with blood upstairs in the pink floral bedroom. There might be, she conceded generously, certain irrational tendencies in her own psyche, but they were as nothing to the inescapable symptoms of insanity that the Kommandant was displaying. She sprang back from him white and gibbering and, seizing an ornamental scimitar that hung on the wall, held it above her old grey head in her two hands.

Kommandant van Heerden was taken totally by surprise. One moment he had been confronted by a dear old lady who held both his hands in hers and gazed tenderly up into his face, and the next she had turned herself into a dancing dervish evidently intent on slicing him in half with a terrible knife.

'Now, now,' he said, unable to adjust his pattern of speech to his new and terrifying predicament. A moment later it was clear that Miss Hazelstone had taken his 'Now, now' as an indication that he wanted his death to be immediate. She was moving crablike towards him.

Miss Hazelstone was, in fact, trying to reach the door into the hall. 'Stand aside,' she ordered, and the Kommandant, anxious to avoid causing her the slightest pretext for bifurcating him with the scimitar, leapt to one side, colliding as he went with a large Chinese pot which toppled from its stand and crashed to the floor. For a second time the expression on Miss Hazelstone's face demonstrated that capacity for rapid change the Kommandant had already noticed. Now she was clearly mad with rage.

'The Ming! The Ming!' she yelled and brought the scimitar crashing down from above her head. But Kommandant van Heerden was no longer there. He was charging across the room leaving in his wake the shattered art treasures of several millennia of Chinese history.

As he plunged across the verandah he could still hear Miss Hazelstone screaming to her brother.

'The Ming! The Ming!' she yelled and judging the Ming to be some indescribably powerful weapon hanging ready to hand on the wall of the gallery, the Kommandant raced across Jacaranda Park yet again, but this time in the direction of the sound of renewed gunfire at the gate, a sound he now welcomed as indications of normal healthy violence. And as he ran, he thanked his lucky stars that dusk was already turning into night, to obscure the path of his flight.

The first indication that Konstabel Els, still smirking at the effects of his marksmanship, had that several new factors had entered the little patch of Western civilization he was defending so manfully, came as dusk began to fall over the Park's contorted gates. He was just having a swig of Old Rhino Skin brandy to keep out the night chill, when he heard a strange scratching noise outside. He thought at first that a porcupine was scratching itself against the armoured door of the blockhouse, but when he opened it there was nothing outside, while the sounds were getting closer. They seemed to emanate from a hedge down the road, and he had just begun to think that they could only be explained by supposing that a rhinoceros suffering from impetigo was seeking relief from its irritation by rolling in a thorn tree when he saw three remarkably agile agglomerations of vegetable matter scuttle across the road. Evidently the next attack was about to begin.

Konstabel Els sat back and considered the position. He had repelled one attack with his revolver. He had decimated a second with the elephant gun. It was time, he felt, to go over to the offensive. In the deepening dusk Konstabel Els left the shelter of the blockhouse, and clutching his revolver crawled silently towards his attackers, whose polyphonic progress drowned any slight noises he might make.

By the time Luitenant Verkramp and his two volunteers had crawled three-quarters of a mile to the top of the hill, Verkramp had begun to wish that he had come up in the armoured car after all, and to doubt the value of the whole exercise. It was already so dark that while he might not be able to miss the bush that was giving so much trouble, he probably wouldn't be able to see it. His hands were scratched and torn, and he had come within spitting distance of two puff-adders and a cobra, which had been an undoubted tribute to his skill in camouflage, but one that he could well have done without. He had never realized before what a profusion of wild life there was in the hedgerows of Piemburg.

The spider that had bitten him on the nose as he tried to disentangle himself from its web had been of a size and malevolence he would never have believed possible if he hadn't seen it with his own one eye, the other being obscured by the spider's three feet which it had fastened there to give it a good foothold while it injected 50 cc of toxic venom into his left nostril. He had almost turned back at that point because the poison spread so fast and with such evident effect that even after the giant spider had been good enough to let go of his cornea he still couldn't see out of it. That side of his face was pulsating alarmingly and his sinus appeared to be filled with some caustic liquid. Realizing that the expedition must proceed with some urgency before his breathing apparatus seized up for good, Luitenant Verkramp and his two men crashed on through the infested undergrowth towards their quarry.

Konstabel Els, crawling with less haste and more anonymity, had, in the meantime, discovered Sir Theophilus' terrible haha and had observed with considerable satisfaction its effects on its latest victims. Els lay back in the grass and debated some further means of satisfying the clearly insatiable appetite of this offspring of Sir Theophilus' anxiety. The sounds reaching him from the hedgerow seemed to indicate that his enemies were already suffering some trepidation. To the sounds of breaking twigs that had accompanied their progress were now added the occasional whimper and what appeared to be chronic catarrh. Konstabel Els waited no longer. Crawling soundlessly he avoided the murderous haha and stationed himself in the grass beside the road.

To Luitenant Verkramp crawling doggedly in the hedge nothing seemed ominous or unusual. His nose was giving him trouble, it was true, and the spider's venom had spread alarmingly so that now his eyes were playing him up and now his ears, but if his interior world was full of flashing lights and strange drumming noises, outside all seemed peaceful and quiet. The night was dark, but overhead the stars shone and the lights of Piemburg in the valley below gave to the sky an orange glow. The lights of Jacaranda House twinkled invitingly across the Park. Crickets sang and the distant murmur of traffic wafted gently to him from the Vlockfontein road. Nothing in the world prepared Luitenant Verkramp for the horror that was to strike him so suddenly.

Not that anything struck him physically. It was worse than that. There was an almost spiritual quality about the scream that exploded in his damaged ear, and about the appallingly crooked and malignant shape that suddenly loomed above him. He couldn't see what it was. He knew only its disgusting breath and with it a banshee yell, malignant beyond belief, and coming, he had no doubt at all, from the very depths of hell. Any doubts Luitenant Verkramp had entertained about the story of the bewitched bush disappeared in a trice, and in another trice Verkramp, hurling himself sideways, dropped into the very pit of hell he suspected the scream came from.

Lying impaled on the iron spikes at the bottom of the haha, his screams echoing across the Park, Luitenant Verkramp, half dead with fear and pain, stared upwards and knew himself eternally damned. In his delirium he saw a face peer down into his grave, a face diabolically satisfied: the face was the face of Els. Luitenant Verkramp passed out.

His two companions had by that time reached the foot of the hill. They had fled, leaving behind them not only the Luitenant but a trail of leaves, branches, helmets, and all the impedimenta of their profession. They need not have hurried. The news of the encounter had preceded them. Konstabel Els' yell, terrible even *diminuendo*, had wafted like some fearful confirmation of doom to the cars that still jammed the Vlock-fontein road.

The policemen lounging by the lorries and armoured cars grew rigid at its import. Men who had been erecting some of the rabies and bubonic plague billboards stopped work and stared into the darkness trying to make out what new horror had sprung from the deadly bush. Even the guard dogs cringed at the sound. And in the middle of Jacaranda Park, Kommandant van Heerden, in terror of his life from the Ming, halted involuntarily at the sound. No one who heard that scream was ever likely to forget it.

If Konstabel Els had been astounded at the effect of the elephant gun, he was even more astounded at the results of his experiment in psychological warfare. His imitation of the awakened dead had borne fruit among his vegetable enemies to an extent he wouldn't have believed possible, but as he stood listening to the ebbing screams from the ditch, a momentary shadow of doubt crossed his mind. There was something about those screams, something about their tone that was vaguely familiar. He went over to the haha and peered down, and was just able to make out through the foliage that covered it, a face, and again there was something familiar about the face. If it hadn't been for the bulbous nose and the puffed-up cheeks, he might have thought it was Luitenant Verkramp down there. He grinned to himself at the thought of the Luitenant lying on those spikes. Serve the bastard right if he had been down there for keeping him hanging around all night when he should have been relieved hours ago, he thought as he entered the blockhouse.

He took another swig of brandy and was just putting the bottle back in his hip pocket when he heard a sound that sent him hurrying to the gun port. Something was coming up the road. Some vehicle, and a touch of familiarity caught his ear. It sounded for all the world like a Saracen armoured car. 'About bloody time too,' Els thought, as the headlights swung round the corner and lit up for a second the bodies lying on the hillside opposite. A moment later a fresh light was thrown on the scene. A searchlight probed through the night and turned the privet hedge into one brilliant spot in an otherwise dark world.

'All right, you bastards, enough's as good as a fucking feast,' Els yelled into the night, and before he could say more the privet hedge began to disintegrate around his shelter. As the bullets tore into the blockhouse walls and the gun port was aflame with tracer bullets, Els knew that he was about to die. This wasn't the relief he expected. In one last desperate move to avert tragedy, Konstabel Els aimed the elephant gun at the armoured car. He held his fire until the Saracen was only ten yards from the gate and then pulled the trigger. Again and again he fired, and with a mixture of awe and satisfaction saw, silhouetted against the searchlight, the great armoured vehicle grind to a halt and begin to disintegrate. Its guns were silenced, its tyres were shreds of rubber and its occupants trickled gently but persistently through a hundred holes drilled in its sides. Only one man was even capable of trying to leave the thing and as he emerged convulsively from the turret-top, Els saw with appalling clarity the familiar uniform and cap of the South African Police. The body slumped back inside the turret, and Els, understanding dimly for the first time the enormity of his offences, knew himself but a stone's throw from the gallows. He fired his last shot. The searchlight exploded into darkness and Els, with desperate energy, gathered up all evidence of his recent occupation and stumbled out of the blockhouse and dragging his awful accomplice, sneaked off across the Park.

Behind him the armoured colander burst into flames and as Els hurled himself towards Jacaranda House the night sky was bright with the flames and the delicate tracery of exploding ammunition.

Chapter 7

In Jacaranda House, Jonathan Hazelstone was singing in his bath. He was wearing a rubber bathing-cap to protect his delicate ears from the water, and partly because of the cap and partly because he was rather deaf, he was singing rather more loudly than he imagined. As a result he heard nothing of the noises of battle that accompanied his rendering of *Onward Christian Soldiers*. Around him the pink water eddied and swirled, assuming strange intricate patterns as the percussion of the elephant gun reached it. But Jonathan Hazelstone had no time for observing such trifles. His mind was preoccupied with his own shortcomings. Shame and a guilty pride at his own achievement mingled in his thoughts and over them both there hung the awful remembrance of things past.

He tried to put the dreadful business out of his mind but it came back insistently. Still, in spite of his remorse he had to smile to himself a little. After all, he thought, there couldn't be many men still alive who could say that they had done what he had and got away with it. Not that he was given to boastfulness, and he certainly was not going to go about broadcasting his deed. On the other hand he had been provoked quite horribly, and in the event he felt that his action had to some extent been excusable. 'Old Rhino Skin', he thought, and shuddered, and was about to remind himself that he must tell the cook never to use the beastly stuff for cooking again, when he remembered that there was in fact no cook to tell.

He looked sadly at the pink ring on the sides of the bath and then hurriedly got out and emptied the water. He sluiced the bath clean, refilled it and added bath salts and then lay down in the hot water to consider what to do next to erase the effects of the afternoon's events. He was faced, he knew, with a terrible problem. True, his sister had promised to make a full confession to the police and that was all right as far as it went, but it wasn't going to help him to escape scot-free. There were bound to be repercussions, and the whole episode was hardly calculated to help his career. It was a ghastly business altogether. Not that he had a great fund of sympathy for that damned cook. If it hadn't been for him, none of this would have happened. Besides, there were some things that Jonathan Hazelstone could never forgive. Perversion was one of them.

Kommandant van Heerden would have shared all these sentiments had he known about them, but by this time his faculties were all focused on one simple realization, that his career as a police officer and probably as a free man had almost certainly been ended by his handling of the Hazelstone Case. The explosion that heralded the end of the armoured car had made that clear as daylight to him. Disgraced, cashiered and convicted of being an accessory before, during, and after the murder of the policeman who had undoubtedly fallen before Els' tornado of gunshot at the main gate, he would share the rest of his life in prison with men who bore him debts of ingratitude no amount of suffering would ever repay. The day he entered Piemburg Prison might not be his last, but it would undoubtedly be his worst. Too many men had signed confessions after being tortured by Konstabel Els in the cells of Piemburg Police Station for him to relish the prospect of their company in prison.

After a brief spell of sobbing Kommandant van Heerden tried to think of some way out of the mess Els had got him into. Only one thing could save him now and that was the successful capture of the murderer of Miss Hazelstone's Zulu cook. Not that he placed much hope in that achievement and it wouldn't help to explain the bloodbath Els had initiated. No, Els would have to stand trial for wholesale murder and there was just a chance that he could be persuaded to plead insanity. Come to think of it, there was no need for the bastard to have to plead. He was obviously insane. The facts spoke for themselves.

Urged forward by this faint hope and certainly not by the exploding ammunition in the once-mobile incinerator, Kommandant van Heerden reached the Park gates. Clambering over the pile of contorted metal the Kommandant stood and looked about him. A pall of black smoke darkened the night sky. It poured from the open turret of the Saracen and issued from the holes in its sides. Even the distracted Kommandant was aware of its smell. It smelt like nothing on earth. Taking a deep breath of the disgusting stuff, Kommandant van Heerden bellowed into the night.

'Konstabel Els,' he yelled, 'Konstabel Els, where in fuck's name are you?' and recognized the stupidity of the question as soon as it was uttered. Els was hardly likely to come forward at this juncture. More likely he would consign his commanding officer to eternity with the same relish he had employed on his other comrades. After a moment's silence punctuated only by the bang and whizz of bullets ricocheting round the interior of the Saracen the Kommandant shouted again.

'This is your commanding officer, I order you to cease fire.'

Down the road the sound of Kommandant van Heerden's strange order puzzled the men in the convoy and brought a warm glow of admiration to their hearts. The Kommandant was up there by the gates and had evidently captured the maniac who had been slaughtering them. They were amazed at this development, for the Kommandant was not known for his physical courage. Slowly but surely in little groups they made their way hesitantly up the road towards him.

Konstabel Els was making off in quite a different direction and racking his brains for a way of getting out of the mess he was in. First of all he had to conceal the elephant gun and then he would have to concoct an alibi. Considering the size of the gun he wasn't sure which was going to be the more impossible task, and he was just debating whether or not to put it back on the stoep, where he had found it, when he ran across another privet hedge. His recent experience of privet hedges had taught him that they were ideal places for hiding things in. In this case the privet hedge hid a swimming-bath. Els peered round the hedge, and after reassuring himself that the swimming-bath was what it purported to be and not yet another of Sir Theophilus' little traps, he stole into the enclosure and across to a small and elegant pavilion which stood at one end. He groped round in the dark for a moment and then struck a match. By its light he saw that the pavilion was a changing-room with pegs along its wall for hanging clothes. To his horror he saw that one of the pegs was being put to good use. A suit of dark clothes was hanging there.

Els doused the match and peered out at the pool. The owner of the black suit must be out there watching him, he thought. But the surface of the swimming-bath was unbroken by any-thing more sinister than reflections of the stars and a new moon which had just begun to rise. The edges of the pool held no unaccountable shadows and Els knew himself to be alone with a suit of dark clothes, an elephant gun, and the need to concoct an alibi.

'Privet hedges seem to bring me luck,' he said to himself and promised himself to plant one in his front garden if he ever got out of this scrape alive.

He lit another match and examined the clothes. He thought at first that he might be able to use them as a disguise but the trousers were much too large for him, while the jacket which he tried on would have done as a winter coat. He was a little puzzled by the black waistcoat with no buttons on it until he spotted the attached dog-collar. Konstabel Els gave up all thought of using the clothes as a disguise. He had too much respect for religion to profane the garments with his own person. Instead he used them to wipe the elephant gun clean of his fingerprints. An expert in removing vital evidence, by the time he had finished there was nothing to connect him with the gun.

Twenty minutes later Konstabel Els stepped jauntily out of the pavilion and sauntered cheerfully across the Park towards Piemburg. Behind him he had left everything that connected him with the massacre at the main gate. The elephant gun was concealed under the clergyman's clothes. In a back pocket of the trousers was his revolver while the jacket pockets bulged with the empty cartridge cases he had carefully collected from the floor of the blockhouse. Each and every article had been meticulously polished. No fingerprint expert could prove that they had been used by Konstabel Els. Finally, and with a touch of whimsy, he had put the half-bottle of Old Rhino Skin into the inside breast pocket of the jacket. It had been quite empty and he had no use for empty bottles anyway.

It was while he was shoving the bottle into the pocket that he made another useful discovery. The pocket contained a wallet and comb. Konstabel Els searched the other pockets and found a handkerchief and several other objects.

'Nothing like doing a job properly,' he thought, pocketing the things and set off for the blockhouse for one final visit. By the time he reached it his confidence had returned. Policemen were wandering around looking at the burning Saracen and no one took any notice of the Konstabel who nipped for a second behind the privet hedge before strolling off down the road in the direction of Piemburg. On the way he stopped to read a notice which was being hammered into place by a group of policemen.

An hour later, foaming at the mouth and exhibiting all the symptoms of rabies, Konstabel Els presented himself at the casualty department of Piemburg Hospital. Before they could get him into bed he had bitten two nurses and a doctor.

At the entrance to Jacaranda Park Kommandant van Heerden was exhibiting similar symptoms to the men who gathered round him under the pall of smoke. The disappearance of Luitenant Verkramp particularly incensed him.

'Missing? What do you mean missing?' he yelled at Sergeant de Kock.

'He came up here to reconnoitre, sir,' answered the Sergeant.

'Any chance he came in that?' asked the Kommandant more hopefully, looking at the burnt-out Saracen.

'No sir. In disguise.'

'In what?' yelled the Kommandant.

'He was disguised as a bush, sir.'

Kommandant van Heerden couldn't believe his ears. 'Disguised as a bush? What sort of bush?'

'Difficult to say, sir. Not a very big one.'

Kommandant van Heerden turned to the men. 'Any of you men seen a small bush round here?'

A hush fell over the policemen. They had all seen a small bush round there.

'There's one just behind you, sir,' a konstabel said.

The Kommandant turned and looked at what remained of the privet hedge. It was obviously nothing like Verkramp disguised or not. 'Not that you fool,' he snarled. 'A walking fucking bush.'

'I don't know about that bush fucking, sir,' said the konstabel. 'And I daresay it can't walk, but I do know the bloody thing can shoot straight.'

'What the hell are you talking about?' snapped the Kommandant as a nervous giggle ran round the crowd.

Sergeant de Kock enlightened him. 'The fellow who knocked out the Saracen took cover behind that bush.'

A moment later Kommandant van Heerden was peering through the doorway into the blockhouse. The interior was still filled with the fumes of burnt powder, but even so Kommandant van Heerden's olfactory nerve could detect a pervasive familiar smell. The blockhouse stank of Old Rhino Skin. On the floor there was further evidence. A wallet, a comb, and a handkerchief lay in the middle of the bunker. The Kommandant picked them up and gingerly held them to his nose. They were practically soaked in brandy. He opened the wallet and saw stamped in gold letters a name he was also familiar with, 'Jonathan Hazelstone'.

Kommandant van Heerden wasted no more time. Leaving the bunker, he gave his orders. The Park was to be surrounded. Road blocks were to be set up on all roads in the vicinity. Searchlights were to illuminate the entire area of the Park. 'We're going in to get him,' he said finally. 'Bring up the other Saracens, and the guard dogs.'

Ten minutes later the five remaining Saracens, a hundred men armed with Sten guns and the sixty-nine tracker dogs were assembled at the Park gates ready for the assault on

Jacaranda House. Kommandant van Heerden climbed aboard a Saracen and addressed the men from its turret.

'Before we start,' he said, 'I think I had better warn you that the man we are after is a dangerous criminal.' He paused. The policeman who had seen the burnt-out armoured car and the corpses littering the hillside needed no telling. 'The house is practically a fortress,' continued the Kommandant, 'and he has at his disposal an armoury of lethal weapons. At the first sign of resistance you have my permission to open fire. Are there any questions?'

'What about the Black Death?' Sergeant de Kock asked anxiously.

'The black's death? Oh yes, caused by gunshot wounds,' replied the Kommandant enigmatically, and disappearing inside the turret slammed the lid. The convoy moved off cautiously down the drive to Jacaranda House.

Chapter 8

Jonathan Hazelstone's musings on his next sermon had taken his mind off the tragic death of Fivepence. He had just decided on the title, 'The Rhinos of Wrath are Whiter than the Horses of Destruction', for a peroration on the evils of alcohol and was drying himself after his bath when he remembered he had left his clothes in the bathing-pavilion. Still groggy from the effects of the brandy he wandered absent-mindedly downstairs wearing the bathing-cap and wrapped only in a voluminous towel. On the steps of the front door he stopped and took a deep breath of cool night air. Headlights were moving slowly down the drive.

'Visitors,' he thought to himself. 'Mustn't be caught like this,' and wrapping the towel more firmly round himself trotted across the drive and disappeared behind the privet hedge as Kommandant van Heerden's convoy approached the house. He went into the bathing-pavilion and a moment later came out again feeling worse than ever. The smell of Old Rhino Skin in the pavilion sent a wave of nausea over him. Standing on the edge of the swimming-pool, he uttered a silent prayer to the Almighty to help him by no matter what drastic methods to avoid the repetition of his wickedness, and a moment later the Bishop of Barotseland plunged through the moon's reflected image into the cool water of the bath. He swam the length of the pool underwater, surfaced momentarily and then swam back and forth along the bottom of the swimming-pool and as he swam it seemed to the Bishop that the Lord was calling to him. Faintly, very faintly it was true, but with a distinctness he had never before experienced he heard through his bathing-cap the voice of the Lord, 'Jonathan Hazelstone, I know you are there. I don't want any resistance. Give yourself up quietly,' and six feet beneath the surface of the water the Right Reverend Jonathan Hazelstone knew for the first time that he was truly destined for great things. The call he had waited so long to hear had come at last. He turned on his back and gave himself up quietly and without any resistance to meditation under the night sky. He knew now that he had been forgiven his lapse of the afternoon.

'O Lord, thou knowest I was provoked,' he murmured, as he floated on the still surface of the pool, and a sense of peace, sweet forgiving peace, descended on him as he prayed.

Peace had not descended on the rest of Jacaranda House. Ringed by one hundred armed men who crouched in the shadows of the garden fingering the triggers of their Sten guns, by sixty-nine German guard dogs snarling and slobbering for a kill and by five Saracen armoured cars which had been driven heedlessly over flowerbeds and lawns to take up their positions, Jacaranda House stood silent and unanswering.

Kommandant van Heerden decided to have one more go at getting the brute out without trouble. The very last thing he wanted was another gun-battle. He peered out of the turret and raised the loudhailer again.

'Jonathan Hazelstone, I am giving you one last chance,' his voice amplified a hundred times boomed into the night. 'If you come out quietly you will be safe. If not, I am coming in to get you.'

The Bishop of Barotseland, lying on his back meditating quietly and staring up into the night sky where a great bird drifted slowly above him, heard the words more distinctly than before. God manifested Himself in many mysterious ways, he knew, but vultures he had never thought of. Now the Almighty had spoken again and more clearly, much more clearly.

The first part of the message had been quite unequivocal. 'Come out quietly and you will be saved,' but the second part had been much less easy to interpret; 'If not, I am coming in to get you.' Jonathan Hazelstone swam to the edge of the pool and climbed out quietly as instructed. Then pausing to look back at the water to see if the Lord had even begun to get in to fetch him out, he noticed the vulture turn and flap horribly away over the blue gums.

'He chased me down the nights and down the days,' he murmured incorrectly, remembering the Hound of Heaven, and he knew that he had been witness that night not only to the voice of God but to his shape as well. If God could come as Doves and Hounds why not as a Vulture? And murmuring another poem his grandfather had taught him as a child, one which he had never understood until these last few minutes, he began to dry himself.

'The harbingers are come. See, see their mark;
Black is their colour, and behold my head.
But must they have my brain? Must they dispark
Those sparkling notions, which therein were bred?
Must dulnesse turn me to a clod?
Yet have they left me. Thou art still my God.'

It was called 'The Forerunners', by George Herbert, and while old Sir Theophilus had revised it by changing white to black in the second line, and had assumed that 'sparkling notions' referred to his murderous haha, the Bishop now saw that it applied perfectly to the vulture and was grateful to note that the harbinger had indeed left him. With a silent prayer

68

to the Lord to assume a less ominous form in future, the Bishop of Barotseland entered the pavilion to fetch his clothes.

Fifty yards away Kommandant van Heerden was making up his mind to give the order to storm the house, when Miss Hazelstone appeared in the main entrance.

'There's no need to shout,' she said demurely. 'There is a bell, you know.'

The Kommandant wasn't in the mood for lessons in etiquette. 'I've come for your brother,' he shouted.

'I'm afraid he's busy just at the moment. You'll have to wait. You can come in if you wipe your boots and promise not to knock anything over.'

The Kommandant could imagine just how busy Jonathan Hazelstone must be and he had every intention of knocking things over if he had to come into the house. He glanced uneasily at the windows on the upper floor.

'What is he so busy about?' as though there was any need to ask.

Miss Hazelstone didn't like the Kommandant's tone of voice. 'He's about his ablutions,' she snapped, and was about to turn away when she remembered the breakage. 'About that Ming...' she began. With a slam of the turret-top Kommandant van Heerden disappeared. From inside the armoured car came the muffled sound of his voice.

'Don't talk to me about the Ming,' he yelled. 'You go in and tell your brother to unblute the fucking thing and come out with his hands up.'

Miss Hazelstone had stood as much as she could take. 'How dare you speak to me like that,' she snarled. 'I'll do no such thing,' and turned to re-enter the house.

'Then I will,' screamed the Kommandant, and ordered his men into the house. 'Get the bastard,' he yelled, and waited for the roar of the deadly Ming. He waited in vain. The men and dogs pouring over Miss Hazelstone's prostrate body encountered no further resistance. The Dobermann, knowing now what lack of foresight it had shown by disputing its patch of lawn with Konstabel Els, lay on the drawing-room floor pretending to be a rug. Around it policemen and dogs charged, searching the house for their quarry. There was no human obstacle to the policemen who dashed upstairs and along corridors into bedrooms in search of the killer. Disconsolate, they reported to the Kommandant who was still cowering in the Saracen.

'He's not there,' they yelled.

'Are you absolutely certain?' he asked before opening the lid. They were, and the Kommandant clambered out. He knew there was only one thing left to do, one slim chance of capturing Jonathan Hazelstone that night.

'The dogs,' he ordered frantically. 'Bring the tracker dogs,' and dashed despairingly into the house and up the stairs followed by the pack of breathless and eager Alsatians. The pink floral bedroom was just as the Kommandant had seen it last – with the notable exception of the naked man. Grabbing the bedspread from the bed he held it out to the dogs to smell. As the dogs sniffed the cloth and passed off down the corridor they read its message loud and clear. The thing reeked of Old Rhino Skin brandy. Ignoring the odour of bath salts on the stairs the dogs bounded down into the hall and out on to the drive. A moment later they had picked up the trail Konstabel Els had left and were off across the Park towards the blockhouse.

Behind them in the privacy of the pavilion the Bishop of Barotseland was having some difficulty in getting dressed. For one thing his clothes seemed to have wrapped themselves round some heavy metallic object and when at last the Bishop had disentangled the thing and had carried it out into the moonlight to see what it was, he was so distressed by its associations with the murder of Fivepence that in his agitation he dropped it and the great gun splashed into the pool and disappeared. Consoling himself with the thought that it could do no more harm down there, he went back into the pavilion to put on the rest of his clothes.

He had some more difficulty with his trousers. There was something large and heavy in his back pocket, and it took him some time to get it out.

'Ah well,' he said to himself as he struggled to pull the

revolver loose, 'these things are sent to try us,' and was trying to imagine how on earth the weapon could have found its way into his trouser pocket when he became aware that he was no longer alone.

With the departure of the dogs in pursuit of Konstabel Els, Kommandant van Heerden found himself with time on his hands. His mood of melancholy had returned with the disappearance of the murderer and, not wishing to share what promised to be his lonely vigil with an irate and unpredictable Miss Hazelstone, he left his hostess still recovering from the novel experience of being used as a doormat by two hundred hobnailed boots and two hundred and seventy-six paws and wandered miserably out into the garden. As the Kommandant sauntered about the lawn viciously kicking the pieces of Sir Theophilus' shattered bust, he came near to cursing the great hero of his yesteryears for having spawned the line of progeny that had brought his career crashing to the ground as effectively as they had the bust of Sir Theophilus himself.

He was just considering what the Viceroy would have done had he found himself in a similar situation when his attention was drawn to one of the blue gums. An odd sort of knocking and ripping sound was coming from its trunk. Kommandant van Heerden peered into the gloom. Something strange was moving there. By bending down so that the creature was silhouetted against the orange glow that coloured the night sky, the Kommandant could make out its shape. In imitation of a woodpecker, the great vulture hung to the trunk of the tree and contented itself with scraps of the late Zulu cook.

For the second time that night the vulture brought a message to a watcher in the garden of Jacaranda House, but if the Bishop of Barotseland had mistaken the bird for the shape of God, Kommandant van Heerden made no such error. What he had seen of the scavenger's hooked profile reminded him too closely for comfort of several prisoners in Piemburg gaol who would welcome his arrival there with just such relish. The Kommandant shuddered and turned hastily away from this vision of his future. And as he turned away he heard a loud splash coming from the back of the house. Loud splashes played no part in the régime he had imposed on Jacaranda Park. There was something, he felt, positively sinister in loud splashes at this time of night, a view which was evidently shared by the vulture which flapped away from its hors d'oeuvres to see if its next course was going to be something drowned.

Kommandant van Heerden followed it less optimistically and found himself beside a privet hedge on the other side of which he could hear something going about some grim business. Whatever was busy behind the hedge was reciting to itself as it worked, work which necessitated the dropping of large heavy objects, weighted no doubt, into deep water. The Kommandant couldn't hear much of the song because from behind him across the Park there came the sound of running feet and a slobbering and snuffling noise which gained intensity from moment to moment. He glanced over his shoulder and saw racing towards him the pack of tracker dogs and dozens of policemen. A few seconds later they were on him and, pinned to the hedge, he watched the tide of animals and men wash past him and round the corner. He sighed with relief and followed in their wake.

The Bishop of Barotseland was less fortunate. His poor hearing and the fact that he was still wearing the bathing-cap prevented him hearing the approach of the dogs. One moment he was standing by the pool looking down at the revolver, and reciting from his grandfather's favourite poem, and the next he was engulfed in dogs. Muzzles raised, fangs bared, with slobbering jowls they came, and the Bishop, overwhelmed by their rush, fell backwards into the swimming-pool, still clutching the revolver. As he went he involuntarily pulled the trigger and a single shot disappeared harmlessly into the night sky. The Bishop surfaced in the middle of the pool and looked around him. The sight was not one to reassure him. The pool was filled with struggling Alsatians and, as he watched, others launched themselves from the edges and joined the hordes already in the water. A particularly ferocious hound just in front of him opened its mouth and the Bishop had just enough time to take a gulp of air and disappear before the dog bit him. He swam the length underwater and surfaced. A dog snapped at him and he swam back. Above him paws thrashed the water into foam as the Bishop pondered this new manifestation of the Almighty. Evidently he had not got out of the pool quietly enough the first time, and God had come in to get him in the shape of dozens of dogs and he was just wondering how this collective appearance could be reconciled with the notion that God was one and indivisible when his arm was seized and he was dragged out of the pool by several policemen. Thankful for this deliverance and too bewildered to wonder how policemen fitted into this spectacle of divinity he stared back at the water. Hardly a foot of the surface of the pool was free of dogs.

The next moment his wrists were handcuffed behind him and he was swung round.

'That is the swine all right. Take him into the house,' said the Kommandant, and the Bishop was frogmarched by several konstabels across the drive and into the family home. Naked and wet, Jonathan Hazelstone stood among the potted plants in the great hall still wearing the bathing-cap. From a great distance and far beyond the frontiers of sanity he heard the Kommandant whisper, 'Jonathan Hazelstone, I charge you with the wilful murder of one Zulu cook and God knows how many policemen, the wilful destruction of Government property and being in unlawful possession of weapons calculated to harm life and limb.'

He was too dazed and too deaf to hear the Kommandant tell Sergeant de Kock to take him down into the cellar and keep him safely under guard until morning.

'Wouldn't he be safer down at the police station?' the Sergeant suggested.

But Kommandant van Heerden was too exhausted to leave Jacaranda House and besides he was looking forward to spending the night in a house renowned throughout South Africa for refined living.

'The place is ringed with men,' he said, 'and besides, we've been having complaints from the neighbours about the screams from the cells. Up here nobody will hear him when he yells. I'll cross-examine him in the morning.'

And as the Bishop of Barotseland was led down into the

cellar of Jacaranda House, Kommandant van Heerden wearily climbed the staircase to find himself a nice comfortable bedroom. He chose one with a blue bedspread on an enormous double bed, and as he stepped naked between the sheets, he considered himself a lucky man.

'To think that I can commandeer the house that once belonged to the Viceroy of Matabeleland,' he said to himself and turning on his side between the remarkably smooth sheets, promptly fell asleep.

Chapter 9

Few other people in Piemburg dropped off to sleep so easily that night. Too many disturbing things were happening around them for their sleep to be anything but fitful. In Upper Piemburg the searchlights swung slowly to and fro around the perimeter of Jacaranda Park, illuminating with quite astonishing brilliance the great hoardings that announced the arrival of death by two of its most awful means. Designed originally for the Army before being turned over to the police force, the searchlights did a great deal more than that. As they traversed the Park, the neighbouring suburbs and the city itself, they turned night into brilliant day with some remarkable results, particularly in the case of a number of chicken farms whose battery hens were driven to the verge of nervous breakdown by finding their already short nights suddenly diminished to something like four minutes.

Families which had taken the precaution of locking their dogs in the backyard and of sprinkling their sheets with DDT and whose bedrooms lay in the path of the searchlights found dawn break upon them with a rapidity and brilliance they had never before experienced, to be succeeded by a duskless night, and the process repeated endlessly while they tossed and turned in their itching beds. Outside along the roads rumbled the armoured cars and trucks of the police and bursts of firing interrupted the silence of the night, as the crews followed the Kommandant's instructions to shoot any small bush resembling Luitenant Verkramp.

The switchboard at the Piemburg Hospital was deluged with calls from agitated callers who wanted to know the symptoms of bubonic plague and rabies and how to treat the diseases. In the end the frantic telephonist refused to take any more calls, a dereliction of duty that had fatal results in two cases of heart attack.

Only Konstabel Els slept soundly in the isolation hospital. Occasionally he twitched in his sleep but only because he was dreaming of battle and sudden death. On the Vlockfontein road families whose cars had broken down in the long queue trudged towards Piemburg. It was a hot night and as they walked they sweated.

Kommandant van Heerden sweated too but for a rather different reason. He had been too exhausted when he climbed into bed to take much notice of his surroundings. He had noticed that the sheets felt peculiar but he had put their smoothness down to the fact that Miss Hazelstone's bed linen would naturally be of the finest quality and unlike his own ordinary sheets.

Kommandant van Heerden slept like a babe for an hour. When he awoke it was to find the bed dripping with moisture. He climbed out of bed horribly enbarrassed.

'It isn't as though I've been on the booze,' he muttered as he grabbed a handtowel from the washbasin and began to mop the bed out, and wondered how he was going to explain the mishap to Miss Hazelstone in the morning. He could imagine the sort of caustic comments she would make.

'Thank heaven the sheets seem to be waterproof,' he said and climbed back into bed to dry them out. 'It's a terribly hot night,' he thought tossing and turning. He just couldn't make himself comfortable. As he drifted off and woke again and drifted off he gained the definite impression that the bed was getting no dryer. If anything it was getting wetter. He could feel the sweat running down his back as he slithered from side to side in the infernally slimy sheets.

75

He began to wonder if he had fallen sick with a fever brought on by the strain of the day. He certainly felt feverish and his thoughts bore all the marks of delirium. Uncertain whether he was dreaming or recalling what had actually happened, pursued by elephant guns, Miss Hazelstone with a scimitar, Mings and a demented Konstabel Els, Kommandant van Heerden thrashed on through the night in a froth of agitation.

At two in the morning he took the blankets off the bed. At three he mopped the bed out again. At four, convinced that he was dying in a raging fever and with a temperature of one hundred and ten he stumbled to the bathroom in search of a thermometer. He had begun to think that he had shown remarkable foresight in ordering the plague notices to be put up round the Park. Whatever disease he had caught he had no doubt it must be both infectious and fatal. But when he took his temperature he found it to be subnormal.

'Odd,' he thought. 'Very odd,' and after drinking several pints of water out of a tooth-mug went back to his room and climbed back into bed. At five o'clock he gave up all idea of sleeping and went along to the bathroom and had a cold bath. He was still debating what was wrong with him as he began to dress. He noticed that the room had a funny sort of smell about it, and for a moment he looked suspiciously at his socks. 'It isn't that sort of smell,' he said to himself and crossing to the windows pulled back the curtains.

Outside the sun was up and the jacaranda trees bright with flowers in the morning light. But Kommandant van Heerden wasn't interested in the view from his window. He was much more concerned with the curtains. They felt just like the sheets. He felt them again. 'The bloody things stretch,' he thought, and found that the sheets were elastic too. He smelt them closely and recognized the smell now. The sheets and the curtains were made of latex. Everything in the room was made of thin blue rubber.

He opened the wardrobe and felt the suits and dresses that hung there. They too were made of rubber. Kommandant van Heerden sat down on the bed astonished. He had never run across anything like this in his life. Certainly his annual

acquaintance with latex had hardly prepared him for this encounter, and as he sat there he began to think that there was
something definitely sinister about the room. Finally he
examined the contents of the chest of drawers and found the
same thing there. Shirts, pants, and socks were all made of
rubber. In one small drawer he found several latex hoods and
two pairs of handcuffs. Very definitely the room had a sinister
purpose, he thought and went downstairs to have breakfast.

'How's the prisoner?' the Kommandant asked Sergeant de
Kock when he had finished his toast and coffee.

'Looks insane to me. Keeps talking about animals all the
time. Seems to think God is a guard dog or a vulture or something,' said the Sergeant.

'Won't do him much good. How many men did we lose
yesterday?'

'Twenty-one.'

'Twenty-one and a Zulu cook. Say twenty-one and a quarter.
No man who shoots twenty-one policemen can plead insanity.'

Sergeant de Kock wasn't convinced. 'Any man who shoots
twenty-one policemen and leaves his wallet behind at the scene
of the crime sounds insane to me.'

'We all make mistakes,' said the Kommandant, and went
upstairs to begin his cross-examination.

Down in the cellar the Bishop of Barotseland had spent the
night chained to a pipe. He had slept even less than the Kommandant and had been guarded by four konstabels and two
dogs. During the sleepless hours he had wrestled with the intellectual and moral problem implied by his predicament and
had finally come to the conclusion that he was being punished
for not getting out of the swimming-bath fast enough. For a
while he had even considered the possibility that what was
apparently happening to him was a symptom of delirium
tremens brought on by drinking a bottle of bad brandy neat.
When finally he was dragged to his feet and taken upstairs and
down the corridor to his father's study he was certain that he
was having hallucinations.

*　　　*　　　*

Kommandant van Heerden had not chosen Judge Hazelstone's study for interrogating the prisoner by accident. His unerring sense of psychology had told him that the study, redolent with judicial severity and the associations of childhood, would prepare Jonathan Hazelstone for the grilling the Kommandant intended to give him. Seating himself at the desk in a large leather-covered chair, the Kommandant assumed a posture and mien he felt sure would remind the prisoner of his father. To this end he toyed with a miniature brass gallows complete with trap and dangling victim which he found on the desk serving as a paperweight. It was a gift, he noted, from 'The Executioner in gratitude for Judge Hazelstone's many favours'. Confident that he looked very much as the great lawmaker must have done when he interrogated his son about some childish misdemeanour, the Kommandant ordered the prisoner to be brought in.

Whatever resemblance there might have been between the Kommandant and Judge Hazelstone of the Supreme Court, and it was practically non-existent, there was absolutely none between the manacled and naked creature that hobbled into the study still wearing the absurd bathing-cap, and any High Church dignitary. Staring wild-eyed at the Kommandant, the Bishop looked the picture of depravity.

'Name?' said the Kommandant putting down the paperweight and reaching for a pen.

'I'm hard of hearing,' said the Bishop.

'So am I,' said the Kommandant. 'Comes of firing that bloody elephant gun.'

'I said I can't hear what you're saying.'

Kommandant van Heerden looked up from the desk. 'What the hell are you wearing that cap for?' he asked, and signalled to a konstabel to take it off. The konstabel laid the bathing-cap on the desk and Kommandant van Heerden looked at it suspiciously. 'Do you make a habit of wearing rubber clothes?' he inquired.

The Bishop chose to ignore the question. It had too much of the nightmare about it and he wanted to get back to the everyday world.

'I must protest against the assaults made on my person,' he

78

began, and was surprised at the reaction this simple statement provoked.

'You want to do what?' yelled the Kommandant.

'I have been assaulted by several of your men,' went on the Bishop. 'They have treated me absolutely abominably.'

Kommandant van Heerden couldn't believe his ears. 'And what do you think you were doing to them yesterday afternoon, playing kiss-in-the-fucking-ring? You butcher half my bloody men, ruin a perfectly good Saracen and murder your sister's Zulu bleeding cook and you've got the nerve to come in here and protest at the assaults on . . .' Kommandant van Heerden was at a loss for words. When he recovered his temper he went on more quietly. 'Anything else you would like to ask me?' he said.

'Yes,' said the Bishop. 'I demand to see my lawyer.'

The Kommandant shook his head. 'Confession first,' he said.

'I'm entitled to see my lawyer.'

Kommandant van Heerden had to smile. 'You're not.'

'I am entitled by law to consult my lawyer.'

'You'll be bleating about Habeas Corpus next.'

'I most certainly will unless you bring me before a magistrate in forty-eight hours.'

Kommandant van Heerden sat back in his chair and grinned cheerfully. 'You think you know your law, don't you? Being the son of a judge, you'd know all about it, wouldn't you?'

The Bishop wasn't going to be drawn. 'I know my basic rights,' he said.

'Well, let me tell you something now. I'm holding you under the Terrorism Act and that means you can see no lawyer and there's no Habeas Corpus, nothing.' He paused to let this sink in. 'I can detain you till the day you die, and you never so much as get a whiff of a lawyer, and as for charging you before a magistrate, that can wait for forty-eight years or four hundred and eighty, for that matter.'

The Bishop tried to say something, but the Kommandant continued, 'I'll tell you something else. Under the Terrorism Act you have to prove yourself innocent. I don't have to go to the bother of proving you guilty. Really rather convenient from my point of view,' and the Kommandant picked up the paperweight with what he hoped was a meaningful gesture.

The Bishop groped for something to say. 'But the Terrorism Act doesn't apply to me. I'm not a terrorist.'

'And what would you call a person who went round murdering twenty-one policemen if not a bloody terrorist?'

'I've no idea what you're talking about.'

'I'll tell you what I am talking about,' shouted the Kommandant, 'I'll spell it out for you. Early yesterday afternoon you attempted to destroy the evidence of a bestial crime committed upon the person of your sister's Zulu cook by shooting him with a monstrous elephant gun. You then forced your sister to confess to the crime to save your skin, while you went up to the main gate and shot down twenty-one of my men as they tried to enter the Park.'

The Bishop looked wildly round the room and tried to pull himself together.

'You've got it all wrong,' he said at last, 'I didn't kill Fivepence—'

Kommandant van Heerden interrupted him quickly. 'Thank you,' he said, and started to write, 'Confesses to killing twenty-one police officers.'

'I didn't say that,' screamed the Bishop. 'I said I didn't kill Fivepence.'

'Denies killing Zulu cook,' continued the Kommandant painstakingly writing it down.

'I deny killing twenty-one policemen too,' shouted the Bishop.

'Retracts previous confession,' said the Kommandant.

'There was no previous confession. I never said anything about killing the policemen.'

Kommandant van Heerden looked at the two konstabels. 'You men heard him confess to killing twenty-one police officers, didn't you?' he said. The two konstabels weren't sure what they heard but they knew better than to disagree with the Kommandant. They nodded.

'There you are,' the Kommandant continued. 'They heard you.'

'But I didn't say it,' the Bishop yelled. 'What would I want to kill twenty-one policemen for?'

The Kommandant considered the question. 'To hide the crime you'd committed on the Zulu cook,' he said at last.

'How would killing twenty-one policemen help to hide Fivepence's murder?' wailed the Bishop.

'You should have thought of that before you did it,' said the Kommandant smugly.

'But I didn't do it, I tell you. I never went anywhere near the main gate yesterday afternoon. I was too drunk to go anywhere.'

The Kommandant started to write again. 'Claims he acted under the influence of alcohol,' he said.

'No I don't. I said I was too drunk to go anywhere. I couldn't have got up to the gate if I had wanted to.'

Kommandant van Heerden put down his pen and looked at the prisoner. 'Then perhaps you'll be good enough to tell me,' he said, 'how it was that sixty-nine tracker dogs when put on your trail followed your scent up to the main gate and then back to the swimming-pool where you were disposing of the murder weapons?'

'I don't know.'

'Expert witnesses, tracker dogs,' said the Kommandant. 'And perhaps you'll explain how your wallet and handkerchief came to be inside a blockhouse from which my men had been shot down.'

'I've got no idea.'

'Right, then if you'll just sign here,' said the Kommandant holding out the statement to him.

The Bishop bent forward and read the statement. It was a confession that he had murdered Fivepence and twenty-one police officers.

'Of course I won't sign it,' he said straightening up at last. 'None of the crimes you mention there have anything to do with me.'

'No? Well then just you tell me who committed them.'

'My sister shot Fivepence . . .' the Bishop began, and realized he was making a mistake. In front of him the Kommandant's face had turned purple.

'You sordid bastard,' he yelled. 'Call yourself an English

gentleman, do you, and try and shift the blame for a murder on your poor dear sister. What sort of a man are you? Doesn't the family name mean a bleeding thing to you?'

At a signal from the Kommandant the two konstabels grabbed the Bishop and hurled him to the floor. In a flurry of boots and truncheons, the Bishop rolled about the floor of the study. Just as he thought he was about to die, he was hauled to his feet in front of the desk.

'We'll continue this conversation when you feel up to it,' the Kommandant said more calmly, and the Bishop thanked the dear Lord for sparing him another encounter with Kommandant van Heerden. He knew he would never feel up to it. 'In the meantime I am sending for Luitenant Verkramp. This is clearly a political case, and in future he will interrogate you,' and with this dire threat the Kommandant ordered the two konstabels to take the prisoner back to the cellar.

As Kommandant van Heerden waited for Miss Hazelstone to be brought to him, he fingered the bathing-cap thoughtfully and wondered what had happened to Luitenant Verkramp. He had no great hope that the Luitenant was dead. 'The crafty swine is probably holed up somewhere,' he thought and idly poked his finger into the bathing-cap. He was beginning to wish the Luitenant was around to consult about the case. Kommandant van Heerden was no great one for theories and the cross-examination had not turned into a confession quite as easily as he had expected. He had to admit, if only to himself, that there were certain aspects of Jonathan's story that had the ring of truth about them. He had been dead drunk on the bed in Jacaranda House. The Kommandant had seen him there with his own eyes and yet the shooting at the gate had started only minutes later. The Kommandant could not see how a man who was dead drunk one minute half a mile from the blockhouse, could the next be firing with remarkable accuracy at the plain-clothes men. And where the hell had Els disappeared to? The whole thing was a bloody mystery.

'Oh well, never look a gift horse in the mouth,' he thought. 'After all my whole career is at stake and it doesn't do to be choosy.'

*   *   *

The Kommandant hadn't been far wrong in his assessment of Luitenant Verkramp's position. He was indeed holed up. Of all the people who slept in Piemburg that night, Luitenant Verkramp was perhaps the least restless and certainly the least refreshed when dawn broke. His sleep had been disturbed, very disturbed, but in spite of his discomfort he had not dared to move. Below him and in some cases actually inside him, the dreadful spikes made the slightest movement an exceedingly unrewarding experience.

Above him the moving finger of an enormous light swung eerily back and forth through a great pall of greasy smoke. A nauseating smell of burning flesh filled the air, and Luitenant Verkramp in his delirium began to believe in the hell his grandfather's sermons had promised for sinners. At intervals during the long night he woke and considered what he had done to deserve this dreadful fate, and his mind was filled with visions of the prisoners he had tortured by tying plastic bags over their heads, or by administering electric shocks to their genitals. If only he were given another chance in life, he promised he would never torture another suspect and realized as he did so that it was a promise he would never be able to keep.

There was only one portion of his anatomy he could move without too much pain. His left arm was free and as he lay staring up into the smoke and flames of hell, he used his hand to feel about him. He felt the iron spikes and underneath him he discovered the body of another damned soul stiff and cold. Luitenant Verkramp envied that man. He had evidently passed on to some other more pleasant place like oblivion, and he envied him all the more a moment later when an extremely unpleasant sound farther down the ditch drew his attention to new and more horrible possibilities.

He thought at first that someone was being undressed in a great hurry, and by a person with little respect for his clothes. Whoever was busy down there certainly wasn't bothering to undo buttons very carefully. It sounded as if some poor devil was having the clothes ripped off him unceremoniously indeed. Luitenant Verkramp was sure they would never be fit to wear again. 'Probably preparing some poor devil for roasting,' he thought and hoped that his camouflage would help to prevent them finding him for some time.

Raising his head inch by inch he peered down the moat. At first it was too dark to see anything. The sound of undressing had ceased and was followed by noises more awful than anything he had ever heard. Whatever was going on down there didn't bear thinking about, but still horribly fascinated he continued to peer into the darkness. Above him the great probing light swung slowly back towards the moat, and as it passed overhead Luitenant Verkramp knew that his encounter with the wildlife of the hedgerow in the shape of the giant spider had been as nothing to the appalling agonies death held in store for him. Down the ditch a great vulture was up to its neck in plain-clothes policemen. Luitenant Verkramp passed out yet again.

When dawn broke over the varied remains of Konstabel Els' defence of Jacaranda Park, the policemen guarding the gate discovered the haha and its inhabitants living and dead and clambered gingerly down to collect what had not already flapped gorged out of the moat. They had some difficulty at first in recognizing Luitenant Verkramp under his vegetation and when they had decided that he was at least partially human, they had even more difficulty deciding whether he was alive or dead. Certainly the creature they hauled onto the grass seemed more dead than alive, and was clearly suffering from a pronounced persecution complex.

'Don't roast me, please don't roast me. I promise I won't do it again,' Luitenant Verkramp yelled and he was still screaming when he was lifted into the ambulance and driven down to the hospital.

Chapter 10

As Luitenant Verkramp was being admitted to Piemburg Hospital, Konstabel Els was being discharged.

'I tell you I've got rabies,' Els shouted at the doctor who told him there was nothing physically wrong with him. 'I've been bitten by a mad dog and I am dying.'

'No such luck,' said the doctor. 'You'll live to bite another day,' and left Els standing on the steps cursing the inefficiency of the medical profession. He was trying to make up his mind what he should do next when the police car that had accompanied the ambulance carrying Luitenant Verkramp to hospital stopped next to him.

'Hey, Els, where the hell have you been?' said the Sergeant next to the driver. 'The old man has been yelling blue murder for you.'

'I've been in hospital,' said Els. 'Suspected rabies.'

'You'd better hop in. We'll go by the station and pick up your little toy.'

'What little toy?' asked Els, hoping it wasn't the elephant gun.

'The electric-shock machine. You've got a customer up at Jacaranda House.'

As they drove up the hill Els sat silent. He wasn't looking forward to seeing the Kommandant and having to explain why he had left his post. As they passed the burnt-out Saracen, Els couldn't restrain a little giggle.

'I don't know what you're laughing at,' said the Sergeant sourly. 'Might have been you in there.'

'Not me,' said Els. 'You wouldn't find me in one of those things. Asking for trouble they are.'

'Safe enough normally.'

'Not when you're up against a good man with the right sort of weapon,' Els said.

'You sound as though you had something to do with it, you know so much about it.'

'Who? Me? Nothing to do with me. Why should I knock out a Saracen?'

'God alone knows,' said the Sergeant, 'but it's just the sort of stupid thing you would get up to.'

Konstabel Els cursed himself for opening his mouth. He would have to be more careful with the Kommandant. He began to wonder what the symptoms of bubonic plague were. He might have to develop them as a last resort.

Kommandant van Heerden's examination of Miss Hazelstone had got off to a bad start. Nothing that he could say would convince her that she hadn't murdered Fivepence.

'All right, suppose for the moment that you did shoot him,' he said for the umpteenth time. 'What was your motive?'

'He was my lover.'

'Most people love their lovers, Miss Hazelstone, yet you say you shot him.'

'Correct. I did.'

'Hardly a normal reaction.'

'I'm not a normal person,' said Miss Hazelstone. 'Nor are you. Nor is the konstabel outside the door. We are none of us normal people.'

'I would have said I was fairly normal,' said the Kommandant smugly.

'That's just the sort of asinine remark I would expect you to make and it only goes to prove how abnormal you are. Most people like to think that they are unique. You evidently don't and since you seem to consider normality to consist of being like other people, in so far as you possess qualities that make you unlike other people, you are abnormal. Do I make myself clear?'

'No,' said the Kommandant, 'you don't.'

'Let me put it another way,' said Miss Hazelstone. 'Normality is a concept. Do you follow me?'

'I'm trying to,' the Kommandant said despairingly.

'Good. As I have said, normality is a concept. It is not a

state of being. You are confusing it with the desire to conform. You have a strong urge to conform. I have none.'

Kommandant van Heerden groped his way after her. He couldn't understand a word of what she was saying but it didn't sound very complimentary.

'What about motive?' he asked, trying to get back on to more familiar ground.

'What about it?' Miss Hazelstone countered.

'If you killed Fivepence you must have had a motive.'

Miss Hazelstone thought for a moment. 'It doesn't follow,' she said at last, 'though I suppose you could argue that a motiveless act is an impossibility because it inevitably presupposes an intention to act without motive which is a motive in itself.'

Kommandant van Heerden looked desperately round the room. The woman was driving him mad.

'You didn't have one then?' he asked after counting to twenty slowly.

'If you insist on my having one, I suppose I'll have to supply it. You can say it was jealousy.'

The Kommandant perked up. This was much better. He was getting on to familiar ground again.

'And who were you jealous of?'

'No one.'

'No one?'

'That's what I said.'

Kommandant van Heerden peered over the edge of an abyss. 'No one,' he almost screamed. 'How in the name of hell can you be jealous of no one?' He paused, and looked at her suspiciously. 'No One is not the name of another kaffir, is it?'

'Of course not. It means exactly what it says. I was jealous of no one.'

'You can't be jealous of no one. It's not possible. You've got to be jealous of somebody else.'

'I haven't, you know.' Miss Hazelstone looked at him pityingly.

Beneath him the Kommandant could feel the abyss yawning. It was the abyss of all abysses.

'No one. No one,' he repeated almost pathetically, shaking his head. 'Someone tell me how somebody can be jealous of no one.'

'Oh it's really quite simple,' Miss Hazelstone continued, 'I was just jealous.'

'Just jealous,' the Kommandant repeated slowly.

'That's right. I didn't want to lose dear Fivepence.'

Teetering above the unfathomable void of abstraction the Kommandant clutched at Fivepence. There had once been something substantial about the Zulu cook and the Kommandant needed something substantial to hang on to.

'You were frightened you were going to lose him?' he pondered aloud, and then realized the terrible contradiction he was stepping into. 'But you say you shot him. Isn't that the best way of losing the brute?' He was almost beside himself.

'It was the only way I had of making sure I kept him,' Miss Hazelstone replied.

Kommandant van Heerden pulled himself back from the void. He was losing control of the interview. He started again at the beginning.

'Let's forget for the moment that you shot Fivepence so that you wouldn't lose him,' he said slowly and very patiently. 'Let's start at the other end. What was your motive for falling in love with him?' It was not a topic he particularly wanted to investigate, not that he believed for a moment that she had ever been in love with the swine, but it was better than harping on about no one. Besides he felt pretty sure she would give herself away now. The Hazelstones couldn't fall in love with Zulu cooks.

'Fivepence and I shared certain mutual interests,' said Miss Hazelstone slowly. 'For one thing we had the same fetish.'

'Oh really. The same fetish?' In his mind the Kommandant conjured up a picture of the little native idols he had seen in the Piemburg Museum.

'Naturally,' said Miss Hazelstone, 'it provided a bond between us.'

'Yes, it must have done, and I suppose you sacrificed goats to it,' the Kommandant said sarcastically.

'What an extraordinary thing to say,' Miss Hazelstone

88

looked puzzled. 'Of course we didn't. It wasn't that sort of fetish.'

'Wasn't it? What sort was it? Wooden or stone?'

'Rubber,' said Miss Hazelstone briefly.

Kommandant van Heerden leant back in his chair angrily. He had had about as much of Miss Hazelstone's leg-pulling as he could take. If the old girl seriously supposed that he was going to believe some cock-and-bull story about a rubber idol, she had another think coming.

'Now listen to me, Miss Hazelstone,' he said seriously. 'I can appreciate what you are trying to do and I must say I admire you for it. Family loyalty is a fine thing and trying to save your brother is a fine thing too, but I have my duty to do and nothing you can say is going to prevent me doing it. Now if you will be good enough to get to the point and admit that you had nothing whatever to do with the murder of your cook and were never approximately in love with him, I will allow you to go. If not I shall be forced to take some drastic action against you. You are obstructing the course of justice and you leave me no alternative. Now then, be sensible and admit that all this talk about fetishes is nonsense.'

Miss Hazelstone looked at him icily.

'Are you easily stimulated?' she asked. 'Sexually, I mean.'

'That has got nothing whatever to do with you.'

'It has got a lot to do with this case,' said Miss Hazelstone, and hesitated. Kommandant van Heerden shifted uneasily in his chair. He had come to recognize that Miss Hazelstone's hesitations tended to augur some new and revolting disclosure.

'I have to admit that I am not easily aroused,' she said at last. The Kommandant was delighted to hear it. 'I need the presence of rubber to stimulate my sexual appetite.'

The Kommandant was just about to say that in his case the presence of rubber had quite the opposite effect, but he thought better of it.

'You see I am a rubber fetishist,' Miss Hazelstone continued.

Kommandant van Heerden tried to grasp the implications of the remark.

'You are?' he said.

'I have a passion for rubber.'

'You have?'

'I can only make love when I am dressed in rubber.'

'You can?'

'It was rubber that drew Fivepence and me together.'

'It was?'

'Fivepence had the same propensity.'

'He did?'

'When I first met him he was working in a garage retreading tyres.'

'He was?'

'I had taken my tyres in for a retread and Fivepence was there. I recognized him at once as the man I had been looking for all my life.'

'You did?'

'I might almost say that our love affair was cemented over a Michelin X.'

'You might?'

Miss Hazelstone stopped. The Kommandant's inability to say more than two words at a time and those two in the form of a question she had already answered was beginning to irritate her.

'Do you have any idea what I am talking about?' she asked.

'No,' said the Kommandant.

'I don't know what more I can do to make my meaning plain,' Miss Hazelstone said. 'I have tried to explain as simply as I can what I found attractive about Fivepence.'

Kommandant van Heerden closed his mouth which had been hanging open and tried to focus his mind on something comprehensible. What Miss Hazelstone had just told him so simply had not, he had to admit, been in the least abstract, but if just before he had hovered over a void of unfathomable abstractions, the simple facts she had placed before him now were so far beyond anything his experience had prepared him to expect that he began to think that on the whole he preferred the conceptual abyss. In an effort to regain his sense of reality, he resorted to healthy vulgarity.

'Are you trying to tell me,' he said, picking the bathing-cap off the desk and dangling it from his finger a few inches in front of Miss Hazelstone's face, 'that this rubber cap gives you an overwhelming desire to lay me?'

In front of him Miss Hazelstone nodded.

'And if I were to wear it you wouldn't be able to control your sexual impulses?' he went on.

'Yes,' said Miss Hazelstone frantically. 'Yes, I would. I mean, no I wouldn't.' Torn between a raging torrent of desire and an overwhelming aversion for the person of the Kommandant, she hardly knew what was happening to her.

'And I suppose you're going to tell me that your Zulu cook had the same taste for rubber?'

Miss Hazelstone nodded again.

'And I suppose all those rubber clothes I found in the bedroom upstairs belong to you too?' Miss Hazelstone agreed that they did. 'And Fivepence would put on a rubber suit and you would wear a rubber nightdress? Is that right?'

Kommandant van Heerden could see from the expression on Miss Hazelstone's face that at long last he had regained the initiative. She was sitting mute and staring at him hypnotized.

'Is that what used to happen?' he continued remorselessly.

Miss Hazelstone shook her head. 'No,' she said, 'it was the other way round.'

'Oh really? What was the other way round?'

'The clothes were.'

'The clothes were the other way round?'

'Yes.'

'Inside out I suppose, or was it back to front?'

'You could put it like that.'

Kommandant van Heerden's experience of rubber clothing during the night hadn't induced in him any desire to put it like anything.

'Like what?' he said.

'I wore the men's suits and Fivepence wore the dresses,' Miss Hazelstone said. 'As you've probably noticed I have some marked masculine characteristics and Fivepence, poor dear, was a transvestite.'

The Kommandant staring at her with increasing disgust could see what she meant. Masculine characteristics indeed! A

91

taste for tall and revolting stories for one thing. And if for one moment he really believed that a fat Zulu cook had been dressing up in his missus' clothes then he was a very lucky Zulu to have gone the way he had. The Kommandant knew what he'd do to any houseboy of his he found prancing around in ladies' clothes, rubber or not, and it included pulling more than his vest tight too.

He dragged his attention back from the prospect and tried to think about the case. He had known there was something sinister about the bedroom with the rubber sheets, and now Miss Hazelstone had explained its purpose.

'It's no good your going on trying to cover up for your brother,' he said. 'We've enough evidence to hang him with already. What you tell me about the rubber clothes merely confirms what we already know. When your brother was arrested last night, he was wearing this cap.' He held it up in front of her again.

'Of course he was,' said Miss Hazelstone. 'He has to when he goes swimming. He has trouble with his ears.'

Kommandant van Heerden smiled. 'Sometimes listening to you, Miss Hazelstone, I fancy there's something wrong with my ears too, but I don't go around with a rubber bathing-cap on all the time.'

'Nor does Jonathan.'

'No? Well then perhaps you'll explain how it came about that when he was brought before me this morning, he was still wearing it. Your brother evidently likes wearing rubber things.'

'He probably forgot to take it off,' Miss Hazelstone said, 'He's very absent-minded you know. He's always forgetting where he's left things.'

'So I've noticed,' said the Kommandant. He paused and leant back in the chair expansively. 'The pattern of the case seems to go like this. Your brother comes home from Rhodesia, probably because things got too hot for him up there.'

'Nonsense,' interrupted Miss Hazelstone. 'Barotseland does get very hot, I know, but Jonathan's used to the heat.'

'You can say that again,' said the Kommandant. 'Well, whatever the reason, he comes home. He brings with him all the rubber clothes he's so fond of and he starts trying to seduce your Zulu cook.'

'What utter rubbish,' said Miss Hazelstone. 'Jonathan wouldn't dream of any such thing. You're forgetting that he is a bishop.'

The Kommandant wasn't forgetting anything of the sort since he had never known it.

'That's maybe what he has told you,' he said. 'Our information is that he is a convicted criminal. There is a file on him down at the station. Luitenant Verkramp has the details.'

'But this is insane. Jonathan is the Bishop of Barotseland.'

'Probably his alias,' said the Kommandant. 'Right. We've got to the part where he tries to make Fivepence. The cook objects and runs out on to the lawn, and your brother shoots him down.'

'You're mad,' Miss Hazelstone shouted and stood up. 'You're quite mad. My brother was in the swimming-bath when I shot Fivepence. He came running when he heard the shot and tried to administer the last rites.'

'Last rites is one way of putting it,' said the Kommandant. 'And I suppose that's how he got blood all over himself?'

'Exactly.'

'And you honestly expect me to believe that a nice old lady like you shot your cook, and that your brother whom I find dead drunk on a bed, naked and covered with blood, is a bishop and had nothing to do with the killing? Really Miss Hazelstone, you must take me for an idiot.'

'I do,' said Miss Hazelstone simply.

'And another thing,' the Kommandant continued hurriedly, 'some maniac shot down twenty-one of my men yesterday afternoon up at the gate to the Park. Now you're not going to try to tell me that you murdered them too, are you?'

'If the wish were father to the thought, yes,' said Miss Hazelstone.

Kommandant van Heerden smiled. 'It's not, I'm afraid. I wish I could hush this whole case up and if it were simply the death of your cook, I daresay it would be possible, but there is nothing I can do now. Justice must run its course.'

He swung his chair round and faced the bookshelves. He

was feeling quite pleased with himself. Everything had sorted itself out in his own mind and he had no doubt that he would be able to convince the State Attorney. Kommandant van Heerden's career had been saved. Behind him Miss Hazelstone acted promptly. Seizing both the opportunity provided by the back of the Kommandant's head, and the brass paperweight, she brought the two together with as much strength as she could muster. The Kommandant slumped to the floor.

Miss Hazelstone stepped nimbly across to the door. 'The Kommandant has had a stroke,' she said to the two konstabels on duty there. 'Help me take him up to his bedroom,' and she led the way upstairs. When the two konstabels had deposited Kommandant van Heerden on the bed in the blue bedroom, she sent them downstairs to ring the hospital for an ambulance and the two men, accustomed to obeying orders without question, dashed down the corridor and told Sergeant de Kock. As soon as they had gone Miss Hazelstone stepped to the door of the bedroom and whistled. A Dobermann Pinscher that had been asleep on the rug in the drawing-room heard the whistle and left its sanctuary. Silently it climbed the stairs and loped down the passage to its mistress.

By the time Sergeant de Kock had telephoned Piemburg Hospital and had arranged for an ambulance to be sent up to the house, a call which necessitated explaining to the telephonist that Kommandant van Heerden was white and didn't need a non-European ambulance, it was clear that van Heerden's condition had taken a turn for the worse.

The Sergeant found Miss Hazelstone waiting for him at the end of the passage. She stood demurely and with that air of melancholy the Kommandant had so much admired the day before, and in her hands she held something that was decidedly melancholy and not in the least demure. It was not the size of the elephant gun and it quite clearly couldn't incapacitate a charging elephant at a thousand yards, but in its own small way it was suited to the purpose Miss Hazelstone very clearly had in mind.

'That's right,' she said as the Sergeant stopped on the landing. 'Stand quite still and you won't get hurt. This is a scatter gun and if you want to find out how many cartridges the magazine holds I suggest you try to rush me. You'll need a lot of men.' Beside her the great Dobermann growled encouragingly. It had obviously had enough of policemen to last it a lifetime. On the landing Sergeant de Kock stood very still. It was obvious from the tone of Miss Hazelstone's voice that whatever the capabilities of the scatter gun, she was not in the habit of repeating herself.

'That's right,' she continued as the Sergeant stared at her. 'Have a good look and while you're about it have a good look at the weapons on the walls. They are all in working order and I have enough ammunition in my bedroom to last me quite some time.' She paused, and the Sergeant obediently looked at the guns. 'Now then, you trot off downstairs and don't attempt to come up again. Toby will tell me if you do.' The dog growled again knowingly. 'And when you get down there,' she went on, 'you are to release my brother. I shall give you ten minutes and then I shall expect to see him walk up the drive freely and without let or hindrance. If not I shall shoot Kommandant van Heerden. If you have any doubts about my ability to kill I suggest you look at the gum trees in the garden. I think you'll find the evidence you need there.' Sergeant de Kock needed no such evidence. He felt sure she could kill. 'Good, it seems you understand me. Now I will remain in intercourse with Kommandant van Heerden until I receive a telephone call from my brother in Barotseland. When I receive that call I will release the Kommandant. If I hear nothing from Jonathan within forty-eight hours I will release the Kommandant dead. Do you understand me?'

The Sergeant nodded.

'Now then, get out.'

Sergeant de Kock dashed downstairs and as he went Miss Hazelstone fired one shot by way of warning down the passage. Its results justified every expectation the Sergeant had entertained about the gun's lethal capacity. Sixty-four large holes appeared suddenly in the bathroom door.

Miss Hazelstone surveyed the holes with satisfaction and went back into the bedroom. Then having fastened the Kommandant by his wrists to the head of the bed with the handcuffs he had noted in the chest of drawers, she walked quietly along the corridor. Five minutes later she had collected a small arsenal from the walls and had erected two formidable barricades which would stop any attempt to rush her long enough for her to start using the scatter gun and other assorted weapons she had piled outside the bedroom door. Finally and for good measure she dragged several mattresses and a chaise-longue down the passage and built herself a bullet-proof barricade.

When she had finished, she surveyed her handiwork and smiled. 'I don't think we're likely to be disturbed just yet, Toby,' she said to the Dobermann which had climbed on to the chaise-longue, and patting the dog on the head she went into the bedroom and began to undress Kommandant van Heerden.

Chapter 11

Downstairs Konstabel Els was having a heated argument with Sergeant de Kock.

'I tell you,' he kept shouting. 'I'm no more like a flaming bishop than—'

'Than he is?' suggested the Sergeant, pointing at the manacled figure of Jonathan. 'He doesn't look like a bishop either.'

Konstabel Els had to admit that this was true. 'I don't care. I'm still not going to walk down the drive dressed up in his clothes. She'd spot me a mile off.'

'So what? She's only an old woman. She couldn't shoot straight if she tried,' said the Sergeant.

'Are you mad?' Els shouted. 'I've seen what that old bird can do with a gun. Why she blew that Zulu cook of hers to pieces without batting an eyelid. I should know. I had to pick the bugger up.'

'Listen to me, Els,' said the Sergeant, 'she won't have time to take a pot shot at you. She'll go to the window to have a look and—'

'And the next moment I'll be scattered in little bits over half the fucking Park. No thank you. If anyone has to pick the bits up afterwards, I'll pick up yours. I've had more experience.'

'If you would let me finish,' said the Sergeant. 'As soon as she goes to the window, we'll rush her down the passage. She won't have time to take a shot at you.'

'In that case, why not make him walk down the drive?' asked Els. 'I'll keep him covered, and as soon as you've got his sister, we'll take him in again.'

Sergeant de Kock wasn't to be persuaded. 'That sod's killed twenty-one men already. I wouldn't let him out of those hand-cuffs if you paid me,' he said.

Konstabel Els had an answer to that one, but he decided not to use it.

'What's going to be happening to the Kommandant while all this is going on?' he asked. 'She'll kill him for sure.'

'Good riddance,' said the Sergeant. 'He got himself into her clutches, let him get himself out.'

'In that case, why don't we just sit tight and starve the old bag out?'

Sergeant de Kock smiled. 'The Kommandant will be pleased when he hears you wanted to let her knock him off. Now then, stop messing about and get into his clothes.'

Konstabel Els realized his mistake. Without Kommandant van Heerden's incompetence he was likely to have to answer a charge of killing twenty-one fellow officers. Els decided he had better see to it that the old man didn't get killed after all. He didn't want an efficient officer taking his place. He started to put on the Bishop's clothes.

Upstairs Miss Hazelstone had been having almost as much difficulty getting Kommandant van Heerden out of his clothes as the Sergeant was in getting Els to put on the Bishop's. It wasn't that he put up any resistance, but his bulk and uncon-scious lack of cooperation hardly helped. When he was finally naked, she went to the wardrobe and picked out a pink rubber nightdress with a matching hood and squeezed him into them. She was just putting the finishing touches to her own ensemble when she heard a movement on the bed. Kommandant van Heerden was coming round.

In the days to come the Kommandant was wont to say that it was this fresh and horrifying experience which had led to the trouble with his heart. As he regained consciousness, the first thought to enter the disordered labyrinth of his mind was that he would never touch a drop again. Nothing less than a bottle of Old Rhino Skin could account for the pain in his head and the horrible sensation of something hot and sticky and tight adhering to his face. It was even worse when he opened his eyes. He had evidently gone down with the DTs or perhaps the fever he had suspected in the night had finally struck him down delirious. He shut his eyes and tried to work out what was wrong. His arms appeared to be tied to something above his head and his body dressed in something very tight and elastic. He tried to open his mouth to speak but some horrible stuff prevented a sound coming out. Unable to move or to speak he lifted his head and peered at the apparition that sat down on the bed beside him.

It appeared to be an elderly man with unspeakable feminine characteristics and it was dressed in a double-breasted suit of salmon-pink rubber with a yellow pinstripe. As if that wasn't bad enough it had on a shirt of off-white latex and a mauve rubber tie complete with polka dots. For a moment the Kommandant gaped at the creature and was horrified to see it leer at him. The Kommandant shut his eyes and tried to conjure the apparition away by thinking about the pain in his head, but when he opened them again it was still there, leering for all it was worth. Kommandant van Heerden couldn't remember when last he had been leered at by an elderly gent but he knew that it must have been a long time since and certainly when and if it had last happened, it had not produced anything like the degree of aversion he felt now. He was shutting his eyes for the second time when he opened them again hurriedly and in horror. A hand had settled gently on his knee and was beginning to tickle his thigh. In his revulsion from its touch the Kommandant jerked his legs into the air and for the first time caught a glimpse of what he was wearing and realized what he was not. He was wearing a pink rubber nightdress with frills along the bottom. The Kommandant shuddered and, aware that he had left himself open by his seizure to whatever depredations the ghastly old man had in mind, he straightened his legs abruptly and vowed that no temptation would make him open them again. The apparition continued to leer and to tickle, and the Kommandant turned his head hurriedly away from the leer and faced the wall.

Directly in front of his face was a small table and on it lay something which made the leer seem preferable if not actually alluring, and which forced the Kommandant into an attempt to scream. He opened his mouth, but nothing like a scream came out. Instead he sucked in a mouthful of thin rubber which immediately popped out again and left him gasping and he was just recovering from the attempt when a growl from the passage attracted the old man's attention. He rose from the bed, picked up a gun and went to the door.

Kommandant van Heerden seized the opportunity to try to break loose from the bed. He bounced and thrashed, oblivious of the pain in his head, and as he thrashed he saw the barrel of the gun point round the door at him. In the face of its menace he lay still and tried to forget what he had seen lying ready for use on the table by the bed. It was a hypodermic syringe and an ampoule marked 'Novocaine'.

The difficulties which from the word go had been attendant on getting Konstabel Els into the Bishop's clothes, had not been lessened by the discovery that they were not quite his size. The jacket was still the greatcoat it had been the night before, and the trousers made him look like a seal. They made his plan to run down the drive utterly impracticable. It was not a plan he had mentioned to the Sergeant who, he felt, would take it amiss, but now that he had flippers where his boots should have been, running was definitely out. At this rate he would be lucky to waddle let alone run, and Els who had once been privileged to shoot a kaffir with a wooden leg knew that waddling targets were as good as dead ones. It was at this point that Els had his second attack of rabies.

It was as ineffectual as his first, and after he had got himself severely kicked for biting Sergeant de Kock in the ankle, and had loosened several teeth by champing on a wrought-iron table leg he had mistaken for wood, he gave up the attempt at deception and was shepherded outside to begin his imitation of a bishop.

'Do it half as well as you do a dog with rabies and they'll make you an archbishop, Els,' said the Sergeant giving him a shove which sent him on his way. As the Sergeant and his men climbed stealthily to the top of the stairs, Els flapped off miserably on what he knew was to be his last walk. His hat was too large for him and made it difficult to see where he was going and when he did try to run he only succeeded in falling flat on his face. He gave up the attempt as more likely to lead to dire consequences than the waddle. Behind him he heard a konstabel snigger. Els felt aggrieved. He knew that he must look like a large black duck. He was certain he would soon be a dead one.

Warned by the Dobermann's growl Miss Hazelstone peered down the corridor and listened to the boots creaking on the stairs. Behind her the Kommandant, evidently in ecstasy at the thought of the pleasures that lay ahead of him, thrashed wildly on the bed. She pointed the gun round the door at him and the anticipatory wriggles ceased abruptly. A voice from the stairs shouted, 'He's on his way. The Bishop is going down the drive now.'

'I'll just go and have a look,' Miss Hazelstone shouted back, and stayed where she was.

It was doubtful who was most astonished by what followed. Certainly Sergeant de Kock was amazed to find himself in the land of the living after Miss Hazelstone had fired her first volley as the assault force tried to breast her first barricade. He wasn't to know that she had fired high less to avoid casualties than to preserve her defences. This time sixty-four large holes appeared in the ceiling and the corridor was filled with a fine fog of powdered plaster. Under cover of this smokescreen the Sergeant and his men fell back thankfully and gathered among the potted plants in the hall.

Miss Hazelstone on the other hand surveyed her handiwork for a moment with satisfaction, and then went back to the bedroom window to watch whatever it was that was trying to run up the drive.

That it was nothing like her brother was obvious at first glance. With the enormous hat wedged down over his ears preventing him from seeing where he was heading and with the trouser bottoms splaying out behind him with each step he took, Els hopped across the Park. Miss Hazelstone burst out laughing and hearing the laughter Konstabel Els redoubled his efforts to win the sack race. As Miss Hazelstone fired, he fell on his face involuntarily. He need not have bothered. Miss Hazelstone was laughing too much to aim straight. Her bullets crashed through the leaves of a tree some distance from him and merely wounded a large and well-fed vulture that had been digesting its breakfast there. As it fluttered to the ground near him and belched, Konstabel Els lying helpless on the grass looked at it speculatively. He could see nothing in the world to laugh at.

Kommandant van Heerden felt the same way about the laughter. It bore too many of the hallmarks of the expert in refined living to leave him in any doubt who the creature in the salmon-pink suit was. Nobody else of his acquaintance laughed like that, shot like that or had such a marked propensity for administering intramuscular injections of novocaine.

Miss Hazelstone returned to her seat on the bed and picked up the hypodermic. 'You won't feel anything,' she said inserting the ampoule. 'Not a thing.'

'I know I won't,' shouted the Kommandant inside the rubber hood. 'That's what's bothering me,' but Miss Hazelstone didn't hear him. The grunts and muffled screams that came out of the hood were quite indistinguishable as words.

'Just a little prick to begin with,' said Miss Hazelstone soothingly. She lifted the skirt of his nightdress and the Kommandant tried to make it even smaller. Eyeing the needle he found was the best way of maintaining his flaccidity, and he concentrated on it with grim determination.

'You'll have to do better than that,' said Miss Hazelstone after a moment's speculation and evidently thinking at cross-purposes to the Kommandant.

Inside the hood the Kommandant continued his attempt to explain that he wasn't afflicted with the same complaint as the Zulu cook.

'It's just the opposite with me,' he yelled. 'I take hours and hours.'

'You are a shy man,' said Miss Hazelstone, and thought for a moment. 'Perhaps you would find a little whipping helpful. Some men do, you know,' and she got up from the bed and rummaged in the wardrobe, emerging at last with a particularly horrid-looking riding crop.

'No I wouldn't,' yelled the Kommandant. 'I wouldn't find it helpful at all.'

'Yes or no?' said Miss Hazelstone as the muffled cries subsided. 'Nod for yes, shake your head for no.'

Kommandant van Heerden shook his head as hard as he could.

'Not your cup of tea, eh?' said Miss Hazelstone. 'Well then, how about some nasty pictures.' This time she fetched a folder from the wardrobe and the Kommandant found himself gazing fascinated at photographs that had evidently been taken by some lunatic with a taste for contortionists and dwarfs.

'Take the disgusting things away,' he yelled as she pressed an exceptionally perverse one on his attention.

'You like that one, do you?' Miss Hazelstone asked. 'It's a position Fivepence was particularly fond of. I'll see if I can get you in the right position.'

'No, I don't,' the Kommandant screamed. 'I loathe it. It's revolting.' But before he could shake his head to indicate his desire not to have his back broken, Miss Hazelstone had seized the hood with one hand and one of his legs with the other, and was trying to bring them together. With a desperate heave he broke loose and sent her spinning across the room.

Out in the Park, Els had recovered his composure. Once he had established that he was not about to become part of the vulture's daily intake of protein, Els decided that his impersonation of the Bishop had gone on long enough. He got up and hobbled to a tree and rid himself of the ridiculous trousers. Then clad in his vest and pants he returned to the house, and found Sergeant de Kock covered in white dust and suffering from shock.

'I don't know what to do,' the Sergeant said. 'She's got barricades up and nothing will get past them.'

'I know something that will,' said Els. 'Where's that elephant gun?'

'You're not using that fucking thing,' Sergeant de Kock told him. 'You'll bring the whole building down round our ears, and besides it's evidence.'

'What does it matter, so long as we get the old bag?'

'Never mind about her, if you fire that gun inside the house, you'll blow the end wall out and probably kill the Kommandant as well.'

Els sat back and thought. 'All right,' he said at last, 'you let me have the machine guns out of the Saracen turrets and I'll fix her for sure.'

Sergeant de Kock was doubtful. 'Go carefully, Els,' he said, 'and try not to shoot the Kommandant.'

'I'll try, but I can't promise anything,' said Els, and when the four Browning machine guns had been taken out of the armoured cars, he silently stole up the stairs with them. He laid the four guns on a small coffee table pointing down the corridor and tied them down. Konstabel Els had learnt the value of overwhelming firepower up at the blockhouse and he was putting his experience of it to good use. True, the Brownings hadn't anything like the power of the elephant gun, but what they lacked in calibre they made up for in rapid fire.

'Five thousand rounds a minute pumped down the passage will make matchwood of all that furniture and mincemeat of the old girl,' he thought happily, and went downstairs to collect more belts of ammunition. On his return he fastened a cord to the triggers of the guns and prepared his next move.

The Dobermann lying asleep on the chaise-longue and dreaming of his battle with Els smelt the Konstabel coming. It had long entertained the hope that it would be able to renew the challenge Els had thrown down to it on the lawn and now it sensed that the chance had come. It stretched lazily and dropped to the floor. With no warning growl and with a stealth and silence surpassing even that of the Konstabel it crept down the corridor and threaded its way through the barricades of furniture.

Miss Hazelstone had not been in the least put out by the Kommandant's rejection of her attempts to get him into an interesting position. The very violence and strength of his effort had increased her admiration for him.

'What a strong boy you are,' she said picking herself up off the floor. 'Quite the little judo expert,' and for the next few minutes the Kommandant had to resist the manual encouragement to virility Miss Hazelstone seemed determined to administer. By dint of concentrating on Konstabel Els as a sexual object, the Kommandant even managed to maintain his lack of interest and finally Miss Hazelstone had to admit herself defeated.

'One can see you're no great shakes as a ladies' man,' she said to the Kommandant, and before he could expostulate with so much as a meaningless grunt that if she must dress as a man she couldn't expect anything else, she had picked up the hypodermic again. 'Perhaps an injection of novocaine will put lead in your pencil,' she said. 'You'll probably feel like a new man afterwards.'

'I feel like a new man now,' the Kommandant shouted through the hood, squirming furiously, but Miss Hazelstone was too intent about her business to take any notice of his protests. As the needle approached the Kommandant shut his eyes and waited, already numb with terror for the jab and at that moment all hell broke loose on the landing. Miss Hazelstone dropped the syringe and seizing her gun made for the door. The sounds emanating from the passage indicated that some terrible and bestial encounter had just begun, and the Kommandant, stung into action by the hypodermic which Miss Hazelstone had dropped in her haste and which had landed like a dart in his groin and was leaking novocaine into some artery or other, made one last desperate attempt to escape. With a herculean effort he managed to reach the floor and dragging the bed behind him leapt out of the window.

* * *

If Kommandant van Heerden and Miss Hazelstone were astonished at the extraordinary turn events had taken, Konstabel Els was even more surprised. He had just finished putting the final touches to what he hoped was going to be Miss Hazelstone's execution when he was vaguely aware that something unforeseen was in the air. Like some dark premonition he glimpsed a black blur as the Dobermann leapt through the mist of powdered plaster that filled the corridor. The dog's mouth was already open and its eye was fastened prematurely on Els' jugular vein. Els dug his chin firmly into his chest and butted the beast's nuzzle with the top of his head. The dog's teeth, missing the vein, fastened on Els' shoulder and a moment later the two animals were locked in their interrupted struggle for supremacy.

As they rolled across the landing, knocking chairs and tables over left, right and centre, as Miss Hazelstone opened up with the scatter gun and the barricades began to disintegrate above them, the Browning machine guns, thrown off target and now pointing up at the ceiling began to pour tracer bullets at the rate of five thousand rounds a minute out through the roof of Jacaranda House. A lame vulture which had only a few minutes before managed to take off after a long and painful run and was flying gamely above the house which had already provided supper, breakfast and very nearly lunch, evaporated in the hail of bullets with an explosion of feathers and odds and ends. It was the only casualty of the gun-battle that raged in Jacaranda House.

The only other person who nearly received a burst of gunfire in his vital parts was Kommandant van Heerden. The sudden eruption of violence on the landing which had allowed him the opportunity to eject himself with double bed attached, out of the window of the bedroom, had found Sergeant de Kock waiting in the garden in the hope of getting a chance to take a pot shot at Miss Hazelstone from below. The Sergeant had been regretting his decision to allow Konstabel Els to use the machine guns and was fully expecting the plan to end in disaster. As the roar of gunfire erupted in the house, the Sergeant threw himself to the ground, and was lying there when there was a clatter of breaking glass followed by an awful thud just above his head. He got to his feet and stared up at the thing that hung dangling from the window above him.

The Sergeant was by no means a squeamish man and not in the least averse to shooting women. Plenty of Zulu widowers could attest to that. And had he been able to imagine for one moment that the corpulent creature in the pink nightdress who squirmed and struggled against the wall of the house some twenty feet up was Miss Hazelstone, he would have shot her without a moment's thought. But it was all too apparent that what was dangling there was not the old lady. She wasn't fat like that, she wasn't hairy like that, and above all, he felt sure she didn't have reproductive organs like that. It was difficult enough for the Sergeant to believe that anything could look like that. Sergeant de Kock stood and wrestled with the problem of the thing's identity. He peered up at its face and saw that it was wearing a mask.

Of all the queer comings and goings Sergeant de Kock had seen since he arrived at the house, this was undoubtedly the queerest. And queer was the word that sprang most naturally to mind. Whatever was hanging hooded and partially dressed up there was exposing itself to him in a manner that was shameful and indecent beyond belief. The Sergeant didn't like pansies at the best of times and he certainly didn't relish being solicited by one in this disgusting fashion. He was just making up his mind to put an end to the obscene display by a burst from his Sten gun when he was stunned by something that dropped out of the sky on to him. Enveloped in a cloud of feathers and draped with what appeared to be the half-digested contents of a stomach that had recently indulged in an enormous meal of raw meat, Sergeant de Kock staggered about the garden in a state of shock.

As he tried desperately to disentangle himself from the mess of entrails and feathers, he was temporarily put off his idea of ridding the world of the raving transvestite jerking spasmodically below the bedroom window. The discovery in the detritus that covered him of several brass buttons and a South African Police cap badge was making him wonder what the hell had hit him. He was still debating the point when a new burst of gunfire above his head told him that the gun-battle was by no means over. He glanced up and saw the mattress above the hooded figure erupt into an enormous cloud of feathers, and as they floated down and adhered to the blood and guts covering him, Sergeant de Kock turned and ran. Behind him a muffled voice yelled 'Chicken'.

Chapter 12

The failure of her rapid fire down the corridor to silence for an instant the roar of the machine guns and the screams and snarls that were part and parcel of all Konstabel Els' encounters with the Dobermann forced Miss Hazelstone to the realization that her plans were not running true to form. As repeated volleys of shot smashed through her Louis Quinze barricades and riddled with new authenticity several pieces of mock-Jacobean furniture and an irreplaceable eighteenth-century escritoire previously inlaid with ivory, the din of battle on the landing increased. Above her head a fountain of tiles hurtled up into the air under the impact of the machine-gun bullets and crashed back on the roof like enormous hailstones. Miss Hazelstone gave up her attempt to peer through the fog of plaster and went back into the bedroom.

It was immediately apparent to her that here too something had gone astray. The room was pitch dark and some large object was completely obscuring the view of the Park she had previously enjoyed from the window. She switched on the light and stood gazing at the underside of the bed on which but a few minutes before she had sat encouraging Kommandant van Heerden to be a man. Looking at the enormous bed she realized for the first time what a tremendously powerful man the Kommandant was. It had taken ten men to manhandle that bed up the stairs and along the corridor, and now one man had lifted it by himself and had carried it to the window where he was evidently standing on the sill holding it at arm's length, a feat of strength she would never have believed possible. As she looked and wondered, a muffled yell came through the mattress.

'Let me down,' the Kommandant was shouting. 'Let me down. Let me down. That bloody woman will be the death of me.' Miss Hazelstone smiled to herself. 'Just as you say,' she murmured and aimed the scatter gun at the bedsprings. As she pulled the trigger she noted how appropriate it was that the Kommandant should meet his Maker strapped in a rubber nightdress to a mattress labelled Everrest and as the bedsprings twanged and the feathers flew, Miss Hazelstone turned and went out into the corridor with a sob.

It was in all likelihood the sound of that sob that led to the death of her beloved Toby. The Dobermann which had until then felt secure in the hold it had fastened on Konstabel Els' face relaxed for one fatal second. It raised its head and pricked its ears for the last faithful time and in that second, Els, half asphyxiated by the dog's persistent hold on his nose, seized his opportunity and clamped his jaws on the dog's throat. With one hand he clasped the dog to him and with the other grabbed the dog's scrotum and squeezed. Squeezed was hardly adequate to describe the immense pressure he exerted.

Unable, thanks to Els' grip on its windpipe, to protest this infringement of the Queensberry rules, the dog hurled itself sideways and scrabbled furiously with all four feet in an attempt to free itself. Dragging the limpet-like Els with it, it accelerated from a standing start, hurtled towards the top of the stairs and a second later the two maddened animals were airborne several feet above the great staircase. As they avalanched into the hall, the portraits of Sir Theophilus and Judge Hazelstone gazed grimly down on the sordid spectacle. Only the wild boar, itself strapped to an unrelenting iron frame, can have appreciated what its modern counterpart was suffering.

Three minutes later Konstabel Els, lying on the marble floor of the hall, knew that he had won. The Dobermann lay still in death and Els relaxed his grip on its throat and rose unsteadily to his feet. Around him the heads of stuffed wart-hogs and buffaloes were his only audience in the moment of triumph. Dragging the dog by the tail Konstabel Els went out into the Park to look for the vulture. It had looked at him ravenously enough, and he thought it might like a change of diet. He had some difficulty in finding it, and when he did, even Konstabel Els could see that it had not died of hunger.

The shots that had indirectly led to the death of Toby had come very near to causing the death of Kommandant van Heerden. Near but rather too high, for the Kommandant had had the good fortune to be hanging by his wrists from what was now the bottom of the bed. He had chewed through the hood and was staring down at Sergeant de Kock who had from the look of him just emerged from a nasty accident in a turkey abattoir. It didn't seem a likely explanation of the Sergeant's condition but after his recent experience of perversion the Kommandant wouldn't have been at all surprised to learn that the Sergeant had been acting out some depraved obsession connected with his name.

He was just speculating on the matter when his thoughts were drowned by the roar of a gun just above his head and a cloud of feathers suddenly obscured his view of the garden. 'Chicken,' he yelled as the Sergeant disappeared round the corner of the house, and he was still screaming abuse some minutes later when the Sergeant followed by several konstabels reappeared. It seemed that his voice issuing through the hole he had managed to chew in the rubber hood carried less than its normal quota of authority. The little group of policemen gathered below him seemed more amused by his orders than likely to obey them.

'Let me down,' yelled the Kommandant. 'Let me down.' Against this background of ignored instructions, Sergeant de Kock was explaining the nastier facts of life to the young konstabels.

'What you see before you,' he said portentously, 'is a transvestite.'

'What's that mean, Sergeant,' inquired a konstabel.

'It means a man who likes dressing up in women's clothes. This transvestite is also a pervert.'

'Let me down, you sod,' yelled the Kommandant.

'It's a pervert,' continued the Sergeant, 'because it is a homosexual and it's a pervert twice over because it's a rubber fetishist.'

'I'll have you stripped of your stripes if you don't get me down.'

'What's a rubber fetishist, Sergeant?'

'It's someone who dresses up in rubber nighties and hangs out of other people's bedroom windows soliciting people below,' continued the Sergeant plucking feathers and lights off his uniform. 'It's also a product of the permissive society and as you all know South Africa is not a permissive society. What this swine is doing is against the law here, and what I suggest is that we shove a bullet or two up his arse and give him the thrill to end all thrills.'

The suggestion was greeted with nods of approval from the konstabels and a crescendo of screams from the hooded dangling figure. Only one naïve konstabel objected.

'But wouldn't that be murder, Sergeant?' he inquired.

Sergeant de Kock looked at him sternly. 'Are you telling me,' he asked, 'that you think that blokes should be allowed to run around the country dressed in women's nighties?'

'No, Sergeant. It's against the law.'

'That's what I just said, so we'd be doing our duty if we put a bullet in him.'

'Couldn't we just arrest him?' the konstabel asked.

'This is your commanding officer, and I order you to let me down.'

'It's guilty of another crime now, Sergeant,' said another konstabel. 'It's impersonating a police officer.'

'You young konstabels know the procedure or you bloody well ought to,' continued the Sergeant. 'In the case of a criminal apprehended in the commission of a crime, what do you do?'

'Arrest him,' chorused the konstabels.

'And if you can't arrest him? If he tries to escape?'

'You give him a warning.'

'And what if he doesn't stop trying to escape?'

'You shoot him, Sergeant.'

'Right,' said the Sergeant. 'Now are you trying to tell me that that bastard isn't a criminal caught in the commission of a crime, and that he isn't trying to escape?'

The konstabels had to agree that the Sergeant was right, and they had just reached this point in their deliberations when Konstabel Els came limping triumphantly round the corner dragging the Dobermann after him.

'Look what I've got,' he said proudly.

Sergeant de Kock's little group were not impressed. 'Look what we've got,' they said, and Konstabel Els had to admit that what was hanging squirming from the window made his own trophy look pretty tame.

'Just doing a queer in,' said Sergeant de Kock. 'Want to join in, Els, should be just up your street?'

'Not my street,' said Els peering up at the figure. 'That's Kommandant van Heerden's street, that's what that is. I'd know it anywhere.'

As the firing party broke up in confusion at the news that it was the Kommandant who was hanging there, the woman largely responsible for his predicament was debating what to do next. She thought that she must have at last got it into the thick head of the Kommandant that she was capable of killing Fivepence and while she realized that Kommandant van Heerden's opinion no longer mattered, she hoped that his successor would have enough sense to arrest her promptly.

She went downstairs to look for a policeman to escort her to her cell in Piemburg Police Station, but the house appeared to be deserted.

'I must have scared them off,' she said to herself and went to fetch her car. Halfway to the garage she realized that Fivepence had the keys with him and instead she climbed into one of the police Land Rovers and started the engine.

As the konstabels on the other side of Jacaranda House assisted the Kommandant down the ladder, they gave no thought to the Land Rover that sailed unsteadily up the drive. At the gate the sentry signalled it out and the car disappeared round the corner and down the road into Piemburg.

*　　　*　　　*

Most of the events of the day had passed clean over the head of the Bishop of Barotseland. Manacled and naked, he lay in the cellar and tried to concentrate on spiritual questions as being less painful than the affairs of the flesh. He wasn't particularly successful in this effort; hunger and pain competed with fear to occupy his attention, and over them all there hung the awful dread that he was going mad. It was less in fact fear at the thought that he was going than that he had already gone. In twenty-four hours he had seen the accepted tenets of his world abused in a way which had, he had to admit, all the hallmarks of insanity.

'I am a bishop and my sister is a murderess,' he said to himself reassuringly. 'If my sister is not a murderess, it is possible that I am not a bishop.' This line of logic didn't seem very helpful and he gave it up as likely to disturb what little balance of mind he had left. 'Someone is mad,' he concluded, and began to wonder if the voices he had heard in the depths of the swimming-bath were not after all symptoms of the insanity he seemed to be suffering from.

On the other hand his firm belief in the intervention of the Lord in the affairs of the world led him to wonder how he had transgressed so gravely as to warrant the punishment that had fallen on him. He came to the conclusion that he had been guilty of *hubris*. 'Pride comes before a fall,' he said, but he couldn't imagine what height of pride could justify the depths to which he had fallen. Certainly the little bit of self-congratulation he had allowed himself on his appointment to Barotseland hardly called for the appalling punishment he was now undergoing. He preferred to believe that his present sufferings were a preparation for better things to come, and a test of his faith. He consoled himself with the thought that there must be some people in the world in even worse plights, though he couldn't think who they were or what they were suffering.

'I shall bear my tribulations gladly and my soul will be renewed,' he said smugly and gave himself up to meditation.

Kommandant van Heerden had come to quite different conclusions. He had borne enough tribulations in the past twenty-four hours to last him a lifetime. He knew now that there were three things he never wanted to see again. Rubber nightdresses, Sergeant de Kock and Jacaranda House. All three had lost whatever charm they had once held for him, and in the case of the first two that was nil.

As for Jacaranda House, he had to admit he had once liked the place, but he could see now that his feelings were not reciprocated. The house evidently reserved its favours for those of impeccable social standing and British descent. For lesser mortals it held terrors. In decreasing order of social standing he placed himself, Els, the Dobermann, Fivepence and the vulture. He himself had been trussed, terrified and threatened with death. Els had been savaged on two separate occasions. The Dobermann had been bitten to death. Fivepence had been deposited all over the garden and the vulture all over Sergeant de Kock. All in all, these indignities had been too closely related to the class of the recipients for there to be any doubt that the reputation for snobbery the Hazelstones enjoyed was not without foundation in fact. On the whole he thought Els had come off pretty lightly, considering his origins and social standing.

On the other hand he had cause to suspect that Els' share of misfortune was yet to come. True, he had been instrumental in saving the Kommandant's life on two occasions. Kommandant van Heerden had to admit that the Konstabel's intervention on the landing had given him time to jump out of the window, and once there it had been Els who had stopped Sergeant de Kock exceeding his duty. But then again, there was the little matter of the fracas up at the gateway. It had too many of the trademarks of Els to be ignored entirely. Els had some explaining to do.

As he dressed in the study Kommandant van Heerden eyed Els warily. The Konstabel was dabbing antiseptic on his nose and playing with the paperweight. By the time he had put on his trousers, the Kommandant had come to some definite conclusions. Miss Hazelstone had made her point, and the Kommandant was convinced that in all probability she had killed Fivepence. Unfortunately, she could not, he knew, have butchered the policemen at the gate. Someone else was responsible for that, and while the evidence pointed to Jonathan Hazelstone, the Kommandant had seen him asleep on the bed just before the firing began. It followed that if Jonathan was innocent, the guilty person was Els. It was but a step from this conclusion to the question of responsibility. Who, it would be asked, had allowed a homicidal maniac like Els to have possession of a multi-barrelled elephant gun, and had given him permission to use it?

Weighing up the various debts he owed to Konstabel Els and the ugly possibilities that faced his career, the Kommandant came to a rapid decision.

'Els,' he said quietly, seating himself behind the desk, 'I want you to think carefully before you answer the next question. Very carefully indeed.'

Konstabel Els looked up nervously. He didn't like the tone of the Kommandant's voice.

'What time was it when you deserted your post at the gate yesterday afternoon?' the Kommandant continued.

'I didn't desert my post, sir,' said Els.

The Kommandant shivered. This was worse than he expected. The idiot was going to claim he stayed there all afternoon.

'I think you did desert your post, Els,' he said. 'In fact, I know you did. At half past three to be precise.'

'No, sir,' said Els, 'I was relieved.'

'Relieved?'

'Yes, sir, by a large black-haired konstabel who had left his revolver at the station.'

'By a large black-haired konstabel who had left his revolver at the station?' the Kommandant repeated slowly, wondering where the trap was.

'That's right. That's what he told me, sir. That he had left his revolver at the station. He asked to borrow mine.'

'He asked to borrow yours?'

'Yes, sir.'

Kommandant van Heerden mulled this statement over in his mind before going on. He had to admit that it had the ring of utility about it.

'Would you be able to identify this large black-haired konstabel again if you saw him?' he asked.

'Oh yes, sir,' Els said. 'He's sitting in the cellar.'

'Sitting in the cellar, is he?' Kommandant van Heerden glanced out of the window and pondered. Outside Sergeant de Kock was patrolling up and down on the path. Looking out at the Sergeant, the Kommandant began to think he might have a use for him after all. He went to the window and shouted.

'Sergeant de Kock,' he ordered, 'I want you in here at the double.'

A moment later the Sergeant was standing in front of the Judge's desk and regretting that he had ever mistaken the Kommandant for a transvestite.

'How many times have I told you, Sergeant,' the Kommandant said sternly, 'that I will not have my men walking about in untidy uniforms. You're supposed to set an example too. Look at your uniform, man. It's disgusting. You're a disgrace to the South African Police.'

'Got dirty in the line of duty, sir,' said the Sergeant. 'Flipping vulture died on me, sir.'

'Birds of a feather, Sergeant de Kock, stick together,' said the Kommandant.

'Very funny, I'm sure, sir,' said the Sergeant unpleasantly.

'Hm,' said the Kommandant. 'Well, as far as I'm concerned, it's inexcusable.'

'I didn't choose to be there.'

'Don't make excuses. I didn't choose to be where I was just now, and I didn't notice any consideration on your part for my state, so you needn't expect any from me. Get out of that filthy uniform at once. Konstabel Els, fetch the prisoner.'

As the Sergeant undressed, the Kommandant continued to lecture him, and by the time he was out of his uniform, he had learnt a great deal about himself that he would have preferred to have remained ignorant about.

'And what do you think I'm going to wear back to the barracks?' he asked.

Kommandant van Heerden tossed him the rubber nightdress. 'Try this for size,' he snarled.

'You don't expect me to go down into town wearing this?'

Sergeant de Kock asked incredulously. The Kommandant nodded.

'What's good for the goose . . .' he said smugly.

'I'm not going to be made the laughing-stock of the barracks,' the Sergeant insisted.

'Nobody will know who you are. You'll be wearing this as well,' and the Kommandant gave him the hood.

Sergeant de Kock hesitated miserably. 'I don't know . . .' he said.

'I bloody well do,' yelled the Kommandant. 'Get into those clothes. That's an order,' and as the Sergeant, bowing before his wrath, squeezed himself into the revolting garments and wondered how he would explain his presence in them to his wife, the Kommandant continued, 'You're incognito now, Sergeant, and provided you keep your trap shut, you'll stay that way.'

'I sure as hell won't,' said the Sergeant. 'I'll be out of the fucking things as quick as I can. I don't know how the hell you expect me to keep discipline when you make me look bloody ridiculous.'

'Nonsense,' said the Kommandant. 'That hood is a perfect disguise. You ought to know that. And another thing, you keep quiet about what you've seen and I'll keep my mouth shut about you. Right?'

'I suppose it will have to be.'

In the next few minutes Sergeant de Kock learnt that he had never so much as seen a vulture and that he hadn't visited Jacaranda Park. He had, it seemed, been away on compassionate leave visiting his sick mother. The fact that his mother had died ten years before didn't seem worth mentioning. With the knowledge that he would be known for the rest of his life as Rubber Cock unless he did what he was told, the Sergeant didn't feel he was in any position to argue with the Kommandant.

The Bishop of Barotseland had reached much the same conclusion. The whole thing was a mistake, and the police would soon discover their error, he told himself as Konstabel Els frogmarched him up to the study. He was delighted to find the

Kommandant in a much friendlier state of mind than he had been earlier in the day.

'You can take the handcuffs off him, Els,' said the Kommandant. 'Now then, Mr Hazelstone,' he continued when this had been done. 'We just want to make a little experiment. It concerns this uniform.' He held Sergeant de Kock's blood-stained tunic up. 'We have reason to believe that the man responsible for the murders yesterday was wearing this uniform. I just want you to try it on for size. If it doesn't fit you, and I don't for one moment suppose that it will, you will be free to leave here.'

The Bishop looked at the uniform doubtfully. It was clearly several sizes too small for him.

'I don't suppose I could get into it,' he said.

'Well, just put it on and we'll see,' said the Kommandant encouragingly and the Bishop climbed into the uniform. In the corner a grim figure in a nightdress and hood smiled to itself. Sergeant de Kock had begun to see daylight.

Finally, the Bishop was ready to prove his innocence. The trousers were too short by a foot. The fly wouldn't do up and the arms of the tunic just covered his elbows. It was obvious that he had never worn the uniform before. He could hardly move in the thing.

He turned cheerfully to the Kommandant. 'There you are,' he said. 'I told you it wouldn't fit.'

Kommandant van Heerden put the Sergeant's cap on his head where it perched precariously. Then he stood back and regarded him appreciatively.

'Just one more thing,' he said. 'We'll have to have an identity parade.'

Five minutes later the Bishop was standing in a row of twenty policemen while Konstabel Els walked slowly down the line. For the sake of verisimilitude, Els chose to hesitate in front of several other men before finally halting before the Bishop.

'This is the man who relieved me, sir,' he said emphatically. 'I'd know him anywhere. I never forget a face.'

'You're quite sure about it?' the Kommandant asked.

'Positive, sir,' said Els.

'Just as I thought,' said the Kommandant. 'Put the handcuffs on the swine.'

Before he knew what was happening the Bishop was manacled once more and being bundled into the back of a police car. Beside him, hooded and hot, sat the grim figure from the study.

'It's a lie. It's a mistake,' the Bishop shouted as the car began to move off. 'I've been framed.'

'You can say that again,' murmured the figure in the hood. The Bishop looked at it. 'Who are you?' he asked.

'I'm the executioner,' said the hooded man and chuckled. In the back of the police car the Bishop of Barotseland fainted.

On the front steps of Jacaranda House, Kommandant van Heerden was giving his orders. They were quite explicit. Find, restrain and transfer Miss Hazelstone to Fort Rapier Lunatic Asylum. Find, collect, and transfer every lethal weapon in Jacaranda House to the police armoury. Find, collect and transfer every piece of rubber including bathmats and rain-coats to the Piemburg Police Station. In short, collect every piece of evidence and get the hell out. No, the Bubonic Plague and Rabies noticeboards could be left up. They were relevant, and if anything understated the dangers Jacaranda Park held for visitors. From now on Kommandant van Heerden was going to conduct the case from a more secure base. His headquarters would be in Piemburg Prison itself where Jonathan Hazelstone couldn't get out, and more important, his sister couldn't get in. And get that damned hypodermic syringe out of his sight. He'd seen enough hypodermics to last a lifetime.

As the men dispersed to carry out his orders, the Kommandant called Konstabel Els back.

'Very good, Els,' he said charitably. 'There was only one little mistake you made.'

'Mistake? What was that?'

The Kommandant smiled. 'It wasn't a konstabel who took over from you at the gate, it was a sergeant.'

'Oh yes, so it was. I remember now. A sergeant.'

Chapter 13

The prison in Piemburg is situated on the edge of town. It is old and looks from the outside not altogether unattractive. An air of faded severity lingers about its stuccoed walls. Above the huge iron doorway are printed the words 'Piemburg Tronk and Gaol', and the door itself is painted a cheerful black. On either side the barred windows of the administrative block break the monotony of the walls whose heights are delicately topped with cast-iron cacti which give the whole building a faintly horticultural air. The visitor to Piemburg who passes the great rectangle of masonry might well imagine that he was in the neighbourhood of some enormous kitchen garden were it not for the frequent and persistent screams that float up over the ornamental ironwork and suggest that something more voracious than a Venus Flytrap has closed upon a victim.

Inside the impression is less deceptive. Opened by Sir Theophilus in 1897, the Viceroy had complimented the architect in his speech at the unveiling of the flogging post for 'creating in this building a sense of security it is hard to find in the world today', a remark which, coming as it did from a man in whom a sense of insecurity was so manifest, spoke for itself. Sir Theophilus' enthusiasm was not shared by most of the people who entered Piemburg Prison. Notorious throughout South Africa for the severity of its warden, Governor Schnapps, it had the reputation for being escape-proof and having the fewest recidivists.

If the prison was escape-proof, the Maximum Security Block was doubly so. Set near the execution shed which was appropriately nicknamed Top, the Security block huddling half underground was known as Bottom.

The Bishop could find no fault with the name. 'I can see it's the bottom,' he said to the warder who pushed him into his tiny cell. 'I don't have to be told.'

'I could tell you a few other things,' said the warder through the grille.

'I'm sure you could,' said the Bishop hastily. His experience with the hooded man in the car had taught him not to ask unnecessary questions.

'I have always kept this cell for murderers,' the warder continued. 'It's convenient for the door, you see.'

'I should have thought that was a disadvantage with prisoners who have such strong motives to escape,' the Bishop said, reconciling himself to the thought that he was a captive audience.

'Oh, no. They didn't escape. It made it easy to take them across to Top. We rushed them along the passage and up the steps and they were gone before they knew it.'

The Bishop was relieved to hear this. 'I am glad you put so much emphasis on the past,' he said. 'I gather there hasn't been a hanging for some time.'

'Not for twenty years. Not in Piemburg, that is. They hang them all in Pretoria these days. Taken all the fun out of life.'

The Bishop was just considering the dreariness of a life that found hangings fun when the warder went on, 'Mind you, it will be different in your case. You're a Hazelstone and you're privileged,' the warder said enviously.

For once in his life the Bishop was thankful to be a Hazelstone. 'Why's that?' he asked hopefully.

'You've got the right to be hanged in Piemburg. It's something to do with your grandfather. Don't know what, but I'll see if I can find out for you,' and he went down the passage and left the Bishop cursing himself for asking yet another silly question. As he paced his cell he heard the sound of vehicles outside and peering out through the tiny barred window saw that the Kommandant had arrived.

The Kommandant had taken the precaution of driving down from Jacaranda House in an armoured car and was busy explaining to Governor Schnapps that he was taking over his office.

'You can't do that,' the Governor protested.

'Can and will,' said the Kommandant. 'Got Emergency

Powers. Now then if you'll be good enough to show me where your office is, I'll have my camp bed moved in and we can get down to business.'

And leaving the Governor to write a letter of complaint to Pretoria, the Kommandant installed himself in Schnapps' office and sent for Konstabel Els.

'Where's Luitenant Verkramp?' he asked. 'That's what I want to know.'

For once Konstabel Els was better informed. 'He's in hospital,' he said. 'Got himself wounded up at the gate.'

'That fellow shot him, did he? Deserves a medal.'

Els was surprised. What he had seen of Luitenant Verkramp's courage didn't seem to him to warrant a medal.

'Who? Verkramp?' he asked.

'No, of course not. The fellow who shot him.'

'He didn't get shot,' said Els. 'Threw himself into a ditch.'

'Typical,' said the Kommandant. 'Anyway, I want you to go and fetch him from the hospital. Tell him he's got to interrogate the prisoner. I want a full confession and quick.'

Konstabel Els hesitated. He was not anxious to renew his acquaintance with the Luitenant.

'He won't take orders from me,' he said. 'Besides he may have hurt himself seriously falling into that ditch.'

'I wish I had your optimism, Els,' said the Kommandant, 'but I doubt it. The swine's malingering.'

'Why not leave him where he is? I don't mind getting a confession out of the prisoner.'

The Kommandant shook his head. The case was too important to have Els botching it up with his dreadful methods.

'It's kind of you to offer,' he said, 'but I think we'll leave it to Luitenant Verkramp.'

'There's gratitude for you,' thought Els, as he went off to fetch Verkramp from the hospital.

He found the Luitenant lying on his stomach taking nourishment through a straw. Verkramp's back, it appeared, made it impossible to eat in any other position.

'Well?' he asked grumpily when Konstabel Els reported to him. 'What do you want?'

'Came to see how you were,' Els said tactfully.

'You can see how I am,' Verkramp answered, regarding Els' dirty boots with disapproval. 'I have been seriously wounded.'

'I can see that,' Els said, grateful that the Luitenant couldn't study his face. He regretted having peered down into the moat now. 'Got you in the back, did he?'

'Came at me from behind,' said the Luitenant who didn't like the imputation that he had been trying to escape.

'Nasty. Very nasty. Well, you'll be glad to know we've got the bastard. The Kommandant wants you to start interrogating him straight away.'

Verkramp choked on his straw. 'He wants what?' he shouted at the Konstabel's boots.

'He says you're to come straight away.'

'Well, he can say what he likes, but I'm not budging. Besides,' he added, 'the doctors wouldn't let me.'

'Would you like to tell him yourself?' asked Els. 'He won't believe me.'

In the end a telephone was brought to the Luitenant's bedside and the Kommandant had a word with him. It was rather more than one word and in the end Luitenant Verkramp was persuaded to report for duty. Short of facing a court martial for cowardice, desertion in the face of the enemy, and incompetence in that he allowed twenty-one policemen under his command to be slaughtered, there didn't seem much he could do to remain in hospital. Verkramp was in a very ugly mood and not altogether clearheaded when he arrived at the prison to question Jonathan Hazelstone.

It was hardly less ugly than the mood Kommandant van Heerden was in. After a momentary spasm of optimism that the case was as good as closed now that the prisoner was in Bottom, the Kommandant had succumbed to a state of extreme pessimism on learning that Miss Hazelstone was still at large. Since leaving the Park she had not been seen. The police Land Rover had been found abandoned but of Miss Hazelstone there was no trace, and while the Kommandant felt pretty sure she wouldn't break into the prison to renew their acquaintance, he had no doubt that what she might do outside was just as likely to jeopardize his future.

For one thing he couldn't afford to allow her to run about the country telling all and sundry that she had had him trussed to a bed in a rubber nightdress and that he hadn't been man enough to take an injection. He was just consoling himself with the thought that Miss Hazelstone's circle of friends was pretty exclusive, when he remembered that among other assets like gold mines, the Hazelstone family owned the local newspaper, whose editor had never shown any great regard for the police. Kommandant van Heerden had no desire whatsoever to provide copy for the *Natal Chronicle* and the thought of headlines like: 'The Tiny Prick. Kommandant in Rubber Nightie says No to Needle', made his blood run cold.

He gave orders that road blocks be set up on all roads leading out of Piemburg and that the homes of all Miss Hazelstone's friends were to be raided. Every hotel and guesthouse in the town was to be checked and plain-clothes men were to mingle with the crowds in the shops. Finally, the Kommandant ordered that notices be put up announcing a large reward for information leading to the capture of Miss Hazelstone, but just to make sure that Miss Hazelstone's confessions did not reach the public, he plucked up courage and left the safety of the prison to pay a personal call on the editor of the *Natal Chronicle*.

'I'm acting under Emergency Powers,' he told the man, 'and I am ordering you to publish nothing Miss Hazelstone may submit. In fact, if anything is submitted by her you're to forward it to me unread,' and the editor had gone off to cancel Miss Hazelstone's current contributions to the women's page which was called, 'How to Convert a Zulu Kraal into a Country Cottage'. He read it through to see if there was anything subversive in it, but apart from the recommendation to use latex for loose covers, he couldn't find anything unusual in it. In any case he had his hands full trying to find out how many victims there were in the bubonic plague and rabies epidemics that had apparently hit the community. As far as he had been able to ascertain, the only people exhibiting symptoms of rabies were the Piemburg police.

Throughout the night and the following day the search for Miss Hazelstone continued. Hundreds of plain-clothes men scoured the town or hung about indecisively in shops making life difficult for store detectives on the lookout for shoplifters. A number of elderly ladies suddenly found themselves in handcuffs and being driven at high speed in police cars to Fort Rapier Mental Hospital, where several had to be admitted with nervous breakdowns as a result of the experience.

On the roads out of Piemburg queues of cars and lorries waited for hours while policemen ransacked each vehicle. There were particularly tiresome delays on the Durban road where trucks carrying offal from the abattoir to the Jojo Dog and Servant Meat Cannery had to be searched. Since Kommandant van Heerden had impressed upon his men the need to search every square inch of every vehicle no matter how unlikely a hiding-place it seemed to be and since the Jojo trucks contained twenty-five tons of pig brains, ox guts and the inedible and doubtless nutritious entrails of every conceivable diseased animal that contributed its share to the liver and love Jojo promised the dogs and servants, the men at the Durban road search-point had to go to considerable trouble to make absolutely sure that Miss Hazelstone was not hiding in the disgusting mess that greeted them every time they stopped one of the lorries. The occupants of the cars piling up behind were astonished to see policemen clad only in bathing-trunks and with facemasks and schnorkels clambering aboard the Jojo lorries and diving into piles of semi-liquid meat so enormous that even the late and unlamented vulture would have been put off its feed. The policemen who finally emerged from their prolonged and fruitless search were hardly a sight to reassure the citizens of Piemburg that the police were looking after their interests, and faced with the prospect of so thorough a search a good many motorists decided to cancel the trips they were making and go quietly home. Those that stayed had the upholstery of their cars irremediably stained by the half-naked and bloodsoaked cops who climbed in and poked under seats and inside glove compartments for the elusive Miss Hazelstone.

In the meantime the homes of Miss Hazelstone's friends were being searched with equal thoroughness, and a good many people, who had boasted of an acquaintanceship with her which they had never enjoyed, found that Miss Hazelstone's friendship carried with it some awesome consequences, not the least of which was the knowledge that they were suspected of harbouring a wanted criminal.

In spite of all these drastic measures, Miss Hazelstone remained at large and cheerfully unaware that she was the object of such a meticulous manhunt.

After driving the police Land Rover through the gates of Jacaranda Park she had followed the main road to town, had parked the car in the main street, and had walked into the Police Station to give herself up.

'I'm Miss Hazelstone of Jacaranda Park, and I've come here to be arrested,' she said to the elderly Konstabel on duty at the desk, who was in fact one of the post-operative cases Kommandant van Heerden had insisted return to duty. Missing his gall bladder and the lower portion of his intestines, he had not lost his wits as well, and he had been in the police long enough to have got used to the queer customers who came in regularly to make false confessions. He looked the old gentleman in the salmon-pink suit up and down for a minute before replying.

'Oh yes,' he said sympathetically. 'So you're Miss Hazelstone are you, sir? And what do you want to be arrested for?'

'I've murdered my cook.'

'Lucky to have one to murder,' said the old Konstabel. 'My old woman cooks for me and if the state of my insides or what remains of them is anything to go by, she's been trying to murder me for years, and it's only thanks to the miracles of modern surgery that she hasn't bloody well succeeded. Do you know,' he went on confidentially, 'it took the surgeons four hours to cut away all the rotten stuff there was in me. They took my gall bladder and then my . . .'

'I have not come here to discuss the state of your health,' Miss Hazelstone snapped. 'It's not of the slightest interest to me.'

Konstabel Oosthuizen wasn't amused. 'If that's the way you want it,' he said, 'that's the way it's going to be. Now hop it.'

Miss Hazelstone wasn't going to be brushed off so easily. 'I have come here to be arrested for murder,' she insisted.

Konstabel Oosthuizen looked up from the medical dictionary he had been reading. 'Look,' he said, 'you've just told me you're not interested in my physical condition. Well, I'm bloody well not interested in your mental state either. So shove off.'

'Are you telling me you refuse to arrest me?'

Konstabel Oosthuizen sighed. 'I'll arrest you for loitering if you don't get out of here double quick,' he said.

'Good, that's what I've come for,' Miss Hazelstone sat down on a bench against the wall.

'You're making a bloody nuisance of yourself, that's what you're doing. All right come on down to the cells,' and leading the way down to the basement he locked her in. 'Give me a shout when you want to come out,' he said, and went back to read about diseases of the intestinal tract. He was still so engrossed in his own pathology when he went off duty that he forgot to mention her presence in the cells to the konstabel who relieved him, and she was still sitting quietly in her rubber suit next morning when he came on duty once more.

It wasn't until mid-morning that he remembered that the old gent was still down in the cells, and he went down to let him out.

'Had enough?' he asked, unlocking the door.

'Have you come to question me?' Miss Hazelstone asked hopefully. She had been looking forward to third degree.

'I haven't come to bring you breakfast if that's what you think.'

'Good,' said Miss Hazelstone. 'Let's get on with it.'

Konstabel Oosthuizen looked bewildered. 'You're a weird old buzzard,' he said. 'Senile if you ask me.'

'What are you going to do?'

'Kick you out,' said the Konstabel. 'I can't have you cluttering up the station.'

'I'm Miss Hazelstone of Jacaranda Park, and I'm wanted for murder. It's your duty to arrest me.'

'And I'm the Queen of England,' said Konstabel Oosthuizen. 'Go on, clear out of here before you get me into trouble.'

'I tell you I'm wanted for murder,' Miss Hazelstone insisted.

'You're certainly not wanted for anything else,' and the Konstabel picked up his medical dictionary and began to read about gynecomastia.

Miss Hazelstone tried to make him see reason. 'What do I have to do to get myself arrested if you won't arrest me for murder?' she asked.

'Try fucking a kaffir for a start,' suggested the Konstabel. 'That usually works wonders.'

'But that's what I've been doing for the last eight years,' Miss Hazelstone told him.

'Get along with you. I doubt if you've got the wherewithal,' was all the answer she got, and with the final comment that she looked as though she might have gynecomastia, which Konstabel Oosthuizen had just learnt was unusual development of the breasts of a male, the Konstabel went back to his book.

'If you won't arrest me, I demand to be taken home,' Miss Hazelstone said.

Konstabel Oosthuizen knew when to compromise. 'Where do you live?' he asked.

'Jacaranda Park of course,' said Miss Hazelstone.

'I might have known it,' said the Konstabel, and glad to be rid of her took her out into the station yard. 'Take the old gent up to Jacaranda Park,' he said to the driver of a police car that was just leaving, and with all the speed and social deference to which she was accustomed, Miss Hazelstone was driven to the gates of Jacaranda Park and deposited there. The car hadn't been stopped at the police checkpoints for obvious reasons.

Chapter 14

When Luitenant Verkramp arrived from hospital to begin his interrogation of the prisoner, he found the Kommandant waiting for him. He hobbled into the Governor's office to report for duty.

'I'm a sick man,' he said grumpily. 'The doctors didn't want me to leave the hospital.'

'Quite so, Luitenant,' said the Kommandant cheerfully. 'Quite so, but now that you're here, let's not waste time. I need your help.'

'What is it this time?' Verkramp asked. Kommandant van Heerden was always needing his help, but this was the first time he had known him acknowledge the fact.

'I have here the Hazelstone family file,' the Kommandant said. 'It includes the security report you submitted to the Bureau of State Security. I've read it through, and I must say, Luitenant, you showed more perspicacity than I gave you credit for.'

Luitenant Verkramp smiled. The Kommandant had never been so complimentary before.

'You say here,' continued the Kommandant, tapping the report, 'that the Hazelstones are noted for their left-wing and Communistic leanings. I would like to know what made you say that.'

'Everybody knows they are Marxists,' said Verkramp.

'I don't,' said the Kommandant, 'and I would like to hear why you do.'

'Well, for one thing Miss Hazelstone's nephew is at the university.'

'Doesn't make him a Commie.'

'He believes in evolution.'

'Hm,' said the Kommandant doubtfully. He knew it was a subversive doctrine, but with Els around it seemed irrefutable to him.

'What else?' he asked.

'I checked the library. It's full of Communist literature. They've got *The Red Badge of Courage*, *Black Beauty*, the collected works of Dostoyevsky, even Bertrand Russell's banned book, *Why I am not a Christian*. I tell you, they are all dangerous books.'

Kommandant van Heerden was impressed. Evidently Verkramp had gone more thoroughly into the matter than he had imagined. 'That seems conclusive enough,' he said. 'What about the brother, Jonathan Hazelstone. You say here he's got a criminal record.'

'That's right. He lives in Rhodesia and he's done time.'

'He says he's a bishop.'

'He can say what he bloody well pleases,' said Verkramp. 'It doesn't alter the facts. I checked them with the Rhodesian Police. You'll find the telegram they sent back in the file.'

Kommandant van Heerden pulled out the telegram. 'I can't make head or tail of it,' he said. 'It's in code or something. You read it,' and he handed the telegram to Verkramp.

The Luitenant peered at the hieroglyphs. 'It's pretty obvious,' he said at last. ' "Jonathan Hazelstone 2 yrs parson Bulawayo 3 yrs·Barotse incumbent at present convocation 3 wks Umtali." Any fool can understand that,' he said.

'Well, this one can't,' snapped the Kommandant. 'You tell me what it means.'

Verkramp sighed. This was what came from having an illiterate Kommandant.

'It's quite simple. He's done two years in Bulawayo Prison for burning a building down. Three years for murdering a Barotse native who was having a nap and three weeks in Umtali for convoking.'

Kommandant van Heerden thought for a moment. 'What's convoking?' he asked.

'You've heard of con men, haven't you? It's fraud and swindling. It's convoking people into buying phoney shares and things.'

'Oh, is that what it is? You would think they'd have given him more than three weeks for a thing like that. After all he got three years for killing the coon boy which was a bit steep,' the Kommandant said, relieved to know that he had got the right man. There was no doubt now in his mind that he could make the case stick. A man who had killed a Barotse while the poor bastard was asleep was hardly likely to hesitate when it came to killing a Zulu cook.

'Well, all we need now is a nice tidy confession,' he said. 'I'll expect you to have it on my desk in the morning.'

Luitenant Verkramp shrugged. 'If you require it so quick you had better ask Els. My methods require that the prisoner be kept awake for at least three days and with a hardened professional like this fellow it will probably take more.'

'I can't ask Els. We can't have a Hazelstone hobbling into court with no toenails and his balls the size of pumpkins. Think what the defence attorney would make of that one. Use your head. No, the interrogation has got to be handled discreetly and I'm putting you in charge of it,' the Kommandant said, resorting to flattery. 'Do what you like with him, but see he's all in one piece when you've finished.'

With this *carte blanche*, the Kommandant ended the interview and ordered his supper.

In the Maximum Security Block, there was no supper for Jonathan Hazelstone, and if there had been it is doubtful if he would have had much appetite for it. He had just learnt from the old warder how it was he enjoyed the unusual privilege of being able to be hanged in Top.

'It's to do with something your grandfather said in his speech when he opened the prison,' the warder told him. 'He said he wanted the gallows to be kept in working order in case his family wanted to use them.'

'I'm sure he meant well,' the Bishop said sadly, wondering at the appalling legacy his grandfather had bequeathed the family.

'Your father, the late Judge, he was a great one for the gallows. Why some of the men who've had their last meal in that cell, where you're standing now, have told me that they were certain they were going to get off free as the air, and damn me if your old dad didn't go and put the black cap on and condemn them.'

'I have always regretted my father's reputation,' said the Bishop.

'I wouldn't worry about it now,' said the warder. 'It's the gallows would put me in a sweat if I were in your shoes.'

'I have every faith in the fairness of the court,' said the Bishop.

'They haven't been used for twenty years,' continued the warder. 'They're not safe.'

'No?' queried the Bishop. 'Is that unusual?'

'They've got the death watch beetle. You'd be lucky to get up the steps alive, if you ask me,' said the warder and shuffled off down the passage to let Luitenant Verkramp and Konstabel Els into Bottom. The interrogation was about to begin.

In spite of the fact that he was still feeling the effects of his injuries, Luitenant Verkramp was determined to apply the standard South African technique to the prisoner.

'I'll butter him up,' he told Konstabel Els, 'and make him feel I'm sympathetic and you can be the hard man and threaten him.'

'Can I use the electric-shock machine?' Els asked eagerly.

'He's too important,' said Verkramp, 'and you're not to beat him up too much either.'

'What are we going to do then?' said Els, who couldn't imagine getting a confession out of an innocent man without some violence.

'Keep him awake until he's ready to drop. I've never known it to fail.'

Luitenant Verkramp seated himself behind the desk and ordering the prisoner to be brought in, assumed what he supposed to be an air of sympathetic understanding. To the Bishop, when he entered the room, the expression on the Luitenant's face suggested only a pained and vicious hostility. In the hours that followed, this first impression proved if anything to have been over-optimistic. Luitenant Verkramp's attempts at sympathetic understanding inspired in the Bishop the conviction that he was locked alone in a room with a sadistic homosexual suffering from an overdose of several powerful hallucinatory drugs. Certainly nothing else could explain the overtures the Luitenant was making nor the distorted version of his own life which Verkramp insisted he corroborate. Everything the Bishop imagined he had done took on an entirely contrary character as seen through the eyes of Verkramp.

He had not for instance been an undergraduate in Cambridge studying theology. He had, he learnt, been indoctrinated in Marxist-Leninist theory by a man whom he had previously imagined to be a leading Anglo-Catholic professor, but who had apparently been a Moscow-trained theoretician. As the hours dragged by the Bishop's faint hold on reality grew fainter. The illusions he had nourished for a lifetime slipped away and were replaced by the new certitudes his deranged interrogator insisted he subscribe to.

By the time they had arrived at the events of the previous day, the Bishop, who had eaten nothing for thirty-six hours, and who had been standing with his hands above his head for six, was prepared to admit to murdering the entire South African Police force, if doing so would allow him to sit down for five minutes.

'I shot them with a multi-barrelled rocket launcher supplied by the Chinese consul in Dar-es-Salaam,' he repeated slowly while Verkramp copied the admission down.

'Good,' said the Luitenant finally, 'that seems pretty conclusive.'

'I'm glad to hear it. Now if you don't mind I would like time to think about my future,' the Bishop said.

'I think you can safely leave that to us,' said the Luitenant. 'There's just one more matter I want to get straightened out. Why did you shoot your sister's cook?'

'I discovered he was a CIA agent,' said the Bishop, who by this time knew the lines along which Verkramp's mind was working. He had long since discovered that there was no point in arguing with the man, and since Verkramp's imagination had evidently been nurtured on spy-thrillers, this seemed the sort of explanation he would swallow.

'Oh, was he?' said Verkramp, and made a mental note to investigate the cooks of Piemburg to discover how many more were in the pay of the Americans.

By the time Verkramp had finished with him, the Bishop had decided that his only hope of escaping execution on the scaffold reserved for him by his grandfather lay in concocting a confession so absurd that it would either be thrown out of court by the judge, or allow him to plead insanity. 'I may as well be hanged for a sheep as a lamb,' he said to himself when Els came to take over the interrogation and wondered what new crimes he could add to the list he had already agreed to. Konstabel Els was glad to suggest some.

'I hear you want us to go around marrying kaffirs,' Els began. He knew he was supposed to be questioning a Communist and the only thing he knew about Communists was that they wanted white people to marry blacks.

'I can't remember having advocated it in public,' the Bishop said cautiously.

'I don't suppose you would in public,' said Els, whose own advocacy of sexual intercourse with blacks had always been undertaken in strictest privacy. 'You'd get arrested for it.'

The Bishop was puzzled. 'For what?' he asked.

'For advocating a black woman in public. What about in private?'

'It's true I have given the matter some thought.'

'Come on, admit it. You haven't just thought about it. You have done it too.'

The Bishop couldn't see much harm in admitting it. 'Well, once or twice I have raised the matter. I've brought it up at meetings of the parish council.'

'At meetings, eh?' said Els. 'Sort of group gropes?'

'I suppose you could put it that way,' said the Bishop who had never heard the expression before.

Els leered at him. 'I suppose you put it other ways too?'

'I put it to them straight, man to man,' said the Bishop, wondering what all this had to do with murdering policemen.

Konstabel Els had difficulty imagining how you could put it man to man and call it straight at the same time.

'I didn't beat about the bush.'

'I don't suppose you'd have to with men,' Els agreed.

'Oh, there were women present too,' said the Bishop. 'It's the sort of question where a woman's viewpoint often helps.'

'You can say that again.'

'Funnily enough, I found the women more receptive to the idea than the men.'

'I should think you would.'

'Of course, it's not something most people will accept at one go. I put it to them gradually, but on the whole they could see there was something to be said for it.'

'Hell,' said Els, 'you must have had some parties.'

'I hope I'm not boring you,' the Bishop said hopefully.

'I'm never bored by sex,' said Els.

'Do you mind if I take a seat?' the Bishop said on the spur of the moment, taking advantage of Els' evident interest.

'Help yourself.' Els couldn't get enough of the Bishop's tales of group gropes and similar perversions.

'Now then,' said the Bishop, when he was seated, 'where was I?'

'You were saying how the women liked it in the tail,' said Els.

'Was I really?' said the Bishop. 'How extraordinary. I had no idea.'

As the night wore on, Konstabel Els sat rapt in admiration for the prisoner. Here at last, was a man after his own heart, a man for whom there was no shame, no remorse, no regret, only a dedication to lust unequalled in Els' experience.

The difficulty for the Bishop was that his imagination was hardly adequate for the task Els set it. Faced with such rapacious curiosity, he stuck to his calling and Els listened fascinated to descriptions of midnight orgies involving chasubles and albs. Among the other invaluable pieces of information that the Konstabel picked up there were three facts which were particularly damning. The Bishop, he learned, wore a frock, possessed a rubric and owned a biretta.

'What the hell is a rubric?' Kommandant van Heerden asked him in the morning when he read the Bishop's signed confession.

'Short for rubber prick,' said Els. 'He uses it for genuflexion.'

'Does he really?' said the Kommandant and read the astonishing document through for the second time. If half of what the Bishop had confessed to was true, thought van Heerden, the sod should have been hanged years ago.

Chapter 15

While the case against Jonathan Hazelstone was being prepared, Kommandant van Heerden wrestled with the problem
posed by the continuing disappearance of the prisoner's sister.
In spite of the most intensive manhunt Miss Hazelstone continued to elude the police. Kommandant van Heerden increased
the reward offered but still no information worth the telling
was telephoned into the Piemburg police station. The only
consolation the Kommandant could find was that Miss Hazelstone had not added to his problems by communicating with
her lawyer or with newspapers outside his province.

'She's a cunning old devil,' he told Luitenant Verkramp, and
was alarmed to note in himself a return of the admiration he
had previously felt for her.

'I wouldn't worry about the old bag, she'll probably turn up
at the trial,' Verkramp answered optimistically. His fall had
not, the Kommandant noted, deprived the Luitenant of his
capacity to say things calculated to upset his commanding
officer.

'If you're so bloody clever, where do you suggest we start
looking for her?' the Kommandant growled.

'Probably sitting in Jacaranda House laughing to herself,'
and Verkramp took himself off to compile a list of black cooks
known to favour Chicken Maryland.

'Sarcastic bastard,' muttered the Kommandant. 'One of these
days somebody will fix him properly.'

It was in fact Konstabel Els whose initiative led to the capture
of Miss Hazelstone. Ever since his battle with the Dobermann,
Els had been regretting his decision to leave the body lying
on the lawn of Jacaranda House.

'I should have had it stuffed. It would look nice in the hall,'
he said to the Kommandant during an idle moment.

'I should have thought it had been stuffed enough already,' the Kommandant had replied. 'Besides, whoever heard of having a dog stuffed.'

'There are lots of stuffed lions and wart-hogs and things in the hall of Jacaranda House. Why shouldn't I have a stuffed dog in my hall?'

'You're getting ideas above your station,' the Kommandant said. Els had gone off to ask the warder in Bottom about getting dogs stuffed. The old man seemed to know about things like that.

'You want to take it to a taxidermist,' the warder told him. 'There's one in the museum but I'd ask for a quote first. Stuffing's a costly business.'

'I don't mind spending a bit of money on it,' Els said and together they went to ask the Bishop about the dog.

'I believe it had a pedigree,' the Bishop told them.

'What's a pedigree?' Els asked.

'A family tree,' said the Bishop, wondering if killing the dog was going to be added to the list of crimes he was supposed to have committed.

'Fussy sort of dog, having a family tree,' Els said to the warder. 'You'd think it would pee against lamp-posts like any other dogs.'

'Spoilt if you ask me,' said the warder. 'Sounds more like a lapdog than a real Dobermann. I'm not surprised you could kill it so easily. Probably died of fright.'

'It bloody well didn't. It fought like mad. Fiercest dog I ever saw,' said Els, annoyed.

'I'll believe it when I see it,' said the warder and Els had promptly made up his mind to fetch the Dobermann to get rid of the slur on his honour.

'Permission to visit Jacaranda House,' he said to the Kommandant, later that day.

'Permission to do what?' the Kommandant asked incredulously.

'To go up to Jacaranda House. I want to get that dog's body.'

'You must be out of your mind, Els,' said the Kommandant. 'I should have thought you'd had enough of that bloody place by now.'

136

'It's not a bad place,' said Els whose own memories of the Park were quite different from those of the Kommandant.

'It's a bloody awful place, and you've done enough harm up there already,' said the Kommandant. 'You keep your nose out of it, do you hear me?' and Els had vented his anger by bullying some black convicts in the prison yard.

That evening Kommandant van Heerden decided to make a spot check on the road blocks around Piemburg. He was beginning to suspect that his enforced absence from the outside world was having a bad effect on the morale of his men, and since he thought it improbable that Miss Hazelstone would be out and about at eleven o'clock at night, and wouldn't be able to see him in the police car if she were, he decided to make his rounds when it seemed most likely his men would be asleep on the job.

'Drive slowly,' he told Els when he was seated in the back of the car. 'I just want to have a look around.' For an hour men on duty at street corners and at the road blocks were harassed by van Heerden's questions.

'How do you know she didn't come through here disguised as a coon?' he asked the sergeant on duty on the Vlockfontein road who had been complaining about the numbers of cars he had had to search.

'We've checked them all, sir,' said the sergeant.

'Checked them? How have you checked them?'

'We give them the skin test, sir.'

'The skin test? Never heard of it.'

'We use a bit of sandpaper, sir. Rub their skin with it and if the black comes off they're white. If it doesn't they're not.'

Kommandant van Heerden was impressed. 'Shows initiative, Sergeant,' he said and they drove on.

It was shortly after this and as they were driving up Town Hill to inspect the road block there that Konstabel Els noticed that the Kommandant had fallen asleep.

'It's only the old man making his rounds,' Els told the konstabel on duty, and was about to turn round and return to the prison when he realized that they were quite close to Jacaranda Park. He looked over his shoulder and regarded the sleeping figure in the back of the car.

'Permission to go up to Jacaranda House, sir,' he said softly. In the back the Kommandant was snoring loudly. 'Thank you, sir,' said Els with a smile and the car moved off past the road block and up the hill to Jacaranda House. On either side of the road the headlights illuminated the billboards which stood like advertisements for macabre holiday resorts: Bubonic Plague, some sinister beach and Rabies, a game reserve. Unaware of his destination, Kommandant van Heerden slept noisily in the back as the car passed through the gate of Jacaranda House, and with a crunch of tyres on gravel, moved slowly down the long drive.

Els parked the car in front of the house and stepped quietly out into the night to collect his trophy. It was dark and clouds obscured the moon, and he had some difficulty finding the Dobermann's corpse.

'That's funny,' he said to himself, as he searched the lawn. 'I could have sworn I left the bugger here,' and continued to look for the beast.

In the back of the car Kommandant van Heerden snored more loudly than ever. He slipped sideways across the seat and bumped his head on the window. The next moment he was wide awake and staring out into the darkness.

'Els,' he said loudly, 'what have you stopped for and why are the headlights off?' From the driver's seat there came no comforting reply and as Kommandant van Heerden sat terrified in the back of the car and wondered where the hell Els had got to, the cloud slipped gently from the moon, and the Kommandant saw before him the front door of Jacaranda House. With a whimper the Kommandant crouched down in the cushions and cursed his own foolishness for leaving the prison. Above him the façade of the great house loomed threateningly, its unlighted windows dark with menace. Moaning with terror, the Kommandant opened the door and stepped on to the forecourt. A moment later he was in the driver's seat and searching for the keys. They had gone.

'I might have known the swine would do something like this,' the Kommandant gibbered and promising himself that more than the Dobermann would get himself stuffed, waited for Els to return. As the minutes passed and Els continued his search for the elusive Toby, the Kommandant's terror grew.

'I can't sit here all night,' he thought. 'I'll have to go and find him,' and he climbed out and moving stealthily stole into the garden. Around him bushes assumed strange and terrifying shapes and the moon which had proved so illuminating but a few minutes before discovered a convenient cloud to hide behind. In the darkness and not daring to shout, Kommandant van Heerden stumbled on a flowerbed and fell flat on his face. 'Dog roses,' he thought bitterly, clutching his face and as he clambered to his feet, Kommandant van Heerden's ears and eyes caught sight and sound of two things that sent his heart racing in his breast. The car's engine had started on the forecourt. Els had found the Dobermann and was departing. As the car's headlights swung round floodlighting the front of Jacaranda House, the Kommandant stood rigid in the flowerbed staring into the night sky at something far more sinister than the house itself. A faint plume of smoke was issuing slowly but steadily from one of the chimneys of the deserted mansion. Kommandant van Heerden was not alone.

Clutching his heart, the Kommandant fell back among the roses and passed out. When he came round from what he chose to call his first heart attack, it was to hear a voice he had hoped never to hear again.

'Nights of wine and roses, Kommandant?' it inquired, and as the Kommandant stared up he saw outlined against the drifting clouds the elegant figure of Miss Hazelstone. She was dressed as he had seen her first, and not, he thanked heaven, in the dreadful salmon-pink suit.

'You're not going to lie there all night, I hope,' Miss Hazelstone continued. 'Come into the house and I'll make you some coffee.'

'Don't want any coffee,' the Kommandant mumbled, disengaging himself from the rose bushes.

'You may not want it, but that's what you obviously need to sober you up. I'm not having drunken policemen stumbling about my garden ruining the flowerbeds at this time of night,' and bowing to that authority he could never resist, Kommandant van Heerden found himself once more in the drawing-room of Jacaranda House. The room was in darkness except for the lamp on a film projector which stood on a small table.

'I was just running through some old films I took, before I burn them,' Miss Hazelstone said, and the Kommandant understood the faint plume of smoke he had seen issuing from the chimney. 'I shan't be able to see them in prison, and besides I think it's better to forget the past, don't you, Kommandant?'

The Kommandant had to agree. The past was something he would have paid a fortune to forget. Unfortunately, it was all too present in his mind's eye. Trapped between his own terror and a sense of deference made all the more persuasive by the erratic beating of his heart, the Kommandant allowed himself to be seated in a low chair from which he expected never to rise, while Miss Hazelstone turned on a reading lamp.

'There's some coffee left over from supper,' Miss Hazelstone said. 'I'll have to heat it up, I'm afraid. In the normal way I would have some fresh made, but I'm rather short of home help at the moment.'

'I don't need any coffee,' the Kommandant said, and regretted his words immediately. He might have had a chance to escape if Miss Hazelstone had gone to the kitchen. Instead she looked at him doubtfully and sat down opposite him in the wing-backed armchair.

'Just as you like,' she said. 'You don't look unusually drunk. Just rather pale.'

'I'm not drunk. It's my heart,' said the Kommandant.

'In that case, coffee is the worst thing for you. It's a stimulant, you know. You should try to avoid any form of stimulation.'

'I know that,' said the Kommandant.

There was a pause, broken finally by Miss Hazelstone.

'I suppose you've finally come to arrest me,' she said. The Kommandant couldn't think of anything he would like to do more, but he didn't seem to have the energy. Mesmerized by the house and the air of gentle melancholy he found so fascinating in the old woman, he sat in his chair listening to his palpitations.

'I suppose Jonathan has confessed already,' Miss Hazelstone said by way of polite conversation. The Kommandant nodded.

'Such a waste,' Miss Hazelstone continued. 'The poor boy

suffers from such a sense of guilt. I can't imagine why. I suspect it's because he had such a blameless childhood. Guilt is so often a substitute for good honest-to-goodness evil. You must find that in your profession, Kommandant.'

In his profession, the Kommandant had to agree it very often was, but he couldn't see the relevance in the case of a man who had several prison sentences behind him. He felt himself once more succumbing not only to deference but also to a sense of unease that Miss Hazelstone's conversation seemed to induce in him.

'I never suffered from the same weakness,' Miss Hazelstone continued primly. 'If anything, I had difficulty finding anything to do that wasn't depressingly good. Like the Devil, I too have felt how awful goodness is. So boring, but I daresay you don't have the same opportunity for being nauseated by it.'

'I daresay you're right,' said the Kommandant whose feeling of nausea sprang from quite different causes.

'As you must have gathered, I have done my best to bring a little gaiety into my life,' Miss Hazelstone went on. 'I write for the papers, you know.'

Kommandant van Heerden knew only too well.

'A little column every now and then on fashion and tasteful living.'

'I have read some of your articles,' said the Kommandant.

'I do hope you didn't follow my advice,' Miss Hazelstone went on. 'They were written with my tongue in my cheek, and I had great fun thinking up the most awful combinations of colours. Everybody took my recommendations seriously too. I think I can honestly say that I have made more homes unliveable in than all the termites in South Africa.'

Kommandant van Heerden gaped at her. 'Why on earth should you want to do that?' he asked.

'A sense of moral duty,' Miss Hazelstone murmured. 'My brother has given his life to spread light and goodness, I have merely sought to redress the balance. If people choose to follow my advice to put maroon wallpaper next to orange curtains, who am I to say them nay? People who believe that having a pink skin makes them civilized, while having a black one makes a man a savage, will believe anything.'

'You mean to say you don't believe in apartheid?' the Kommandant asked in astonishment.

'Really, Kommandant, what a silly question,' Miss Hazelstone replied. 'Do I behave as though I believed in it?'

Kommandant van Heerden had to admit that she didn't.

'You can't live with a Zulu for eight years and still believe in segregation,' Miss Hazelstone went on. 'As a matter of fact, the films I have just been looking at are ones I took of Fivepence. I wonder if you would care to see one.'

Kommandant van Heerden hesitated. What he had already seen of the cook didn't dispose him to want to see any more.

'I admire your delicacy of feeling,' Miss Hazelstone said, 'but you need not hesitate. I don't in the least mind sharing my memories with you,' and she started the projector.

A moment later the Kommandant saw on a screen at the far end of the room, the object of Miss Hazelstone's passion, moving about the garden of Jacaranda House as it had been in the summer some years before. The film had been shot from the same angle and in the same corner of the garden as had its actor nearly a decade later. At first sight the Kommandant had the illusion that there had been no murder and that he had dreamt the events of the preceding days. It was an illusion that did not last. As the image of Fivepence grew larger on the screen, the Kommandant decided that he preferred the reality he had known to the fantastic scene he was now witnessing. There had, he noted, been something almost healthy about the corpse of Fivepence. Living, the Zulu cook had quite clearly been diseased.

Tall and heavily built, he cavorted about the lawn like some appalling black nymph, and paused a moment to caress the bust of Sir Theophilus before kissing it passionately upon its unresponding mouth. Then he was off again, flitting about the garden and displaying his repulsive charms in a series of swirls and flounces designed to show off his garments to their very worst advantage. He was wearing a very short crimson frock trimmed with violet; as the Kommandant might have anticipated, it was made of rubber. As Fivepence executed his last pirouette and ended his performance with a curtsy, the Kommandant understood why Miss Hazelstone had murdered him. If the film was anything to go by, he had asked for it.

The film ended and Miss Hazelstone switched off the projector. 'Well?' she said.

'I can see why you shot him,' said the Kommandant.

'You can see nothing,' Miss Hazelstone snapped. 'What you have just seen appears to your crude mind to be quite horrible. To me it is beautiful.' She paused. 'That is life, a black man pretending to be a white woman, dancing steps of a ballet he has never seen, dressed in clothes made of a material totally unsuited to a hot climate on a lawn which was imported from England, and kissing the stone face of a man who destroyed his nation, filmed by a woman who is widely regarded as the arbiter of good taste. Nothing could better express the quality of life in South Africa.'

Kommandant van Heerden was about to say that he didn't think she was very patriotic, when Miss Hazelstone stood up.

'I'll get my suitcase. I have one packed ready,' she said, and was moving towards the door when a dark shape hurtled through the french windows and threw her to the ground.

It had taken Konstabel Els some time to locate the body of the Dobermann in the darkness, and in the end he had been guided more by smell than sight to the rubbish dump behind the house where Miss Hazelstone had deposited the dog. Carrying it carefully Els went back to the car and put the body in the boot. He climbed in and started the engine, and drove slowly off thankful that the Kommandant had not woken. It wasn't until he had got halfway down the hill into town that the absence of snores from the back led him to realize that he had been mistaken.

With a curse he turned the car and headed back to the Park. He stopped in the drive and looked about. Kommandant van Heerden was nowhere to be seen. Els left the car and walked round the house and found himself looking into the lighted drawing-room where the Kommandant and Miss Hazelstone were talking. In the darkness Els wondered what the hell was going on. 'The sly old devil,' he thought to himself at last. 'No wonder he wouldn't give me permission to come up here,' and

Els began to think he understood how it was that the Kommandant should be sitting chatting in a very friendly way with a woman who had a reward on her head. He knew now why the Kommandant had been so eager to pin the murder of Fivepence on Jonathan Hazelstone.

'The old sod's courting her,' he thought, and a new respect for the Kommandant grew in Konstabel Els' mind. His own courtships were always accompanied by threats of violence or blackmail and it seemed obvious that the Kommandant, whose own lack of charm almost equalled that of Els, would have to employ pretty drastic methods to make himself at all attractive to a woman of Miss Hazelstone's wealth and social standing.

'He goes and arrests her brother for murder, and then puts a price on the old bag's head. What a way to get a dowry,' Els exclaimed, and immediately thought how he could forestall the plan. With a rush he was across the lawn and into the room. As he hurled himself on the Kommandant's fiancée he yelled, 'I claim the reward. I captured her,' and from the floor looked up and wondered why the Kommandant was looking so relieved.

Chapter 16

To Kommandant van Heerden the transition of Miss Hazelstone from the mistress of Jacaranda House to the inmate of Fort Rapier Mental Hospital was a sad affair. As he watched the stretcher on which the old lady lay carried for the last time past the portraits of her ancestors in the fern-infested hall, he knew that an epoch was ending. No longer would Jacaranda House stand supreme in the eyes of Zululand society, the symbol of all that was best in the British occupation of Africa and an emblem of an aristocratic way of life. No more garden parties, no more grand balls, no more of those dinner parties for which Miss Hazelstone had such a reputation, nothing of

144

importance would happen within these walls. The house would stand empty and sepulchral until the white ants or the demolition men cleared it away to make room for a new suburb. As Kommandant van Heerden turned off the lights and the house stood dark under the moon, he was filled with a great sense of loss. The old arrogance on which he had relied to sharpen his servility was gone. He was a free man, and the architect of his own freedom. It was the last thing that he wanted.

It was a cortège which passed up the drive and out the contorted gates, a funeral cortège of motorcycles and police cars accompanying the ambulance in which Miss Hazelstone slept the sleep of the heavily sedated. In the driver's seat of the leading car sat Konstabel Els, happy in the knowledge that he had earned his just reward, and behind him in the darkness Kommandant van Heerden wondered at the strangeness of fate which had made a creature like Els the instrument of the fall of the house of Hazelstone.

It was not as if Els was clever, the Kommandant thought, as the procession wound its way through the unlighted streets of Piemburg, nor was there anything vaguely intentional about his activities which would explain their effect. Els was merely chance, random and trivial in its ways.

'Entropy made man,' the Kommandant said to himself, and opened the window. The car had begun to smell quite intolerable.

'Els,' said the Kommandant, 'you need a bath.'

'Me, sir?' said Els.

'You, Els. You stink.'

'Not me, sir. That's Toby.'

'Who the hell's Toby?'

'The Dobermann, sir. He's a bit high.'

'You mean you've got the carcase of a rotting dog in the car?' shouted the Kommandant.

'Oh no, sir,' said Els. 'He's in the boot.'

The Kommandant was about to say that he wasn't going to share his car with a putrefying Dobermann, when they passed through the gates of Fort Rapier and drove up the drive to the hospital.

In the moonlight the buildings of Fort Rapier looked much as they had done when the garrison occupied the barracks. A few bars had been added here and there to convert an establishment which had been designed to keep people out into one that served to keep them in, but the atmosphere had not altered. Irrationality had kept its hold on the place.

'Old traditions die hard,' the Kommandant thought as the car stopped at the edge of the parade ground. He stepped out and patted a field gun that had once seen service at Paardeberg where his grandfather had slept through its bombardment and which now stood like an iron pensioner overlooking the lunacies of another generation.

While Miss Hazelstone was taken into a ward reserved for the criminally insane, Kommandant van Heerden explained her case to the Superintendent, Dr Herzog, who had been summoned from his bed to deal with the case.

'Couldn't you have waited till morning?' he asked grumpily. 'I didn't get to bed until one.'

'I haven't been to bed at all,' said the Kommandant, 'and in any case this is an emergency. Miss Hazelstone is something of a celebrity and her committal may arouse public comment.'

'She certainly is, and it certainly will,' said the doctor. 'She happens to be the chief benefactress of this hospital.'

'She has evidently been providing for her own future which will be to remain here until she decides to die,' said the Kommandant.

'Who has diagnosed her?' asked Dr Herzog.

'I have,' said the Kommandant.

'I wouldn't have thought you were qualified to.'

'I know a criminal lunatic when I see one. The police surgeon and her own doctor will be up in the morning, and committal papers will arrive in due course.'

'It seems rather irregular,' said the doctor.

'As a matter of fact, it is irregular,' said the Kommandant. 'But if you really want to know, we have pretty incontrovertible evidence that she has murdered someone. I won't go into details but I can assure you that we have enough evidence to have her tried for murder. I think you understand that the

146

trial of such a prominent person would not be in the public interest.'

'Good God,' said the doctor, 'what is Zululand coming to? First her brother and now Miss Hazelstone.

'Quite,' said the Kommandant. 'It's a reflection on our times.'

Having ensured that Miss Hazelstone would be allowed no visitors and that she would have no access to the Press or to her lawyers, the Kommandant took his leave. Dawn had broken when he crossed the great parade ground, and a few grey figures had emerged from the wards and were shuffling about sadly in the early sunlight.

'To think it had to end like this,' the Kommandant thought and his mind dwelt not so much on Miss Hazelstone as on the Imperial splendour that had once marched red-coated and supreme across the square. He stood for a moment imagining the regiments that had passed the saluting base on which Miss Hazelstone's grandfather had stood before going to their deaths on Majuba Hill and Spion Kop and then he turned away and climbed into his reeking car.

When Miss Hazelstone woke to find herself in bed in a ward, she had difficulty understanding where she was. The decor and the row of beds brought back to her memories of her boarding school but her companions were hardly the gay carefree girls of her youth. Not that they were really gay, she thought lying back and studying the ceiling, merely expectant, which passed for gaiety. There was nothing remotely gay or expectant about the figures she could see now. Withdrawn into remote provinces of their own imaginations the patients wandered listlessly among the obstacles presented by reality. Miss Hazelstone looked at them and was tempted to follow their example. Only a sense of pride prevented her. 'Such lack of style,' she said to herself, and sitting on the edge of her bed looked round for her clothes.

In the days that followed she clung grimly to her arrogance, firmly rejecting the unreal worlds the other patients pressed on her.

'You may be,' she told a patient who introduced himself as

147

Napoleon, 'though I doubt it. I am Miss Hazelstone of Jacaranda House,' and even the staff learnt that it was unwise to address her simply as Hazelstone.

'Miss Hazelstone to you,' she snapped at a sister who made the mistake.

'One must keep up appearances,' she told Dr von Blimenstein, the psychiatrist who had been assigned to deal with the new patient, and who was trying vainly to get Miss Hazelstone to recognize the sexual origins of her illness. Dr von Blimenstein was so wildly eclectic in her approach that it was difficult to tell which school of psychology she most favoured. She was known to prescribe electric-shock therapy in unlimited doses to the black patients, but with whites placed particular stress on sexual guilt as the cause of psychoses. She was so successful in this approach that she had once even managed to cure a keeper at the Durban Snake Park of his anxiety neurosis about snakes. His phobia had, he claimed, been brought on by his having been bitten on forty-eight separate occasions by snakes as venomous and varied as puff-adders, cobras, Gabon vipers, ringhals and asps, each of which had brought him to the verge of death. Dr von Blimenstein had convinced the poor man that his fears were purely sexual in origin and resulted from a feeling of inadequacy brought on by the realization that his penis was neither so long nor so potent as a mature python and had sent him back to work at the Snake Park where three weeks later he had been bitten, this time with fatal results, by a black mamba whose length he had been trying to measure by comparing it with his own erect member which he knew to be six inches long. 'Nine feet three inches,' he had just concluded, laying the mamba's head against his *glans penis*. It was practically the last thing he could conclude, as the mamba with a ferocity fully justified by the absurd comparison plunged its fangs into its symbolic counterpart. After that Dr von Blimenstein had turned away from psychoanalysis and had favoured a more behaviourist approach.

With Miss Hazelstone she decided there was no danger of such tragic results and she had encouraged the patient to record her dreams so that these could be examined for the symbolic meaning which would explain all her problems. The trouble was that Miss Hazelstone never dreamt and the concocted dreams that she supplied the doctor with were down-to-earth in the extreme. They were for one thing punctuated with phalluses and vaginas which no amount of symbolic interpretation could turn into anything else.

'How about snakes, or steeples?' Miss Hazelstone inquired when the doctor explained how difficult it was.

'I've never heard of people having dreams about penises before,' said the doctor.

'Probably wish-fulfilment dreams,' Miss Hazelstone said and went on to describe a dream in which a creature called Els had struggled with a black dog on a lawn.

'Extraordinary,' said von Blimenstein, 'absolutely archetypal,' and had begun to talk about the Shadow struggling with Instinctual Libido.

'Yes, it struck me like that at the time,' said Miss Hazelstone cryptically. After several weeks of these dreams the doctor had begun to think she would be able to write a monograph on 'The Policeman Archetype in South African Psychology' using this material.

For Miss Hazelstone these interviews provided a break from the boredom of life in Fort Rapier.

'Madness is so monotonous,' she told the doctor. 'You would think that fantasies would be more interesting, but really one has to conclude that insanity is a poor substitute for reality.'

Then again, when she looked around her, there didn't seem to be any significant difference between life in the mental hospital and life in South Africa as a whole. Black madmen did all the work, while white lunatics lounged about imagining they were God.

'I'm sure the Almighty has more dignity,' Miss Hazelstone said to herself, as she watched the shuffling figures moving aimlessly about the grounds. 'And I'm sure He hasn't delusions of grandeur.'

The news that his sister had finally been found and was now an inmate in Fort Rapier Mental Hospital came as no surprise to the Bishop of Barotseland.

'She was never very sane,' he told the Kommandant who

came to see him personally to break the news, and demonstrated once more that lack of family loyalty the Kommandant found so deplorable in one who belonged to such an illustrious line, by adding, 'The best place for her. She should have been certified years ago.' The Bishop was shedding all his illusions, it seemed, and certainly he had ceased to feel kindly towards his sister and had stopped thinking she was merely mildly eccentric.

'I have a great admiration for Miss Hazelstone,' said the Kommandant coldly. 'She was a remarkable woman and Zululand will be the poorer for her passing.'

'You speak of her as though she were already dead,' said the Bishop, whose thoughts about mortality were markedly more frequent since he had moved into Bottom. 'I suppose in a way she has gone to a better life.'

'She won't be leaving there until she is dead,' said the Kommandant grimly. 'By the way, your trial starts next week so if you have anything to say in your defence you had better start thinking about it now,' and the Kommandant had gone away convinced that Jonathan Hazelstone deserved his fate.

The Bishop, left alone in his cell, decided that there was really nothing he could do to add to the confession he had made. It seemed to him a perfectly adequate defence in itself. Nobody on earth could possibly believe he had committed the crimes he had admitted to, and he doubted if any but an expert on High Church ritual could disentangle criminal offences from ecclesiastical practices. No judge worth his salt could ever condemn him for latitudinarianism. The Bishop lay down on the mat on the floor of his cell which served as his bed and looked forward to the verdict he was sure would free him.

'It probably won't even come to that,' he thought cheerfully. 'The judge will throw the prosecution case out of court.'

As usual with the Bishop of Barotseland's prognostications events were to prove him entirely wrong. The Judge chosen to hear the case was Justice Schalkwyk, whose mother had died in a British concentration camp and who was noted both for his deafness and his loathing for all things British. The attorney for the defence, Mr Leopold Jackson, was likewise handicapped physically by a cleft palate which made his speeches almost inaudible, and who was in any case known for his tendency to defer to the authority of judges. He had been chosen to conduct the defence by the accused man's heirs, distant cousins who lived in a poor section of Capetown and who hoped by speeding the course of justice to avoid any further unwelcome publicity which would besmirch the family name. Mr Jackson was only allowed to see his client a few days before the trial began, and then only in the presence of Konstabel Els.

The interview took place in Bottom and was marked by an almost complete misunderstanding from the start.

'You thay you've thigned a confethion. Motht unfortunate,' said Mr Jackson.

'It was made under duress,' said the Bishop.

'It wasn't,' said Els. 'It was made in here.'

'Under dureth,' said Mr Jackson. 'Then it won't thtand up.'

'I don't expect it to,' said the Bishop.

'It can't,' said Els. 'Confessions never do.'

'How wath it forthed out of you?'

'I was made to stand up.'

'You weren't,' said Els. 'I let you sit down.'

'So you did,' said the Bishop.

'Tho it wathn't made under dureth,' said Mr Jackson.

'I told you just now. It was made in here,' said Els.

'It was partly made under duress,' said the Bishop.

'Don't listen to him,' said Els. 'I know where it was made. It was made in here.'

'Wath it made in here?' asked Mr Jackson.

'Yeth,' said the Bishop, lapsing into legal jargon.

'There you are. I told you it was,' said Els.

'There theemth to be thome confuthion,' said Mr Jackson. 'What did you confeth to?'

'Genuflexion with a rubber prick,' said Els hurriedly fore-stalling lesser crimes.

'Genuflecthion with a what?' Mr Jackson asked.

'He means a rubric, I think,' said the Bishop.

'I don't. I mean a rubber prick,' said Els indignantly.

'Thoundth a thrange thort of offenth,' said Mr Jackson.

'You're telling me,' said Els.

'I thought thith wath a capital cathe,' said Mr Jackson.

'It is,' said Els, 'I'm enjoying it no end.'

'Genuflecthing ithn't a crime under Thouth African law.'

'It is with a rubber prick,' said Els.

'There were some other crimes in my confession,' said the Bishop.

'Thuthch ath?'

'Murder,' said the Bishop.

'Lesbianism,' said Els.

'Lethbianithm? Thatth impothible. A man can't commit lethbianithm. Are you thure you've got the right cathe?'

'Positive,' said Els.

'Would you mind allowing my client to thpeak for himthelf?' Mr Jackson asked Els.

'I'm just trying to help,' said Els aggrieved.

'Now then,' Mr Jackson went on, 'ith it true that you have admitted to being a lethbian?'

'As a matter of fact, yes,' said the Bishop.

'And a murderer?'

'It does seem strange, doesn't it?' said the Bishop.

'It thoundth fantathtic. What elth did you confeth?'

The Bishop hesitated. He did not want Mr Jackson to object to his confession before it was read out in court. Everything depended on the absurdity of the document and Mr Jackson did not look like a lawyer who would understand that.

'I think I would prefer the case to go forward as it is,' he said, and excusing himself on the ground that he was tired, ushered the attorney out of the cell.

'Thee you on the day,' Mr Jackson said cheerily, and left Bottom.

It was not due to Mr Jackson however, that Jonathan Hazelstone's confession never reached the court in its unabridged version. It was thanks rather to the conscientiousness of Luitenant Verkramp who, eager for praise, had sent a copy of the confession to BOSS in Pretoria. The head of the Bureau of State Security found the document on his desk one morning and read the thing through with a growing sense of disbelief. It wasn't that he was unused to reading extravagant confessions. After all the Security Branch existed to manufacture them and he could boast that it had a reputation in this respect second to none. One hundred and eighty days in solitary confinement and days of standing up without sleep while being questioned had the tendency to produce some pretty damning admissions from the suspects, but the confession that Verkramp had sent him made all previous ones look positively tame.

'The man's out of his mind,' he said after ploughing through a catalogue of crimes that included necrophilia, flagellation and liturgy, but it was not certain which man he was referring to. After a conference with leading members of the Government, BOSS decided to intervene in the interests of Western civilization incarnate in the Republic of South Africa and using the powers bestowed on it by Parliament, ordered the suppression of nine-tenths of the confession. Judge Schalkwyk was to try, convict, and condemn the prisoner, with no opportunity to appeal, on charges of murdering one Zulu cook and twenty-one policemen. No other charges were to be preferred and no evidence prejudicial to State security was to be presented in court. Grumbling furiously, the old Judge was forced in accordance with South African law to obey. Jonathan Hazelstone was to be hanged, there must be no miscarriage of justice, but he was after all to be hanged for a lamb.

The trial took place in Piemburg and in the very courtroom in which the accused's father had made such a great reputation.

'The old order changeth,' Jonathan murmured to his lawyer as he took his seat in the dock. Mr Jackson was not amused.

'It hardly becometh you to make mockery of my defect,' he said. 'Bethideth from what I have heard you would do better to thay "The wortht ith yet to come."'

Mr Jackson for once was right. The discovery that his confession had been expurgated came as the real shock of the trial to the Bishop. In the adjournment that followed the announcement that he was only to be tried for murder, Jonathan consulted with his attorney.

'I thould plead inthanity. It theemth your only chanth,' was Mr Jackson's advice.

'But I'm entirely innocent. I had nothing to do with the murder of twenty-one policemen.'

'I darethay but it ith an unfortunate fact that you have confethed to killing them.'

'I was forced to. Why on earth should I want to murder them?'

'I have no idea,' said Mr Jackson. 'My clienth motiveth are alwayth a mythtery to me. The point ith that the evidenth againtht you theemth pretty concluthive. You had the opportunity and the weaponth were found in your pothethion. Furthermore you have admitted in a thigned confethion to having killed them. I thuggetht you change your plea from not guilty to guilty but inthane.'

'I'm not inthane,' shouted the Bishop.

'I haven't come here to be inthulted,' said Mr Jackson.

'I'm thorry,' said the Bishop. 'I mean I'm sorry.'

'I shall change the plea,' said Mr Jackson finally. 'Inthanity it ith.'

'I suppose so,' said the Bishop.

'It'th better than being hanged,' said Mr Jackson. They went back into the courtroom.

The trial proceeded rapidly. By the end of the afternoon the prosecution's case had been presented and Mr Jackson had made no attempt at a reasoned defence. He was relying on the leniency of the court in the face of the accused's obvious insanity.

In his summing-up to a jury handpicked from close relatives of the murdered policemen, Judge Schalkwyk spoke with a brevity and degree of impartiality quite unusual for him.

'You have heard it said,' he mumbled, though it was certain that thanks to his own deafness he hadn't, 'by the prosecuting counsel that the accused committed these crimes. You have seen the accused's confession with your own eyes, and you have heard the defence counsel's plea that his client is insane. Now you may think that there is something to be said for the hypothesis that a man who murders twenty-one policemen and then signs a confession saying that he has done so is manifestly not of his right mind. It is my duty however to point out to you that to plead insanity in the light of the overwhelming evidence against him is not the action of an insane person. It is a highly rational action and one that indicates a degree of perception only to be found in an intelligent and healthy mind. I think therefore that you can disregard the question of insanity altogether in your deliberations. You need only concern yourselves with the matter of guilt. There is in my mind no shadow of doubt that the defendant committed the murders of which he is accused. He possessed, as we have heard from the expert evidence presented by the prosecution, both the opportunity and the means. He was found in possession of the murder weapons and in the act of disposing of them. His wallet and handkerchief were found at the scene of the crime, and he has given no adequate explanation of how they got there. Finally, he has admitted in a signed confession that he was responsible for the murders. I think I need say no more. You and I both know that the defendant is guilty. Now go away and come back and say so.'

The jury filed out of the courtroom. Two minutes later they returned. Their verdict was unanimous. Jonathan Hazelstone was guilty of murder twenty-one and a quarter times over.

In passing sentence Judge Schalkwyk allowed himself to depart from the lack of bias he had shown in his summing-up. He took into account a previous conviction which concerned a motoring offence. The convicted man had failed to give adequate notice of intention to make a left-hand turn at an intersection and as the Judge pointed out, this threatened the very existence of the South African constitution which was based on a series of consistent moves to the right.

'You are a threat to the values of Western civilization,' said the Judge, 'and it is the duty of this court to stamp Communism out,' and he ordered the prisoner to be taken from the court and hanged by the neck until he was dead. He was about to leave the courtroom when Mr Jackson asked to have a word with him in private.

'I would like to draw your Honour'th attention to a privilege which belongth to the Hazelthtone family,' he gurgled.

'The Hazelstone family doesn't have any privileges any more, I'm glad to say,' said the Judge.

'It'th a prerogative of long thtanding. It dateth back to the dayth of Thir Theophiluth.'

'Long standing, what do you mean? There's no question of his standing long. He'll be hanged shortly.'

'I mean the privilege of being hanged in Piemburg Prithon. It wath conferred on the family for perpetuity,' Mr Jackson tried to explain.

'Mr Jackson,' the Judge shouted, 'you are wasting my time and that of this court, not to mention that of your client who has little enough left of it as it is. Perpetuity means the quality of preserving something from oblivion. The quality of the sentence I have just passed is in intent quite the opposite. I think I need say no more, and I should advise you to do the same.'

Mr Jackson made one last effort. 'Can my client be hanged in Piemburg Prithon?' he shouted.

'Of course he can,' the Judge yelled. 'He has to be. It's a long-standing privilege of the Hazelstone family.'

'Thank you,' said Mr Jackson. As the court was cleared Jonathan Hazelstone was taken back to his cell in a state of numbed shock.

Chapter 17

It was with something of the same sense of shock that Governor Schnapps learnt that it had fallen to him to preside over the first hanging Piemburg Prison had seen for twenty years. Not that he was in the least squeamish or upset at the thought of having to attend an execution. He had in his time as a prison officer attended any number of hangings, mostly unofficial ones carried out by black convicts anxious to escape once and for all from the régime he had prescribed for them, but none the less hangings and the prospect of having at least one official execution to his credit filled him with a feeling of satisfaction. The sense of shock stemmed from quite other considerations.

There was for instance the question of the gallows which had not been used for twenty years except as a convenient place in which to store odds and ends. Governor Schnapps inspected Top himself and, from the little of it he could see across the buckets and garden rollers that were packed inside, came to the conclusion that the scaffold was in no shape to hang anyone. The same might well be said of the prospective executioners. The old warder volunteered to advise whoever was chosen as hangman but adamantly refused to attend the execution in person on the grounds that the Death House was unsafe, and the Governor's attempts to persuade one of the other warders to accept the job of executioner met with no success. No one it seemed was anxious to join Jonathan Hazelstone on his last walk if this entailed climbing the rickety steps up to Top.

In desperation Governor Schnapps telephoned the official executioner in Pretoria to ask him if he could come down to Piemburg for the day but the executioner was far too busy.

'Out of the question,' he told Schnapps, 'I've got thirty-two customers that day and besides I never hang singles. I can't remember when I last did one man. I always do mine in batches of six at a time and in any case I have my reputation to think of. I hang more people every year than any other executioner in the world, more than all the other executioners in the free world put together as a matter of fact, and if it once got about that I hanged a single man, people would think I was losing my touch.'

As a last resort Governor Schnapps raised the question of privilege with the State Attorney.

'I can't see why this man Hazelstone should be privileged,' he said. 'Everyone else is hanged in Pretoria. It seems wrong to me that a fellow who knocks off twenty-one policemen should be entitled to privileges which are denied to ordinary common-or-garden murderers.'

'I'm afraid there's nothing I can do about it,' the State Attorney told him. 'Judge Schalkwyk allowed the privilege to stand and I can't alter his decision.'

'But how did the Hazelstone family ever get the right to be hanged in Piemburg in the first place?'

The State Attorney looked up the records.

'It dates from the speech made by Sir Theophilus at the opening of the prison in 1888,' he told the Governor. 'In the course of that speech Sir Theophilus said, and I quote, "Capital punishment and flogging are essential to the peace and tranquillity of Zululand. They confer upon the native races a sense of the innate superiority of the white man and in declaring this prison open I should like to say that it is my considered opinion that the very future of white civilization in this dark continent depends, one might almost say, hangs, on the frequent use of the scaffold we have been privileged to see here today. It will be a sad day for this country when the gallows trap falls for the last time and one that I trust no member of my family will live to see." Unquote.'

'All very commendable,' said the Governor, 'but I don't see that it necessarily means that we have to keep the gallows for the exclusive use of the Hazelstone family.'

The State Attorney picked up another document.

'Now here we have the statement of the late Judge Hazelstone made at the time all executions were transferred to Pretoria. The Judge was asked what he thought his father had meant in his speech. His answer was, I quote "It's perfectly obvious. The gallows and the Hazelstone family stand or fall together. My father believed and rightly believed that our family should set an example to Zululand. I can think of no finer example than that of having our own private gallows in Piemburg Prison." Unquote. Pretty conclusive, don't you think?'

Governor Schnapps had to concede that it was and returned to the prison still faced with the problem of finding an executioner.

In the end it was Konstabel Els who became the official hangman. The Konstabel was still happily contemplating how he was going to spend the reward money he had earned from the capture of Miss Hazelstone and was looking forward to the ceremony in the police drill hall when he would be presented with the cheque by the Commissioner of Police. He had decided it was worth the price asked by the taxidermist at the Piemburg Museum to have Toby stuffed.

'I'm having the Dobermann stuffed,' he announced to Kommandant van Heerden one day.

'Then I expect you wouldn't mind earning some pocket money,' said the Kommandant.

'How?' asked Els suspiciously.

'Nothing arduous,' said the Kommandant. 'It certainly doesn't require any effort on your part. In fact when I come to think of it I wonder you haven't tried your hand at it already. I can't think of a better man for the job.'

'Hm,' said Els who didn't like the Kommandant's beguiling tone.

'I'd say you've probably got a natural talent for it.'

Els tried to think what dirty jobs needed doing round the police station. 'What is it?' he asked shortly.

'It's the sort of job you'd really like,' said the Kommandant, 'and for once you would be doing it legally.'

Els tried to think of something he would really like which wasn't legal. Having it off with black women seemed the most obvious thing.

'Of course you'd get the usual fee,' continued the Kommandant.

'The usual fee?'

'Twenty-five rand, I think it is,' said the Kommandant, 'though it may have gone up.'

'Hm,' said Els who was beginning to think his ears were deceiving him.

'Not bad for a bit of fun,' said the Kommandant, who knew that Konstabel Els had shot at least fifteen people in the course of duty and twenty-one for pure pleasure. 'Of course the method would take some getting used to.'

Konstabel Els searched his memory to find some method he hadn't used. As far as he knew he'd used every position in the book and a few more besides.

'What method had you in mind?' he inquired.

The Kommandant was getting fed up with Els' diffidence.

'With a rope round the neck and a ten-foot drop,' he snapped. 'That ought to do for a start.'

Els was appalled. If that was how it was going to start, he hated to think what the finish would be like.

'Wouldn't that be a bit dangerous?' he said.

'Of course not. Safe as houses.'

It was not as safe as any house Konstabel Els could think of.

'Of course if you're scared,' began the Kommandant.

'I'm not scared,' said Els. 'If you really want me to do it, I will, but I'm not taking any responsibility for what will happen to the poor bitch. I mean you can't drop a woman ten feet with a rope tied round her neck without doing her some injury, not even a kaffir woman. And as for stuffing—'

'What the hell are you talking about, Els?' the Kommandant asked. 'Who said anything about women? I'm talking about hanging Jonathan Hazelstone. I'm offering you the job of hangman and you keep going on like a maniac about women. Are you feeling all right?'

'Yes sir. I am now,' said Els.

'Well, then will you do it or not?'

'Oh yes. I'll hang him all right. I don't mind doing that,' and Els had gone off to practise on the gallows at Piemburg Prison.

'I'm Executioner Els,' he announced grandly to the warder at the gate. 'I'm the official hangman.'

Left alone in his office Kommandant van Heerden listened to his heart. Ever since the night he had found himself alone in the garden of Jacaranda House, he had known that there was something seriously wrong with it.

'It's all that running about and jumping out of windows,' he said to himself. 'Bound to be bad for a man of my age.' He had visited his doctor several times only to be told that he needed to take more exercise.

'You must be mad,' the Kommandant told him. 'I've been running about all over the place.'

'You're overweight. That's the only thing wrong with you,' said the doctor.

'I've collapsed twice,' the Kommandant insisted. 'Once at Jacaranda House and the second time in court.'

'Probably bad conscience,' said the doctor cheerfully, and the Kommandant had gone away in a foul temper to take it out on Luitenant Verkramp.

Kommandant van Heerden's third seizure came during the ceremony in the drill hall at which the Commissioner of Police presented the reward to Konstabel Els. The Kommandant had regretted giving Els the reward as soon as he heard that it would be presented by the Commissioner before an audience of five hundred and seventy-nine policemen and their families. The prospect of Els standing up and making a speech of thanks was not one that Kommandant van Heerden could look forward to with any enthusiasm.

'Listen, Els,' he said before climbing on to the platform where the Commissioner was waiting. 'You don't have to say anything more than "Thank you very much." I don't want to listen to a long speech.'

Konstabel Els nodded. He wasn't given to making speeches, long or short. The two men entered the hall.

In the event, the evening was worse than even the Kommandant had anticipated. The Commissioner had just heard of the new honour conferred on Konstabel Els and he had decided to end his speech by announcing the news to the assembled men.

'And so I call on Konstabel Els to come up and receive his reward,' he said finally, 'or should I say, Executioner Els.'

A wild burst of laughter and applause greeted the remark. 'That's right, call him Executioner Els,' someone shouted, and another voice yelled, 'Kaffir-Killer Els.'

The Commissioner held up his hand for silence as Els scrambled on to the platform.

'We all know what a vital contribution Konstabel Els has made to the solution of the racial problem in South Africa,' he continued amid laughter. 'I think I can honestly say that there can be few men in the South African Police force who have disposed of more obstacles to the establishment of a racially pure and truly white South Africa than Konstabel Els. But I am not referring now to Konstabel Els' excellence of aim nor to the sacrifices he has seen fit to make in pursuit of our common dream, a South Africa with no blacks in it. I speak now of his new duty. Konstabel Els has been chosen to carry out the duty of hanging the man whom we have to thank for our depleted ranks here tonight.' He paused and turned to Konstabel Els. 'I have great pleasure in presenting you with this cheque in reward for the capture of a dangerous criminal,' he said shaking Els by the hand. 'Hangman Els, you have done your fellow policemen proud.'

A great round of applause greeted the news of Els' appointment. Els took the cheque and turned to go back to his seat.

'Thank God for that,' said the Kommandant out loud, but the next moment there were shouts of 'Speech. Speech. You've got to make a speech,' and 'Tell us how you're going to kill the bastard,' and Els standing awkwardly on the edge of the platform was finally persuaded to say something.

'Well,' he said hesitantly, when the shouting had died down, 'I expect you all want to know how I'm going to spend the money.' He paused and the Kommandant shut his eyes. 'Well, first of all I'm going to stuff a Dobermann.'

The audience roared its approval, and the Kommandant opened his eyes for a moment to see how the Commissioner of Police was taking it. The Commissioner was not laughing.

'It's a dog, sir,' whispered the Kommandant hurriedly.

'I know it's a dog. I know what a Dobermann is,' said the Commissioner icily, and before the Kommandant could explain the true nature of Els' intentions the Konstabel had started again.

'It's a big black one,' said Els, 'and it's been dead a few weeks now, so it's not going to be an easy job.'

The audience was delighted. Shouts and the stamping of boots greeted Els' news.

'Do your men make a habit of stuffing dogs?' asked the Commissioner.

'He's not using the word in its usual sense, sir,' said the Kommandant desperately.

'I'm fully aware of that,' said the Commisioner. 'I know exactly what he means.'

'I don't think you do, sir,' the Kommandant began, but Els had started to speak again and he had to keep quiet.

'It's sort of stiff,' said Els, 'and that's what makes it difficult to get at its insides.'

'You've got to stop him,' the Commissioner shouted at Kommandant van Heerden, as the hall erupted with hysterical laughter.

'You don't understand, sir,' the Kommandant shouted back. 'He killed the dog and—'

'I'm not at all surprised. It's a pity he didn't kill himself in the process.'

Around them in the hall pandemonium raged. Konstabel Els couldn't see anything in what he had said to laugh at.

'You can laugh,' he shouted above the din, 'you can bloody laugh, but I bet you haven't got a dog with a family tree. My dog had a special tree ...' The rest of his sentence was drowned in the laughter.

'I'm not sitting here listening to any more of this filth,' shouted the Commissioner.

'If you'd just wait for a moment, sir,' the Kommandant screamed. 'I can explain what he means. He's going to take the dog to a taxidermist.'

But the Commissioner had already risen from his seat and had left the platform.

'Damned disgusting,' he said to his adjutant as he entered his car. 'The fellow's a sexual maniac.'

Behind him in the hall Els had left the stage and was telling a plain-clothes cop in the front row how he would stuff him if he went on laughing. On the platform Kommandant van Heerden had had his third heart attack.

In Piemburg Prison Jonathan did not share his sister's belief in the dignity of God. After a lifetime spent in the service of the Lord and a month in Bottom he felt unable any longer to believe that whatever had chosen to reveal itself to him in the depths of the swimming-pool had been even vaguely beneficent. As to its having been sane, his view of the world and its ways led him to suppose that its Maker must have been out of His mind.

'I thould think He must have needed a rest on the seventh day,' he told the old warder who insisted on bringing him consolation, 'and as for its being good, I think the facts speak for themselves. Whatever was responsible for the Creation cannot possibly have had anything good in mind. Quite the opposite if you ask me.'

The old warder was shocked. 'You're the first man to occupy that cell,' he said, 'that didn't come round to being converted before he was hanged.'

'It may have something to do with the fact that I am innocent,' said the Bishop.

'Oh is that what it is,' said the old warder with a yawn. 'They all say that,' and shuffled off to give his advice to Konstabel Els who was practising in Top. Alone in his cell the Bishop lay on the floor and listened to the noises that reached him from the gallows. By the sound of things he was less likely to die from a broken neck than from some appalling form of hernia.

Executioner Els wasn't finding his new job at all easy. For one thing he was fed up with all the work it entailed. He had had to empty the Gallows Shed of all the junk that had accumulated there for the past twenty years. With the help of half a dozen black convicts, he had moved several tons of old furniture, garden rollers, disused cat-o'-nine-tails, and corroded lavatory buckets before he could begin to get the scaffold ready for its task, and when the shed was empty he was not sure what to do.

'Pull the lever,' the old warder told him when Els asked him how the thing worked, and the new hangman had returned to the shed and had pulled the lever. After falling twenty feet to the floor of the shed as the trap opened beneath him, Els began to think he was getting the hang of the contraption. He tried it out with several unsuspecting black convicts standing there, and they seemed to disappear quite satisfactorily. He was disappointed that he wasn't allowed to try it out properly.

'You can't do that,' the old warder told him, 'it's not legal. The best thing I can suggest is a sack filled with sand.'

'Fussy old sod,' thought Els and sent the convicts off to fill some sacks with sand. They were quite satisfactory as stand-ins and didn't complain when the noose was fitted round their necks which was more than could be said for the black convicts. The trouble was that the bottom dropped out every time one was hanged. Els went back into Bottom to consult the old warder.

'He's not here any longer,' the Bishop told him.

'Where's he gone to?' Els asked.

'He's applied for sick leave,' the Bishop said. 'He's got stomach trouble.'

'It's the same with those sacks,' said Els and left the Bishop wondering which was worse, hanging or disembowelling.

'I don't suppose it makes a great deal of difference,' he thought finally. 'In any case there is nothing I can do about it.'

Kommandant van Heerden did not share the Bishop's fatalism. His third heart attack had convinced him that he too was under sentence of death, but he had decided that there was something he could do about it. He had been assisted in reaching this conclusion by Konstabel Oosthuizen whose experience of major surgery made him an unrivalled source of medical information.

'The most important thing is to have a healthy donor,' the Konstabel told him, 'after that it's a piece of cake, compared to my operation.' Kommandant van Heerden had hurried off to avoid having to listen to a description of the operation in which the greater portion of Konstabel Oosthuizen's digestive tract figured so memorably.

Sitting in his office he listened to Luitenant Verkramp discussing very loudly the case of his uncle who had died of heart trouble. The Kommandant had noticed recently that an extraordinarily large proportion of the Verkramp family had succumbed to what was evidently an hereditary defect and the manner of their passing had been uniformly so atrocious that he could only hope that Verkramp would go the same way. The Luitenant's solicitude was getting on his nerves, and he was equally tired of inquiries about how he felt.

'I feel all right, damn it,' he told Verkramp a hundred times.

'Ah,' Verkramp said sadly, 'that's often the way it seems.

Now my Uncle Piet said he was feeling fine the day he died but it came on all of a sudden.'

'I don't suppose it was quick,' the Kommandant said.

'Oh no. Very slow and agonizing.'

'I thought it would be,' said the Kommandant.

'A dreadful business,' said Verkramp. 'He—'

'I don't want to hear any more,' the Kommandant shouted.

'I just thought you'd like to know,' said Verkramp and went out to tell Konstabel Oosthuizen that irritability was a sure sign of incurable heart disease.

In the meantime the Kommandant had tried to occupy his mind by devising a suitably caustic reply to the Commissioner of Police, who had written ordering him to see that the men under his command got plenty of outdoor exercise and had even hinted that it might be a good thing to organize a brothel for the police barracks in Piemburg. The Kommandant could see that Konstabel Els' confession was still preying on the mind of the Police Commissioner.

'How do you spell taxidermist?' he asked Konstabel Oosthuizen.

'Oh, I wouldn't go to one of them,' the Konstabel replied. 'You need a proper surgeon.'

'I wasn't thinking of going to a taxidermist,' the Kommandant shouted. 'I just want to know how to spell the word.'

'The first thing to do is to find a suitable donor,' the Konstabel went on, and the Kommandant had given up the attempt to finish the letter. 'Why don't you have a word with Els? He should be able to fix you up with one.'

'I'm not having a kaffir,' said the Kommandant firmly. 'I'd rather die.'

'That's what my cousin said the very day he passed on,' Verkramp began.

'Shut up,' snarled the Kommandant, and went into his office and shut the door. He sat down at his desk and began to think about Konstabel Els' capacity for supplying a donor. Half an hour later he picked up the phone.

It was with some surprise that Jonathan Hazelstone learnt that Kommandant van Heerden had put in a request to see him.

'Come to gloat, I suppose,' he said when the Governor brought him the note from the Kommandant. He was even more astonished at the way the request had been worded. Kommandant van Heerden did not actually beg an audience with the Bishop, but his note spoke of 'a meeting perhaps in the privacy of the prison chapel, to discuss a matter of mutual interest to us both'. Jonathan racked his brains to think of some matter of mutual interest, and apart from his coming execution which Kommandant van Heerden must have had considerable interest in if his pains to achieve it were anything to go by, he couldn't think of any interests he might share with the Kommandant. At first he was inclined to refuse the request, but he was persuaded to go by the old warder, whose bowel trouble had stopped, now that Els had ceased rupturing the sacks.

'You never know. He might have some good news for you,' the warder said, and the Bishop had agreed to the meeting.

They met in the prison chapel one afternoon just a week before the execution was due to take place. The Bishop clanked over firmly chained and manacled to find the Kommandant sitting in a pew waiting for him. At the Kommandant's suggestion the two men made their way up the aisle and knelt side by side at the altar rail, out of hearing of the warders at the chapel door. Above them in the windows scenes of edifying horror done in late nineteenth-century stained glass filtered the sunlight that managed to penetrate the dense colours and the bars behind the glass, until the whole chapel was glowing with maroon gore.

While Kommandant van Heerden offered a short prayer the Bishop, having declined the Kommandant's invitation to say one, gazed up at the windows awestruck. He had never realized before how many ways there were of putting people to death. The windows provided a comprehensive catalogue of executions and ranged from simple crucifixion to burning at the stake. St Catherine on the wheel entirely merited her fame as a firework, the Bishop decided, while St Sebastian would have made an ideal trademark for pincushions. One after another the martyrs met their terrible ends with a degree of realism that seemed to mark the artist out as a genius and an insane one at that. The Bishop particularly liked the electric chair in one window. With a truly Victorian obsession for naturalism combined with high drama, the figure in the chair was portrayed encased in an aura of electric-blue sparks. Looking up at it, the Bishop was glad that he had agreed to the meeting. To have seen these windows was to know that his own end on the gallows, no matter how badly bungled by the incompetent Els, would be positively enjoyable by comparison with the sufferings portrayed here.

'I suppose I can be grateful for small mercies,' he said to himself as the Kommandant mumbled his final prayer which in the circumstances the Bishop thought was rather curiously worded.

'For what we are about to receive may the good Lord make us truly thankful, Amen,' said the Kommandant.

'Well?' said the Bishop after a short pause.

'You'll be glad to hear that your sister is doing very well at Fort Rapier,' the Kommandant whispered.

'It's nice to know.'

'Yes, she is in the best of health,' said the Kommandant.

'Hm,' said the Bishop.

'She has put on some weight,' said the Kommandant. 'But that is only to be expected with hospital food.' He paused, and the Bishop began to wonder when he was coming to the point.

'Overweight is something to be avoided,' said the Kommandant. 'Obesity is the cause of more premature deaths than cancer.'

'I daresay,' said the Bishop, who had lost two stone since he had been in prison.

'Particularly in middle age,' whispered the Kommandant. The Bishop turned his head and looked at him. He was beginning to suspect that the Kommandant was indulging in a rather tasteless joke.

'You haven't come here to lecture me on the dangers of being overweight, I hope,' he said. 'I thought your note said that you wanted to discuss something of interest to us both, and frankly obesity isn't one of my problems.'

'I don't suppose it is,' said the Kommandant sadly.

'Well then?'

'I have trouble with it myself.'

'I don't see what that has to do with me,' said the Bishop.

'It can lead to all sorts of complications. It's one of the main causes of heart disease,' said the Kommandant.

'Anyone would think from the way you go on that I was in danger of having a coronary when in fact I don't think I am going to be allowed that particular luxury.'

'I wasn't really thinking of you,' said the Kommandant.

'I didn't suppose you were.'

'It's more my own obesity I'm thinking of,' continued van Heerden.

'Well, if that's the only thing you've come here to talk to me about, I think I'll go back to my cell, I have something better to think about in the hours left to me than the state of your health.'

'I was afraid you'd say that,' said the Kommandant mournfully.

'I can't think what else you supposed I would do. You surely didn't come here for sympathy. Have a heart.'

'Thank you,' said the Kommandant.

'What did you say?'

'Thank you,' said the Kommandant.

'Thank you for what?'

'For a heart.'

'For a what?'

'A heart.'

The Bishop looked at him incredulously. 'A heart?' he said finally. 'What the hell are you talking about?'

Kommandant van Heerden hesitated before continuing. 'I need a new heart,' he said finally.

'It hasn't escaped my notice,' said the Bishop, 'that a change of heart would do you a power of good, but to be frank I think you're too far gone for any prayers of mine to help you. In any case I am afraid that I have lost faith in the power of prayer.'

'I've tried prayer already,' said the Kommandant, 'but it hasn't done any good. I still get palpitations.'

'Perhaps if you truly repented,' the Bishop said.

'It's no good. I'm a doomed man,' said the Kommandant.

'Metaphorically I suppose we all are,' said the Bishop. 'It

happens to be part of the condition of man, but if you don't mind my saying so I'm a damned sight more doomed than you are, and it's thanks to you that I'm going to be hanged next Friday.'

There was a long silence in the chapel while the two men considered their futures. It was broken by the Kommandant.

'I don't suppose you'd do something for me,' he said at last. 'A last bequest.'

'A last bequest?'

'A small thing really and nothing you'll have much use for.'

'You've got a nerve coming here and asking to be included in my will,' the Bishop said irritably.

'It's not in your will,' the Kommandant said desperately.

'No? Well where the hell is it?'

'In your chest.'

'What is?'

'Your heart.'

'You keep going on about my heart,' said the Bishop. 'I wish you would stop it. It's bad enough knowing you're going to die without having someone harp on about your heart. Anyone would think you wanted the thing.'

'I do,' said the Kommandant simply.

'What?' screamed the Bishop, struggling to his feet with a clanking of chains. 'You want what?'

'Only your heart,' said the Kommandant. 'I need it for a transplant.'

'I'm going insane,' shouted the Bishop. 'I must be. It isn't possible. Do you mean to tell me that you've gone to all this trouble just so you could have my heart for a transplant operation?'

'It was no trouble,' said the Kommandant. 'I hadn't got anything to do this afternoon.'

'I'm not talking about this afternoon,' the Bishop screamed. 'I'm talking about the murders and the trial and having me condemned to death for crimes you knew I couldn't have committed. You did all that just so that you could hoik my heart out of my body to stick it in your own? It's incredible. You're a ghoul. You're . . .' The Bishop couldn't find words to express his horror.

Kommandant van Heerden was horrified too. He had never been accused of anything so disgraceful in his life.

'Good God,' he shouted back. 'What do you take me for?'

He could see it was the wrong thing to ask. It was perfectly obvious what the Bishop took him for. For one terrible moment it looked as if the manacled and chained prisoner was going to hurl himself on him. Then quite suddenly the Bishop's fury evaporated and the Kommandant saw that he was staring up at óne of the stained-glass windows. Following the Bishop's gaze he found himself looking at the particularly grisly portrayal of a martyr in the process of being hanged, drawn and quartered. To Kommandant van Heerden the change in the prisoner's demeanour could only be explained by miraculous intervention. In some strange way the stained-glass window had communicated a sense of peace and tranquillity to his soul.

And this in its own way was true, for Jonathan Hazelstone had suddenly realized that the second verse of 'The Forerunners' needed revising. It wasn't his brain they wanted. It was his heart.

'Good men ye be, to leave me my best room,
Ev'n all my heart, and what is lodged there.'

Turning back to the Kommandant, the Bishop was a picture of truly Christian generosity.

'Yes,' he said quietly. 'If you want my heart, of course you can have it,' and without another word he turned from the altar rail and clanked down the aisle towards the door. And as he went he composed the lines afresh.

'Bad men ye be, to pilfer my best room
Ev'n all my heart . . .'

The Bishop smiled happily to himself. It was extraordinarily appropriate, he thought, and he was still smiling beatifically when Kommandant van Heerden caught up with him and overcome with emotion grabbed his manacled hand and shook it as vigorously as the handcuffs would allow.

'You're a real gentleman,' he gasped, 'a real English gentleman.'

'*Noblesse oblige*,' murmured the Bishop, whose heart had been chronically weak since he had suffered from rheumatic fever as a child.

Chapter 18

The Bishop was still in a cheerful frame of mind when Hangman Els visited him to weigh him for the drop.

'You can smile,' Els said as he dragged him out of the cell and shoved him on to the weighing machine. 'It's all right for you. You don't have to do anything. I'm the one who has to do all the work.'

'Each of us has his little part to play,' said the Bishop.

'Play?' said Els. 'I don't call what I'm doing playing. I'm having to work my guts out.'

'Just so long as you don't achieve the same result in my case,' said the Bishop uneasily. 'By the way, how are you getting on with those sacks?'

'I've practised with them till I'm fit to drop,' Els said, 'and I still don't seem to get it right. It's got to do with the weight how far you have to fall.' He tried to read the scales. 'I can't make these things out at all,' he said finally. 'What do you make your weight out to be?'

The Bishop came to his assistance.

'Three hundred and ninety-eight pounds,' he said.

Els consulted a little black book entitled, *The Hangman's Handbook*, which he had borrowed from the old warder.

'You're too heavy,' he said at last. 'It only goes up to three hundred pounds. Are you sure that's what the weighing machine said?'

The Bishop checked. 'Three hundred and ninety-eight pounds exactly.'

'Well I don't know what I'm going to do. It doesn't look as if you need any drop at all.'

'That's a nice thought,' Jonathan said, adding hopefully, 'Perhaps fat men don't commit murders.'

'Well, if they do, nobody seems to hang them,' said Els. 'Perhaps they shoot them.' On the whole he much preferred shooting. It was quicker and involved a lot less effort on his part.

'No, no,' said the Bishop hurriedly. 'They definitely have to be hanged.' He thought for a moment. 'What does it say is the drop for a man weighing two hundred pounds?' he asked.

Els consulted his little compendium. 'Six feet,' he said at last.

'Then three feet should be just about right,' said the Bishop.

'Why?' Els didn't like the sound of a shortened drop at all. It smacked too much of an attempt to avoid death.

'Double the weight and halve the drop,' the Bishop explained.

Els wasn't fool enough to fall into that trap. 'Double the weight and double the drop, you mean.'

The Bishop tried to explain. 'The heavier someone is the shorter the fall needed to break his neck. The light man needs a much longer drop to achieve the necessary momentum.'

Els tried to work it out. He found it very difficult.

'Why is a momentum necessary?' he asked. 'Nobody told me to get one.'

'Momentum is the product of a moving body's mass by its velocity.'

'I thought death was,' said Els.

'Yes, but you won't get death without momentum. It's not possible.'

'Oh, isn't it?' said Els. 'Well, I'll have a bloody good shot at it, don't you worry.'

Alarmed by the constant reference to shots, the Bishop tried again.

'When a man is hanged, how does he die?' he asked.

Els thought about it. 'By hanging,' he said finally.

'And hanging means doing what to him?'

'Dropping him down a hole with a rope round his neck.'

'And what happens then?'

'He dies.'

'Yes,' said the Bishop patiently, 'but what does the rope do?'

'Holds him up.'

'No, no. It breaks his neck.'

Els knew better than that. 'Oh no, it doesn't,' he said. 'I've been practising with sacks and it doesn't break their necks. Their bottoms drop out. It makes no end of a mess.'

The Bishop shuddered. 'I'm sure it must,' he said. 'Now we don't want that to happen to me, do we? That's why we've got to get the length of the drop right.'

'Oh, it wouldn't happen to you,' Els assured him. 'The old warder says it's the other way round with you. He says your head would . . .'

The Bishop didn't want to know what the old warder had said. He had had enough of his morbid interest in anatomy already.

'Look, if you're really so keen to get a permanent job as a hangman, you'll have to make a success of this execution. Nobody is going to employ you if you don't make a go of your first hanging.'

Els looked pathetically at the Bishop. 'I know that,' he said, 'but what can I do if your weight isn't in the handbook?'

'You could make me lighter,' the Bishop suggested looking at his manacles and chains.

'Done,' said Els delighted. 'I'll have you put on a nil diet at once.'

'I didn't mean that,' said the Bishop who couldn't imagine anything niller than the diet he was already on. 'What I had in mind was taking all these chains off and weighing me without them. I think you might find me a lot lighter.'

'I doubt if I'd find you at all,' said Els.

'Well, if you won't take these chains off I don't see how I can help you,' said the Bishop wearily.

'If I were to take them off, I'm damned sure you would not help me either,' said Els.

'In that case I don't know what to suggest. You're not going to find my proper weight with the chains on and if you won't take them off . . .' He paused as he remembered another scene in the chapel window. 'You don't surely intend to hang me in chains?' he asked.

'No,' said Els, 'there's a special set of leather straps and a cloth bag for your head.'

'Dear God what a way to go,' murmured the Bishop.

'I've put boot polish on the straps and shone them up. They look quite smart,' Els went on. The Bishop wasn't listening to him. He had suddenly thought of a way round the problem of weight.

'I know what we can do,' he said. 'You go and get another set of chains and manacles and bring them here, and we'll weigh them by themselves.'

'I don't see how that's going to help,' said Els. 'I've just told you we won't be using chains on the day. You don't think I've been polishing those straps for nothing, do you?'

The Bishop was beginning to think that he would never be able to get Els to understand anything.

'Once we know how much the chains weigh by themselves we can subtract their weight from three hundred and ninety-eight pounds and then we'll know how much I weigh by myself.'

Els considered the proposal for a moment, but in the end he shook his head.

'It wouldn't work,' he said.

'Why on earth not?'

'I could never do subtraction at school,' Els confessed finally.

'Never mind,' said the Bishop. 'I was very good at it and I'll do the sum myself.'

'How do I know you won't cheat?'

'My dear Hangman Els,' said the Bishop. 'I can think of two good reasons why I am as anxious as you are that this hanging should go with a swing. Possibly three. One is that if you make the drop too short, I shall strangle to death and I really don't want to. Two is that if you make it too long you'll probably decapitate me.'

'I won't,' said Els. 'Your head will come off.'

'Quite,' said the Bishop hurriedly. 'Nothing like calling a spade a bloody shovel, is there?'

'What's three?' asked Els, who didn't care what a bloody shovel was called.

'Oh yes, three. I had almost forgotten three. Well three is

that you are obviously a born executioner and while you've got a lot to learn about hanging, I like to see a man make use of the gifts he's been given. Yes, I know about the cloth bag,' the Bishop continued, as Els tried to interrupt with the news that he wouldn't see anything on the scaffold, 'but I am speaking metaphorically, and speaking metaphorically I hope you'll go on to greater things, one might almost say to the top of your profession.'

'You really think I'll make a good hangman?' Els asked eagerly.

'I'm sure of it,' said the Bishop. 'I can feel it in my bones that you will make a name for yourself among executioners the world over,' and having given the hangman the reassurance Els so desperately needed the Bishop went back to his cell while Els went off to fetch another set of chains and manacles. In the end they discovered that Jonathan Hazelstone weighed one hundred and eighty pounds and needed a seven-foot drop.

If the Bishop was having difficulty persuading Els to kill him properly, Kommandant van Heerden was finding it almost as difficult to persuade the surgeons at Piemburg Hospital to undertake the operation he needed to save his life. They seemed to insist on raising quite irrelevant objections, and the Kommandant found particularly irritating their insistence that there was nothing wrong with his heart. When he had disposed of that difficulty by threatening to charge them with attempted murder if they didn't agree with his diagnosis, they spent another hour discussing the ethical problems involved in transferring the heart of a murderer into the body of a man, who, as they pointed out, was so manifestly non-homicidal. The Kommandant soon set their minds at rest on that score, and it was only when they raised the technical problems of tissue typing and rejection and tried to explain how unlikely it was that the condemned man's tissues would match those of a purebred Afrikaaner, like Kommandant van Heerden, that he lost his temper.

'Are you telling me that I'm not a human being?' the Kommandant yelled at Dr Erasmus who led the transplant team. 'Are you telling me I'm a bloody baboon?'

'I'm not saying anything of the sort,' Dr Erasmus protested. 'You don't seem to understand. Each human being has a different type of tissue and yours may not be the same type as that of the donor.'

'You're telling me I've got coloured blood in me,' the Kommandant yelled. 'You're saying I can't have an Englishman's heart because I'm part-kaffir. Is that what you're saying?'

'I'm not saying anything of the sort. There's no reason at all why you shouldn't have a kaffir's heart,' Dr Erasmus said desperately. He found Kommandant van Heerden's violence positively unnerving.

'There you are. You said it. You said I could have a kaffir's heart,' shouted the Kommandant.

'I didn't mean that you had to have one. There's no reason why a black man's heart should not be put into a white man's body any more than there is any reason why a white man's organs shouldn't be transferred to a black man.'

Kommandant van Heerden had never heard such a flagrant violation of the basic concepts of apartheid in his life.

'There's every bloody reason,' he shouted, 'why a white man's organs shouldn't be put into a black man. No white man is allowed to put any portion of his body into a black man. It's against the fucking law.'

Dr Erasmus had never heard of the Fucking Law but he assumed it was police slang for the Immorality Act.

'You misunderstand me,' he said. 'I wasn't referring to sexual organs.'

'There you go again,' bellowed the Kommandant. 'I'll charge you with incitement to inter-racial homosexuality if you don't shut up.'

Dr Erasmus was silenced.

'Calm yourself, Kommandant,' he said soothingly. 'For goodness sake calm yourself. You'll do yourself an injury carrying on like this.'

'I'll do you an injury, you bastard,' yelled the Kommandant who wasn't going to be ordered about by any pig of a doctor who told him he had coloured blood. 'I know your sort. You're an enemy of South Africa, that's what you are. You're a bloody

Communist. I'll have you in under the Terrorist Act and we'll soon see how you like organ transplants.'

'For the sake of your health, please stop shouting,' the doctor pleaded.

'My health? You talk about my health? It's your health you should be worrying about if you don't do as I say,' the Kommandant screamed before he realized just what Dr Erasmus had meant. With a tremendous effort of will he calmed himself. Now he had not the slightest doubt that his heart needed changing. Dr Erasmus had admitted it in so many words.

In a quiet voice and with the authority he still possessed under Emergency Powers, Kommandant van Heerden gave his orders to the surgical team. They were to make all the necessary preparations for the transplant operation and were ordered not to divulge any information to the Press, the public or their families. The whole operation was to be conducted in the utmost secrecy. It was the only welcome piece of news the doctors could glean from the Kommandant's brief.

The only other consolation was the knowledge that Kommandant van Heerden's body would almost certainly reject the new heart. As Dr Erasmus pointed out to him, he was probably committing suicide. The Kommandant knew better. He had been eating in the police canteen for years and if his stomach could keep down the food they served there, he couldn't imagine that his body would reject a perfectly good heart.

Leaving the hospital still smarting at the affront to his origins and the good name of his family, but pleased with the way he had handled the situation, Kommandant van Heerden decided the time had come to pay a visit to Fort Rapier. His interest in the fortunes of Miss Hazelstone was undimmed by the events of the past month and his respect had if anything been increased by the old lady's remarkable resilience in the face of the misfortunes which had overtaken the Hazelstone family. The reports that had reached him from Fort Rapier indicated that Miss Hazelstone had maintained her dignity and sense of social prerogative in a situation which would have induced a feeling of despondency if not of inferiority in a less vigorous woman. Miss Hazelstone had succumbed to none of the temptations of madness. She neither shuffled lost in some interior wilderness nor imagined herself to be other than she was.

'I am Miss Hazelstone of Jacaranda Park,' she insisted in the face of attempts to turn her into a model patient with problems amenable to psychotherapy, and instead of conforming to the indolence that marked the lives of the other patients, she had found plenty of interest to occupy her time. The history of Fort Rapier and the part played by her ancestors in the creation of the garrison particularly fascinated her.

'My grandfather was C-in-C Zululand when this fort was built,' she told Dr Herzog when she met him one day crossing the parade ground, and had astonished the Superintendent by her grasp of military history.

'On this very parade ground in 1876 the Greys, the Welsh Regiment and the 12th Hussars marched past my grandfather before leaving for the Zulu War,' she told the astonished doctor, and went on to give details of the uniforms of the various branches and the character of the officers in command.

'What a remarkable memory you have,' he said, 'to remember these things.'

'Part of the family history,' said Miss Hazelstone and had gone on to explain the mistakes made in the campaign, and in particular at the Battle of Isandhlwana. Dr Herzog was so impressed with her interest, and especially by her knowledge of the Boer War and the part played in it by Dr Herzog's own grandfather, that he invited her to his house for tea and the discussion was continued until supper.

'Quite extraordinary,' he said to his wife when Miss Hazelstone went back to the ward. 'I had no idea my grandfather was responsible for our victory at Magersfontein.'

The following day he sent a memorandum to the staff, instructing them that Miss Hazelstone was to be given all the help and encouragement she needed to continue her study of military history and the part played in it by Fort Rapier.

'We have a duty to encourage patients to pursue their hobbies, particularly when they may well be of benefit to the hospital,' he told Dr von Blimenstein who complained that Miss Hazelstone had stopped attending her therapy classes.

'Miss Hazelstone hopes to publish the history of Fort Rapier and any publicity must surely redound to our credit. It's not every day that lunatics publish military history.'

Dr von Blimenstein had reservations on that score, but she kept her thoughts to herself and Miss Hazelstone had continued her researches with growing enthusiasm. She had discovered regimental records in a trunk in the basement of what was now the staff canteen, but which had in earlier days been the officers' mess. These had led her to unearth even more interesting relics in the shape of discarded uniforms in the quartermaster's stores.

'We really ought to hold a pageant,' she told the Superintendent. 'The uniforms are there and while they do need patching up in places, because the cockroaches have got at them you see, there's no doubt they are authentic and it will give all the patients something to work for. It's so important for morale to create a common aim and something to look forward to.'

Dr Herzog had been impressed by the idea.

'A pageant of Fort Rapier's history,' he said, 'what a splendid idea,' and his mind toyed with the idea of an open day in which the public and the Press could see the wonderful work being done on behalf of mental health in Zululand.

'I thought we might start with a march-past,' Miss Hazelstone continued, 'followed by several tableaux commemorating particularly memorable feats of courage in the history of South Africa.'

Dr Herzog was hesitant. 'I don't want any mock battles,' he said anxiously.

'Oh no, nothing like that,' Miss Hazelstone assured him, 'I was thinking more of purely stationary representations of the events.'

'We can't have the patients getting too excited.'

'Quite,' said Miss Hazelstone who had long since ceased to think of herself as a patient. 'I take your point. We shall have to see that the whole affair is conducted with truly military discipline. I was thinking of including as one of the set-pieces your great-grandfather's heroic defence of his homestead in the 6th Kaffir War.'

Dr Herzog was flattered. 'Were you really?' he said. 'I had

no idea my family played such an important role in the military history of the country.'

'The Herzogs were practically the Afrikaans counterpart of the Hazelstones,' Miss Hazelstone told him, and with the knowledge that the pageant would enhance the reputation of the Herzog family as well as that of the hospital, the Superintendent gave his permission for the event to be held.

In the weeks that followed Miss Hazelstone threw herself into the preparations with an enthusiasm that communicated itself to the other inmates of Fort Rapier. She took command of the organization with all the natural authority of Sir Theophilus' granddaughter and with an attention to detail made possible by her wealth. Bales of red cloth were ordered from Durban on Miss Hazelstone's account, and the patients in the sewing-rooms were kept busy making new uniforms.

'It certainly brightens the place up,' Dr Herzog said to Dr von Blimenstein as they watched Miss Hazelstone drilling a squad of manic depressives on the parade ground one day.

'I can't help feeling uneasy,' Dr von Blimenstein said. 'Is it really necessary to include the Battle of Blood River in the programme? I'm sure it will have an unfortunate effect on the black patients.'

'Our chief responsibility is to the whites,' said Dr Herzog, 'and it can only help them to see the great events of the past re-enacted here. I have every hope that by participating in them our patients will come to see that there is still a place for the mentally sick in modern South Africa. I like to think of this pageant as drama therapy on a vast scale.'

'But surely, Doctor, you don't consider insanity to be simply a matter of morale?' Dr von Blimenstein said.

'Yes, I do, and if it isn't it ought to be. Besides,' said the Superintendent, 'the pageant will help to sublimate some of their aggression.'

On the parade ground Miss Hazelstone's squad marched past the saluting base which the carpenters had erected between the two field guns.

'Eyes right,' Miss Hazelstone shouted, and two hundred pairs of eyes fixed themselves manically on Dr Herzog. The Superintendent saluted.

'Eyes front,' and the squad marched on.

'Most impressive,' said Dr Herzog. 'What a pity we didn't think of this before.'

'I just hope we don't have cause to regret it,' said Dr von Blimenstein pessimistically.

As the day of the pageant approached, Miss Hazelstone had to deal with several problems. One was the question of assegais for the Zulu warriors. Dr Herzog was adamant.

'I'm not having hundreds of black patients running around brandishing spears. God alone knows what would happen.'

In the end the problem was solved by the purchase of one thousand rubber spears which had been used in the making of a film a year or two before.

Another problem centred round the question of the music and the sound effects to accompany the tableaux.

'I was thinking of the *1812 Overture*,' Miss Hazelstone explained to the conductor of the hospital band.

'We can't reach those heights,' the bandmaster objected, 'and in any case we haven't got a cannon.'

'We could use the field guns,' Miss Hazelstone said.

'We can't go round letting off loud bangs in the hospital grounds. It would have a terrible effect on the anxiety cases.'

In the end it was agreed that the band would restrict itself to simple marches like *Colonel Bogey* and tunes like *Goodbye Dolly Gray* and that a recording of the *1812 Overture* should be played over loudspeakers to accompany the battle scenes.

A dress rehearsal was held the day before the pageant and Superintendent Herzog and the staff attended.

'Simply splendid,' Dr Herzog said afterwards. 'One has the feeling that one is actually present, it's so real.'

It was quite by chance that Kommandant van Heerden chose the afternoon of the pageant for his visit to the hospital. Unlike the Mayor of Piemburg and other notables, he had not been invited because it was felt that Miss Hazelstone might not like it.

'We don't want anything to put the old lady off her stride, and having the police here would only remind her of her brother's execution,' the Superintendent said.

As his car passed into the grounds of Fort Rapier Kommandant van Heerden noticed that a new air of festivity seemed to have come to the hospital.

'I hope it isn't too open,' he said to the driver who had replaced Konstabel Els, as the car passed under a banner which announced Open Day. They drove up to the parade ground which was decked with regimental flags and Kommandant van Heerden got out.

'Glad you could make it Kommandant,' Dr Herzog said, and led the way to the saluting base, where the Mayor and his party were already seated. The Kommandant looked nervously around as he took his seat.

'What's going on?' he asked one of the aldermen.

'It's some sort of publicity stunt to foster public interest in mental health,' the alderman said.

'Funny place to hold it,' said the Kommandant. 'I thought everyone up here was supposed to be barmy. Good heavens, look at those kaffirs.'

A detachment of schizophrenic Zulus marched across the parade ground to take up their position for the tableaux.

'Who the hell gave them those spears?'

'Oh it's all right, they're only rubber,' said the councillor.

The Kommandant sank down in his chair in horror. 'Don't tell me,' he said, 'this whole thing has been organized by Miss Hazelstone.'

'Right first time,' said the councillor. 'Put up the money herself. Just as well she did too. I hate to think what this little lot cost.'

Kommandant van Heerden wasn't listening. He rose from his chair and looked desperately round for some way of escaping, but the crowd round the saluting base was too dense to pass through, and in front the march-past had already begun. He sank back into his chair in despair.

As the band played the regiments formed up and marched towards the stand. Red-coated and surprisingly well drilled for their mental health, they swung past the Superintendent and at their head there marched the familiar figure of Miss Hazelstone. For a moment the Kommandant thought he was back in the hall at Jacaranda House, and staring once more at the portrait of Sir Theophilus. Miss Hazelstone's uniform was a replica of the one the Viceroy had worn in the painting. Her face was partially obscured by a plumed pith helmet but on her chest were the stars and medals of her grandfather's disastrous campaigns. Behind the first regiment which was the Welsh Guards, came the others, the county regiments of England, appropriately less in step than the Guards (it had been difficult to find enough compulsive cases to be really smart) but shuffling along with determination all the time. After them came the Scots regiments recruited from women patients wearing kilts and led by a chronic depressive playing the bagpipes. Last of all was a small detachment of frogmen in rubber suits with flippers who had difficulty keeping in step.

'A nice touch of modernity, don't you think?' Dr Herzog murmured to the Mayor as twenty crazed faces turned their masks towards the stand.

'I hope those kaffirs aren't going to come too close,' said the Mayor anxiously. There was no need to worry. The black lunatics were not allowed the privilege of marching past the stand. Miss Hazelstone was arranging them for the first tableau.

In the interval Kommandant van Heerden left his seat and spoke to the Superintendent.

'I thought I told you to keep Miss Hazelstone under close surveillance,' he said angrily.

'She's made remarkable progress since she has been here,' Dr Herzog answered. 'We like to see our patients taking an interest in their hobbies.'

'You may,' said the Kommandant, 'but I don't. Miss Hazelstone's hobbies happen to include murder and you go and let her organize a military parade. You must be out of your mind.'

'Nothing like allowing the patients to dramatize their aggressive tendencies,' said the Superintendent.

'She's done that quite enough already,' said the Kommandant. 'My advice is to stop this thing before it's too late.'

But already the first tableau had begun. A square of cardboard ox wagons stood in the centre of the parade ground and around them gathered the Zulu schizophrenics brandishing their spears. After several minutes the Zulus lay down on the tarmac in attitudes supposed to represent agonizing death.

'Blood River,' said the Superintendent.

'Very realistic,' said the Mayor.

'Bloody insane,' said Kommandant van Heerden.

A polite round of clapping greeted the end of the battle. For the next hour the history of South Africa unfurled before the spectators in a series of blood-curdling battles in which the blacks were invariably massacred by the whites.

'You would think they'd get tired of lying down and getting up and lying down again,' the Mayor said when the Zulus had gone through their death agonies for the umpteenth time. 'Must keep them physically fit, I suppose.'

'So long as the bastards don't win, I'm happy,' said the Kommandant.

'I think they do have a moment of triumph in the finale,' said Dr Herzog. 'It's the Battle of Isandhlwana. The British ran out of ammunition and were massacred.'

'Do you mean to tell me,' said the Kommandant, 'that you have allowed white men to be defeated by blacks? It's insane. What's more it's illegal. You are encouraging racial hatred.'

Dr Herzog was nonplussed. 'I hadn't thought of it like that,' he said.

'Well, you had better think of it now. You're breaking the law. You've got to put a stop to it. I'm not prepared to sit here and watch anything so outrageous,' the Kommandant said firmly.

'Nor am I,' said the Mayor. Several councillors nodded in agreement.

'I don't really see how I can,' Dr Herzog said. 'They're about to begin.'

In the middle of the parade ground Miss Hazelstone had organized the British camp and was superintending the placement of the two old field guns. Several hundred yards away the Zulu army was gathered ready for its moment of triumph.

'I insist that you stop the battle,' said the Kommandant.

'So do I,' said the Mayor, who still didn't feel very comfortable about the rubber spears.

Dr Herzog hesitated. 'Oh dear, I do wish you had told me it was illegal before. I don't see what I can do now,' he said anxiously.

'Well, if you won't stop it, I will,' said the Kommandant.

'Good man,' said the Mayor, seconded by the councillors.

Before he could think about the likely consequences of his intervention, Kommandant van Heerden found himself being helped off the saluting base and on to the parade ground. He marched slowly towards the two armies, and as he went the realization of his position slowly dawned on him. In the middle of the square halfway between the two opposing forces of lunatics, he began to regret his precipitate decision to intervene. On one side of him five hundred Zulu schizophrenics pawed the ground and waved their spears ferociously, while on the other, an equal number of white madmen awaited defeat with a determination made all the more awful by foreknowledge.

Kommandant van Heerden halted and raised his hand. Silence fell over the two armies.

'This is Kommandant van Heerden speaking,' he shouted. 'I am ordering you to disperse and return to your wards. This is an illegal gathering and contravenes the Riotous Assemblies Act.'

He stopped and waited for the armies to retire. There was no sign of their doing anything of the sort. As his words echoed away, both sides stared insanely at their adversaries and there were murmurs in the ranks. Miss Hazelstone finished sighting the field guns and stepped forward. On the Zulu side an enormous warrior followed suit.

'What is the meaning of this nonsense?' Miss Hazelstone shouted.

'You heard me,' said the Kommandant. 'This battle constitutes a breach of the peace. I insist you disperse.'

In the space between the armies Kommandant van Heerden found his new role as keeper of the peace becoming more difficult.

'You've no right to come here and interfere with our pageant,' Miss Hazelstone insisted. 'And it's not a breach of the peace.'

'We won,' said the Zulu chief. 'We won the battle of Isandhlwana and now we win it again.'

'Over my dead body,' said the Kommandant and regretted

the words as soon as he had said them. The murmurs in the ranks of the two armies indicated all too clearly that the spirit of belligerency was spreading.

On the saluting base the spectators were growing as restless as the lunatics.

'Are those axes made of rubber too?' the Mayor asked as he watched several Zulus flourishing choppers in place of their spears.

'I certainly hope so,' said the Superintendent.

'The British appear to be loading those field guns,' said the Mayor.

'Impossible,' said the Superintendent. 'They've nothing to load them with.'

'They're putting something up the spout,' said the Mayor. 'And those Zulus seem to be putting something on the ends of their spears. They look like knitting needles to me. Either that or bicycle spokes.'

The alarm of the Mayor was as nothing to the panic that Kommandant van Heerden was beginning to feel. Miss Hazelstone and the Zulu chief were engaged in a fierce argument about who had won the Battle of Isandhlwana.

'My grandfather was there,' said Miss Hazelstone.

'So was mine,' said the Zulu.

'Mine wasn't,' said the Kommandant, 'and in any case I don't care a stuff who won the battle, no one is going to win it here. I demand you withdraw your forces.'

'We're going to win,' said the Zulu. 'We've been losing all afternoon and we've a right to win.'

'Nonsense,' said Miss Hazelstone. 'My grandfather won the victory and that's all there is to be said.'

'My grandfather told my father and my father told me that your grandfather ran away,' the Zulu said.

'How dare you?' Miss Hazelstone shrieked. 'How dare you insult a Hazelstone?'

Kommandant van Heerden was horrified too. He knew from experience what was likely to be the result of any altercation between Miss Hazelstone and a Zulu. As the old lady wrestled with the sword that hung from her belt and the Zulu took refuge behind his enormous shield, Kommandant van Heerden made one last effort to restore harmony.

'I order you to leave this parade ground,' he yelled, drawing his revolver from its holster, but it was already too late. With an upward sweep of her sword Miss Hazelstone knocked the Kommandant's arm into the air. The revolver fired harmlessly into the sky and with a great roar the two armies of the insane surged towards one another.

As Miss Hazelstone's sword swept through the air and the Zulu parried with his shield, Kommandant van Heerden turned to flee. One glance at the Zulu schizophrenics convinced him that if safety lay anywhere, it was with the British Army and he dashed towards the advancing lines of redcoats. A moment later he regretted his decision. Advancing at a run, a regiment of paranoid women in kilts still headed by the depressed piper playing *The Road to the Isles*, swept over the Kommandant and he had just time to turn and run with them before he was bowled over and thrown to the ground. He lay still and was trodden on several times before the regiment was past. Then raising his head, he surveyed the scene around him.

It was immediately clear that the Zulus had no intention of forgoing their victory. Nonplussed for a moment by the charge of the paranoid women, they had recovered their nerve and had counter-attacked to good effect. Using their short rubber spears now tipped with knitting needles, they were stabbing their way forward very successfully. On the left flank the Welsh Guards were making a desperate defence but their wooden rifles were no match for the assegais. As the Black Watch wavered and began to retreat Kommandant van Heerden scrambled to his feet and ran before them. Around him the parade ground echoed to the war-cry of the Zulu hordes, the screams of the wounded women, and the weird noises coming from the bagpipes. To add to the din a tape-recorder struck up the *1812 Overture* through the loudspeakers. In the middle of the battle, Miss Hazelstone's pith helmet could be seen bobbing about. Kommandant van Heerden made it to the British camp and collapsed inside one of the tents.

To the spectators on the stand the re-enactment of history

appeared at first to be entirely convincing. The valiant charge of the British and their subsequent retreat had an air of authenticity about them which the previous tableaux had lacked.

'Amazing realism,' said the Mayor, who had just seen a Guardsman run through with a spear.

'I think the music helps too,' said the Superintendent.

The Mayor had to agree. 'People seem to be screaming rather a lot,' he said.

'I'm sure this sort of thing helps the patients,' Dr Herzog continued. 'Tends to take their minds off their problems.'

'I suppose it must,' said the Mayor. 'Certainly takes other things off. There's a fellow over there who seems to have lost a leg.'

On the square in front of them glimpses of a terrible reality were beginning to appear through the pageant of history. Increasingly it was becoming difficult to tell what was illusion from what was fact. History and present tragedy mingled inextricably. In some places, death was being mimed with a series of violent contortions whose realism far surpassed the agonies of those whose deaths were in no way rehearsed. To the strains of Tchaikovsky a number of patients in the Black Watch found themselves being raped by Zulu warriors while a detachment of frogmen who had never been anywhere near Isandhlwana threw themselves into the fray with all the vigour their flippers would allow.

From the shelter of the tent into which he had crawled the Kommandant watched as the crew of a field gun aimed the weapon into the crowd of struggling combatants and was horrified to see Miss Hazelstone, minus her pith helmet and stained with blood, superintending the operation.

'More chlorate and less sugar,' he heard her say to a man who was filling what appeared to be a pillowcase with powder. The Kommandant waited no longer. He knew too well Miss Hazelstone's remarkable skill with large-calibre weapons to risk being in the line of fire. Disentangling himself from the canvas and refusing the passionate overtures of a private of the Black Watch who had crawled in beside him, the Kommandant dashed for shelter towards the saluting base. He had covered some twenty yards when he heard Miss Hazelstone give the order to fire, and a moment later a sheet of flame enveloped the British camp. As an enormous explosion threw him to the ground and the blast slid him across the tarmac the Kommandant shut his eyes and prayed. Above his head portions of field gun mingled with combatants interrupted in their struggles. Miss Hazelstone had not merely fired the gun, she had exploded it. As he slid to a halt under the saluting base, Kommandant van Heerden raised his head and looked around at the subsiding chaos. The actors in the tableau had assumed a new and altogether convincing stillness and it was clear that nobody had won the Battle of Isandhlwana.

The parade ground was littered with black and white bodies while what survivors there were had lost all interest in history. With all the marks of an entirely sane instinct for self-preservation, they crawled towards the sick bay.

Only the staff seemed to have taken leave of their senses. On the stand above him the Kommandant could hear Dr Herzog still trying to reassure the late Mayor that the spears were made of rubber. To Kommandant van Heerden the assurance seemed quite unnecessary. Whatever had hit the Mayor had been made of something much more lethal.

The Kommandant waited until Dr Herzog had been taken away before crawling from his hiding-place. He stood up and looked around. History had not merely been portrayed, he thought, it had been made. Not only the past but the present and future of South Africa was to be seen in the devastation that greeted his eyes. Picking his way over the bodies, the Kommandant made his way towards a large crater which had been blown in the middle of the parade ground. Beside it, there lay the remains of a plumed pith helmet and the Star Miss Hazelstone had been wearing.

'A last memento,' he murmured, and picked them up. Then still dazed and shaken he turned and made his way back to the car.

Chapter 19

On the morning of his execution Jonathan Hazelstone was denied the usual privilege of choosing a hearty breakfast on the grounds that before all major operations patients had to do with light refreshment. Instead of the bacon and eggs he had ordered, he was allowed a cup of coffee and a visit from an Anglican chaplain. Jonathan found it difficult to decide which was the more unpleasant. On the whole he thought he preferred the coffee.

His ties with the Church had been severed at the time of his trial and the Bishop had reached the conclusion that the refusal of the Church authorities to testify on his behalf had been due to the jealousy he knew to exist among his colleagues at the rapidity of his promotion to a bishopric. He had no idea that parts of his confession, particularly those chosen by Konstabel Els, had been shown to the Archbishop.

'I knew the fellow was progressive,' the Archbishop muttered as he read the extraordinary document, 'but really this time he has gone too far,' and he recalled Jonathan's admission that he had used every possible method to attract people into the Church. 'High Church in ritual, Low Church in approach, that's my way,' Jonathan had said and the Archbishop could see that he had meant it. To combine sodomy with genuflection was to be High Church and Low with a vengeance and it was hardly surprising his congregations had grown so quickly.

'I think the least said the soonest mended,' the Archbishop had decided, and in short the Church had disowned him.

The Chaplain who came to visit him in his last hours was not a South African. It had been impossible to persuade any self-respecting parson to minister to the needs of a man who had brought disgrace on his cloth and even the Bishop of Piemburg had declined the invitation.

'There are moments when a man needs to be alone,' he explained to Governor Schnapps over the telephone, 'and this is surely one of them,' and had gone back to compose a sermon on the Brotherhood of Man.

In the end it was the Chaplain of a Cambridge college who was visiting Piemburg during the long vacation who was inveigled into Piemburg Prison to attend to the prisoner's spiritual needs.

'I understand there is a particularly fine display of prickly pears in the prison garden,' the Vicar of Piemburg explained to the Chaplain who was far more interested in the physical needs of rock plants than in the spiritual ones of his fellow men and the Chaplain had jumped at the opportunity afforded by the hanging to see a riot of prickly pears.

Standing in the cell, the Chaplain found it difficult to know what to say.

'You weren't by any chance in the Navy?' he asked finally.

Jonathan shook his head.

'I just wondered,' the Chaplain continued. 'There was a middy on HMS *Clodius* in '43 I think it was, or it might have been '44. His name was Hazelnut.'

'Mine's Hazelstone,' said the Bishop.

'So it is. How forgetful of me. One meets so many people in my profession.'

'I suppose so,' said the Bishop.

The Chaplain paused, and looked at the manacles and chains. 'Do you wear those all the time?' he asked. 'They must be frightfully uncomfortable.'

'Only when I'm going to be hanged,' said the Bishop.

The Chaplain thought he detected a note of bitterness in the remark, and recollected the reason for his visit.

'Is there anything you would like to tell me?' he asked.

The Bishop could think of a great many things he would like to tell him, but there didn't seem much point.

'No,' he said, 'I have made my confession.'

The Chaplain sighed with relief. These occasions are so embarrassing, he thought.

'I've never actually attended an execution before,' he mumbled at last.

'Nor have I,' said the Bishop.

'Nasty things,' continued the Chaplain, 'nasty but necessary. Still they do say hanging is quick and painless. I daresay you'll be quite relieved when it is all over.'

The Bishop, whose hope of eternal life had vanished along with his faith, doubted if relieved was quite the right word. He tried to change the subject.

'Do you come here often?' he asked.

'To the prison?'

'To South Africa, though it's much the same thing.'

The Chaplain ignored the remark. He was a staunch supporter of the South African point of view at high table in his college, and had no time for liberals.

'I try to get away to summer climes at least once a year,' he said. 'Undergraduates are so irreligious these days and my real interest lies in gardening. South Africa is full of lovely gardens.'

'Then perhaps you'll appreciate this poem,' said the Bishop and began to recite 'The Forerunners'.

> 'Lovely enchanting language, sugar cane,
> Hony of roses, whither wilt thou flie?'

He was still reciting when Governor Schnapps and Hangman Els arrived. As the chains were removed and he was strapped into the harness that held his arms, the Bishop continued:

> 'True beautie dwells on high: ours is a flame
> But borrow'd thence to light us thither.
> Beautie and beauteous words should go together.'

'Bugger these buckles,' said Els, who was having difficulty with the straps.

The solemn procession passed out of Bottom into the bright sunshine of the prison courtyard. Stumbling between Els and the old warder, Jonathan looked round him for the last time. Incongruous against the dead black paint of the Death House stood a white ambulance. To everyone's amazement, the condemned man laughed.

'Bleak paleness chalkes the doore,' he shouted,

193

> 'The harbingers are come. See, see their mark
> White is their colour and behold my head.'

The two ambulance men stared in horror at the shouting figure whose corpse they had been sent to collect for the transplant operation.

> 'But must they have my heart? Must they dispark
> Those sparkling feelings which thereine were bred?'

The little group hurried on up the steps to the scaffold. The old warder helped Els to get the Bishop on to the trap and then rushed down the ladder and across the courtyard to his office. It wasn't that he was squeamish but he had no intention of being anywhere near the gallows when Els pulled the lever, and besides he had a good excuse for his absence. He had to phone the hospital the moment the ambulance left the prison.

Standing on the trap the Bishop continued his recitation. Governor Schnapps asked the Chaplain what a harbinger was. The Chaplain said he thought it was probably a member of the hydrangea family though he seemed to remember having served under a Captain Harbinger during the war. Els was trying to get the cloth bag over the Bishop's head. He was having some difficulty because the Bishop was so tall and the bag had evidently been made for a much smaller head. Els couldn't get the Bishop to bend his legs because the straps prevented any movement. In the end Governor Schnapps had to give Els a lift up before he could drag the hood down into position. He had to repeat the performance when it came to putting the noose round the condemned man's neck, and then Els pulled the rope so tight the Bishop was forced to stop his recitation.

'Must dulnesse turn me to a clo—' He ground to a halt.

'For goodness sake, Els, loosen the bloody thing,' Governor Schnapps shouted as the poem throttled to a stop. 'You're supposed to hang him down there, not strangle him up here.'

'They seem to grow best in sandy soil,' said the Chaplain.

'Is that loose enough for you?' Els asked after he had pulled the rope and loosened the noose so that it hung limply on the Bishop's shoulders. He was sick of people telling him how to do his job. If the Governor was so bloody knowledgeable about hangings, why didn't he do the job himself.

'What do?' Governor Schnapps said to the Chaplain.

'Hydrangeas.'

'Clod,' said the Bishop resuming his recital.

Els stepped over to the lever.

'Yet have they left me,' the Bishop's muffled voice came through the cloth bag. Els pulled the lever and the hooded figure disappeared through the trap into the well below, and his voice, already indistinct, was silenced by the dreadful thud that followed. As the trapdoor slammed and the scaffold rocked alarmingly under the impact, the Chaplain, recalled to the purpose of his visit by the intimations of mortality he had just witnessed, offered a prayer for the dead man.

'Let us pray for the soul of the departed wherever it may be,' he said, and lowered his head. Governor Schnapps and Els closed their eyes and listened with bowed heads as he prayed. For several minutes the Chaplain mumbled on before ending, 'And may Thy Servant depart in Peace, Amen.'

'Amen,' said Governor Schnapps and Els together. The men on the scaffold raised their heads and Els stepped forward to peer down into the well. The rope had stopped swinging and hung rather limply, Els thought, considering the weight of its burden. As his eyes became accustomed to the darkness below Els began to realize that something was missing. The noose on the rope hung loose and empty. The Chaplain's prayer had been answered. Wherever God's servant might be, he had certainly departed and evidently in one piece too. The well of the scaffold was absolutely empty.

As the Bishop dropped into eternity he thought how appropriate his last words had been and was glad he hadn't reached the next line which went, 'Thou art still my God,' because he no longer believed. He braced himself for the awful shock to his neck, but the pain came from another extremity altogether. 'Corns,' he thought, as he hit the ground with a tremendous crash and rolled sideways, through the door and out into the sunlit courtyard. His cloth bag was ripped and his legs felt decidedly painful, but it was evident that whatever else had been broken, his neck had not. He lay still, waiting for Els to fetch him for a second attempt and wasn't surprised when he felt hands lifting his feet and shoulders.

A moment later he was lying on a stretcher and had been lifted into the ambulance. As the doors were slammed the ambulance moved off hurriedly, stopped for a moment while the prison gates were opened, and hurtled out into the street, its siren whirring.

Behind it the Death House had begun to fulfil the predictions of the old warder. Under the impact of the stampede that followed on the scaffold when the distraught hangman peering into the well slipped and grabbed Governor Schnapps' legs to prevent himself falling, the walls of the gallows slowly toppled inwards and with a roar of falling masonry, Governors, Hangmen and Chaplains, disappeared from view in a dense cloud of black dust. The old warder sat in his office and thanked his lucky stars. 'I said it wasn't safe,' he murmured and picked up the phone to dial the hospital.

As the ambulance sped through the streets of Piemburg, Jonathan Hazelstone felt the attendant undoing the straps that held his arms and legs. A hand slid inside his shirt and felt his chest.

'It's all right. It's still beating,' he heard the attendant tell the driver. Jonathan held his breath until the hand went away. Then he relaxed slowly. Around him the sounds of the city filtered through the canvas bag and as he lay there Jonathan Hazelstone realized for the first time that what lay in store for him might make death by hanging seem infinitely preferable.

'I'll be hanged if anyone is going to cut my heart out now,' he thought to himself as the ambulance swung through the gates of Piemburg Hospital, and stopped outside the mortuary.

Inside the hospital the news of the execution had been accompanied by the old warder's insistence that several more ambulances be sent to the prison to deal with the victims of the disastrous collapse of the Death House. The air of tension that was already present in the hospital developed into a state of wholesale panic. The Kommandant, already prepared for the operation, was given a general anaesthetic and wheeled unconscious into the operating theatre. While the surgeons prepared for the transplant, ambulance drivers rushed to their vehicles and preparations were made to receive the expected influx of victims from the prison. Nurses already distraught at having to deal with scores of lunatics injured in the massacre at Fort Rapier tried to ready themselves for this fresh disaster. When the ambulance carrying Jonathan Hazelstone arrived at the mortuary it was caught up in the general confusion.

'Get back to the prison,' yelled an orderly from a window when the two attendants carried the donor into the mortuary and deposited him on a trolley. 'There's been a major catastrophe there.' The two men dashed back to their ambulance and drove off. Alone in the mortuary for a moment the Bishop leapt off his trolley and snatched the cloth bag from his head and looked around him. Under the sheets that covered still forms on their slabs he found what he was looking for, and by the time two orderlies arrived to fetch the donor for the transplant, the body lying snugly under its white sheet and with its head covered by a grey cloth bag contained a heart that was far too cold and still to be of much assistance to Kommandant van Heerden.

As the operation got under way, what remained of the late Bishop of Barotseland was strolling with the faint suggestion of a limp up the hill towards Jacaranda House, and as it strolled it was singing:

> 'Yet if you go, I passe not; take your way:
> For Thou art still my God, is all that ye
> Perhaps with more embellishment can say.
> Go birds of spring: let winter have his fee.
> Let a bleak paleness chalke the door.
> So all within be livelier than before.'

Jonathan Hazelstone had begun to think that there might, after all, be reasons for recovering his faith.

The state of panic that reigned at Piemburg Hospital when the ambulance containing the Bishop arrived was as nothing to the chaos and hysteria which began in the operating theatre when the body of the donor arrived on the trolley. An incision had already been made in Kommandant van Heerden's chest when it was discovered that whoever had been responsible for the execution had made an altogether too thorough job of it. The corpse on the trolley had multiple injuries of the most appalling sort. The only thing that didn't appear to be broken on it was the neck. Not only was it fractured in a score of places but it had been dead for at least forty-eight hours. And when it was further revealed to be the corpse of a woman of eighty-nine, the surgeons knew that what they had considered stupid from the start, not to say criminal, had degenerated now to the point of sheer lunacy.

Dr Erasmus was frantic. 'Who said this was beating?' he yelled, slapping the withered object that hung out of the old lady's chest. (She had in fact been run over by a twenty-five-ton truck while crossing the road.) 'This hasn't beaten for days and, when it last worked, it didn't bloody beat. It winced once in a while. I wouldn't feed this heart to a starving dog let alone put it into that maniac's body.' He sat down and wept.

After half an hour during which the mortuary was searched again and again, and various possible donors in the hospital wards had their deaths hastened by teams of desperate surgeons who came masked and predatory to stare at them and feel their pulses hopefully, Dr Erasmus pulled himself together and taking a quick tot of ether addressed the heart team.

'Gentlemen and ladies,' he said, 'what we have all been witness to this afternoon is of such a regrettable and dreadful nature that the sooner we forget about it the better. As you know I never wanted to undertake this transplant in the first place. We were forced to agree to it by that bloody lunatic there.' He pointed to Kommandant van Heerden's unconscious body. 'We acted under immense pressure and, thank heaven, in absolute secrecy. And now owing to the prison authorities' delay in letting us have the donor, and looking at her injuries

198

I can fully appreciate why there was this delay, we are quite unable to proceed with the operation. I intend to stitch the patient's chest up and leave his own heart beating perfectly healthily in place.'

There were murmurs of protest from the other members of the transplant team.

'Yes, I know how you feel and given any further provocation I would agree to remove his heart and let the bastard rot. But I have decided against it. Thanks to the secrecy that surrounds this whole irregular business I have a better plan. I think it will be better to allow the Kommandant to remain in complete ignorance of the good fortune that has prevented him from getting this,' and Dr Erasmus slapped the old woman's heart again. 'We will simply maintain the fiction that the transplant has been completed successfully and I have every confidence that his stupidity is so colossal that it will never cross his mind to question our statement that he has a new heart.'

Amid congratulations and a few cheers, the eminent surgeon turned to Kommandant van Heerden and stitched him up.

An hour later the Kommandant woke up in his room. He felt rather sick and the wound in his chest hurt when he moved but otherwise he didn't seem to feel any ill-effects from his operation. He took a deep tentative breath and listened to his new heart. It sounded perfect.

Chapter 20

As the great cloud of black dust swelled out in the centre of the prison courtyard and the last piece of rotten masonry fell with a final thud, an awestruck silence settled on the black convicts cowering in their cells. Konstabel Els, treading on Governor Schnapps' scrotum as a last tribute to the man who had ruined his career as a hangman, clambered painfully to the top of the pile of debris and stared into the murk. It was hardly a peak in Darien and the prospect ahead could hardly be called pacific but in his own way ex-Hangman Els was a proud man. At the very centre of a slowly expanding ball of black dust, Konstabel Els knew that he had once again put his great gifts of annihilation to good use. Below him lay the bodies of Governor Schnapps, the Chaplain and, he still hoped, the man he had attempted to hang. He, Hangman Els, had topped them all and no one would ever forget the day that Els had hanged a man in Piemburg Prison. He had made more than a reputation for himself, he had made a name, a great name. And as Els clambered down from the mound of debris and emerged dazed from the black cloud, he had no regrets.

Naked, bruised and black as the ace of spades, Els stepped forth to meet the world. He walked slowly and unsteadily up the great courtyard and as he walked men began to pour out of their prison cells where they had been waiting in silent fear, while the first hanging Piemburg Prison had known for twenty years took place. From every doorway overlooking the courtyard the convicts poured to gaze at the scene of disaster.

At first they stood and stared in silent wonder, and then a great cry went up, followed by shouts of joy and presently a man broke into song and a moment later the great courtyard was a mass of dancing and singing men who stamped their feet and clapped their hands in an ecstatic and triumphant dance. One thousand black convicts, Zulus to a man, danced as they had never danced before round the mound that had once been the dreaded Death House. Rank after rank they stamped and swayed and as the earth and sky reverberated to their dance they sang.

And their song was a great requiem of joy at the passing of Els, Kaffir-Killer Els, Hangman Els, the scourge of the Zulus. In their midst stamping and dancing and singing for dear life, naked and black as the best of them, was Els.

Someone threw a match on to the pile of masonry and rotten wood and a moment later the remains of the scaffold were ablaze. As the dust slowly subsided a plume of black smoke arose into the cloudless sky. Rising almost vertically in the still air the black plume signalled far and wide that some-thing extraordinary and significant had occurred.

The swaying convicts, advancing with their knees raised high for the emphatic stamp of their feet and backing again for another triumphant surge, accompanied the flames and the roar of the fire with their endless chant.

> *'Els is dead, Kaffir-Killer Els,*
> *Gone to the devil where his soul belongs*
> *Raper of our women, killer of our men*
> *We won't see the swine again.'*

The song was picked up by the Zulus in the street outside the prison and they took up the refrain. From house to house, from street to street, the chant spread like wildfire as servants poured into the streets to watch the smoke of the funeral pyre rise over Piemburg Prison. Within an hour all Piemburg reverberated to the Zulus' chant. Lying in his bed in Piemburg Hospital Kommandant van Heerden dozily caught the refrain and smiled. It seemed a good omen. He began to hum it cheer-fully. It put him in good heart.

As dusk fell the convicts were still dancing and singing. In the administrative block the warders cowered in terror and peered fearfully through the bars at the black figures silhouetted against the flames. The old warder cursed Els and his bloody hanging but he knew better than to try to put a stop to the celebrations. He wasn't going to get himself torn to bits by the mob by trying to intervene and when he rang the police station to ask for reinforcements he had been told by Luitenant Verkramp that the police station was itself under siege and he would have to pray and wait for the exuberance to die down of its own accord. Verkramp had not been exaggerating. The streets of Piemburg were filled with dancing crowds. Traffic ground to a halt and white drivers walked home or spent the night in their offices rather than risk trying to drive through the excited mobs. Not that there was any sign of anger among the crowds, only a great sense of liberation and joy.

*   *   *

As the plane for London passed low over Piemburg that night a large cheerful clergyman drew the attention of his companion to the fire and the crowds dancing in the streets.

'So all within is livelier than before,' he remarked enigmatically.

His companion put down the catalogue of rubber goods she had been reading. 'I'm sure you'll make a very good college chaplain,' she said and sighed, 'but I doubt if I'll find a Zulu cook in London.'

It was only a month before Kommandant van Heerden was well enough to leave hospital. His new heart had shown no signs of being rejected and the doctors were delighted with his progress. There had been a little trouble over the matter of injections and it had taken six male nurses all their strength to hold the Kommandant down, but apart from that he had been a model patient. After a fortnight he had been allowed out of bed and only then had he learnt the full story of the tragedy at Piemburg Prison.

'It was a miracle the ambulance men managed to get the body away in time,' he told Dr Erasmus. 'Another minute and I wouldn't be here today.'

Dr Erasmus had to agree. 'A genuine miracle,' he said.

'You're quite certain there won't be any rejection of the new heart?' the Kommandant asked, and was relieved that the doctor was so confident all would be well.

'I can honestly say,' said Dr Erasmus, 'that to all intents and purposes the heart that beats in your chest at this moment might well have been the one you were born with,' and with this assurance that there would be no rejection, the Kommandant smiled happily to himself.

When he finally left hospital, the Kommandant took a month's leave and spent it on the beach at Umhloti acquiring a healthy tan and reading books about the Hazelstone family. For a while he toyed with the idea of changing his name to van Heerden-Hazelstone. 'After all, I'm practically one of the family,' he thought, but he gave up the idea finally as being not in the best of taste. Instead he cultivated an air of arrogance which irritated Luitenant Verkramp and was ignored by everybody else. The doctors had told him that his new heart needed plenty of exercise and the Kommandant tried to get out of his office and walk about the town as much as possible.

His favourite stroll took him up Town Hill to Jacaranda Park where he would wander down the drive to the house. It was still empty and there was talk of turning it into a museum or even a National Park. In the meantime Kommandant van Heerden liked to go and sit on the stoep and recall the events of the week that had changed his life so momentously.

He often thought of Konstabel Els and now that Els was dead he felt quite sorry. There had been a good side to the Konstabel's nature, he supposed, and he had to admit that Els had saved his life more than once.

'If it hadn't been for Els and that damned gun, I wouldn't be here today,' he said to himself before remembering that it had been Els' lunacy that had caused his heart trouble in the first place. Still he could afford to be magnanimous now. Els died as he had lived, killing people. 'He went with a swing,' he thought, and recalled nostalgically the Konstabel's epic struggle with the Dobermann. It reminded him of a case he had read about in the paper recently. It concerned a coloured convict on a prison farm in Northern Zululand who had bitten a guard dog to death before hanging it. The fellow's name had been Harbinger, which the Kommandant thought sounded vaguely familiar. Anyway he had been given twenty lashes for indecent assault and the Kommandant thought he deserved them.

He settled himself comfortably in a wicker chair and looked out over the lawn at the new bust of Sir Theophilus which he had had erected at his own expense – or rather at the expense of the reward money Els no longer had any use for. He had paid the taxidermist too for his trouble, and had taken the stuffed Toby and put it in his office at the police station where it gave him an opportunity to wax eloquent to the new konstabels on the virtues of Konstabel Els who had killed the dog to save his Kommandant's life.

All in all, the Kommandant reflected, he had good cause to be happy. The world was a good place to be in. South Africa was white still and would remain so. But above all he knew that he merited the high place he held in Piemburg and that his greatest ambition had finally been achieved. Within his chest there beat the heart of an English gentleman.

Tom Sharpe
Wilt 75p

'Henry Wilt works humbly at his Polytechnic dinning Eng. Lit. into the unreceptive skulls of rude mechanicals, his nights in fantasies of murdering his gargantuan, feather-brained wife, half-consummated when he dumps a life-sized inflatable doll in a building site hole, and is grilled by the police, his wife being missing, stranded on a mud bank with a gruesome American dyke' GUARDIAN

'Superb farce' TRIBUNE

'. . . triumphs by a slicing wit' DAILY MIRROR

Indecent Exposure 75p

The brilliant follow-up to *Riotous Assembly* . . . another of Tom Sharpe's hilarious and savage satires on South Africa . . .

'Explosively funny, fiendishly inventive' SUNDAY TIMES

'A lusty and delightfully lunatic fantasy' SUNDAY EXPRESS

Stephen Vizinczey
In Praise of Older Women 80p

'A cool, comic survey of the sexual education of a young Hungarian, from his first encounter, as a twelve-year-old refugee with the American forces, to his unsatisfactory liaison with a reporter's wife in Canada at "the belated end of his youth", when he was twenty-three . . . elegantly erotic, with masses of that indefinable quality, style . . . this has the real stuff of immortality' PUNCH

Leslie Thomas
Bare Nell 90p

Little Nell Luscombe, paddling naked in her native Devon streams, was the delight of the local GIs. She grew up into BARE NELL, learning that there was a good living to be made from her substantial charms. From servicing the Weymouth fishermen, she progressed to the pinnacle of her profession . . . running a high class establishment – within earshot of the division bells at Westminster . . .

'A most disarming heroine, guileless and open-hearted, innocent and lascivious . . . it is all good fun. And Nelly's a love!' DAILY TELEGRAPH

Leslie Thomas
Dangerous Davies, The Last Detective 80p

When Dangerous gets a murder case, it's a twenty-five year-old sex crime. His witnesses range from a veteran of the Zulu wars to a mad policeman who thinks he's Peter the Great . . . and the mightily endowed Ena Lind, catsuit-wearer and crème-de-menthe drinker.
Exhibit A is the pair of pale green knickers that the victim wasn't wearing . . .

'Cheerfully vulgar . . . sharply observed' THE TIMES

His Lordship 75p

His Lordship was what the girls in a posh boarding school called William their handsome tennis coach. They laid traps for him. They teased him. They were very fond of him. Very fond. That is why William is in a prison cell when the story opens . . .

'A girls' school that makes St Trinians sound like a nunnery'
THE LISTENER

'High jinks and low jinks . . . Ripe comedy, very funny and an ingenious pay-off' DAILY EXPRESS

Tropic of Ruislip 75p

'A romp among the adulteries, daydreams and nasty woodsheds of an executive housing estate . . . there are Peeping Toms, clandestine couplings, miscegenation on the wrong side of the tracks, the spilling of gin and home truths on the G-Plan furniture and the steady susurrus of doffed knickers' THE GUARDIAN

'Extremely funny . . . for sheer pace, invention, gusto and accuracy, Leslie Thomas takes some beating' SUNDAY TIMES

Christy Brown
Wild Grow the Lilies 90p

'Will probably be every bit as successful as *Down All The Days* . . . Never before has so much alcohol been consumed between book covers!' TIMES LITERARY SUPPLEMENT

'Hilarious and randy' THE TIMES

A. G. Macdonell
England, their England 80p

One of the great classics of English humour . . . The story of Donald Cameron, returning home from the First World War and setting out to write his book about the curious habits and traditional customs of the English. En route there are superb scenes of village life, a weekend-country-house-party at the redoubtable Lady Ormerode's, international conferences, and a description of village cricket that is immortal in the annals of English humour.

'Praise be for a book that is really funny' SPECTATOR

'A joy to read' SUNDAY TIMES

George MacDonald Fraser
Flashman 80p

This fascinating first instalment of the Flashman Papers solves the mystery of what happened to Harry Flashman – that cad and bully from *Tom Brown's Schooldays* – after he was expelled from Rugby . . . here is the story of his early career in Lord Cardigan's 11th Light Dragoons, told by a self-confessed rotter, liar, womanizer and coward.

J. D Gilman and John Clive
KG 200 95p

They flew Flying Fortresses. They wore American uniforms . . . but they were Germans! KG 200 – the phantom arm of Hitler's Luftwaffe. From a secret base in occupied Norway these crack pilots plan their ultimate mission, the raid that would bring Allied defeat crashing down from the exploding skies . . .

Inspired by the best-kept secret of World War Two, this is one of the most enthralling novels of air warfare, espionage and manhunt ever written.

Joe Eszterhas
F.I.S.T. 80p

Now a sensational film starring Sylvester 'Rocky' Stallone . . . F.I.S.T. is the Federation of InterState Truckers . . . F.I.S.T. is the story of Johnny Kovak, whose combination of punch and persuasion took him to the top of the truckers' union . . . of the wife he betrayed and the ambitions he tarnished . . . and of the dangerous allies who brought him down. A story peopled with characters as big and powerful as the trucks they drive.

Walter Macken
Sunset on the Window Panes 80p

Whenever misfortune befell anyone of the Irish country village of Bolla, you could be certain that Bart O'Breen was not far away . . . strong, wilful and callous, though not intending harm. How long was it to be before Bart realized how much he'd done to mar the lives of others, as he walked his own long road, as proud as the Devil and as lonely as Hell . . .?